To Bob an
Bob

Creatively
Dave Daines

MW00984418

What A Line!

HIGHLIGHTING 50 Years of Adventure, Artistry, Wit and Wisdom

FROM THE ULTIMATE "OLD SCHOOL"
FREEHAND ARTIST ENTREPRENEUR

DAVE DAVIES

Copyright © 2016 by Dave Davies

DAVIESCUSTOMPAINT.COM

ISBN 978-1-4958-1157-9

Printed in the United States of America

Published August 2016

INFINITY PUBLISHING
1094 New DeHaven Street, Suite 100
West Conshohocken, PA 19428-2713
Toll-free (877) BUY BOOK
Local Phone (610) 941-9999
Fax (610) 941-9959
Info@buybooksontheweb.com
www.buybooksontheweb.com

(ABOVE) *The author sits aboard a 1906 Maxwell*

(BELOW) *Freehand Pinstriping lines on the Maxwell*
Owner: Ron Davis Cobleskill, NY

I would like to thank Elma and Ron Phillips for their encouragement in pushing me to complete this book. Many thanks also to Martin Kelly for his editing, and to Judy Hicks of Plush Design for the layout and cover design.

I must also acknowledge my illustrators Bill Carney, SueAnn Summers Griessler, and Darla for their beautiful work.

We're certain to mention the late "Miss Vikki" for her help in laying out the first pages and helping get this project rolling.

PREFACE

In my mind it has always been as if there were two worlds. From the world I was living in there was a clear view off in the distance another world, the Competitive World, a world of *dog eat dog, kill or be killed, swim with the sharks, crush the competition.* Although being well aware of that world, I was content not having to live in it. I resided in the Creative World. A very different place which, from as far back as I can remember, introduced me to adventure, artistry, diverse knowledge and wisdom.

This book is about the Creative world, what is held therein, and through experiences and adventures, the creative value and development of ideas.

I have had very little interest in the competitive environment; its education, techniques and philosophies, and haven't invested much time there. I believe we are born "creative creatures" but are taught to think competitively. After living over six decades in a world so fascinating and wonderful, I am surprised that more people don't seem to know about it. Common sense reveals the sharp contrast between the two worlds. An example would be, in the creative world... the older you are, the **more valuable**. From what I have observed, that doesn't hold true in the competitive environment and seems unnatural to me.

The creative world is governed by very basic and natural principles. Every blade of grass, every tree, every animal, every human, and every idea begins with a seed. I don't know of anything that has its beginning in a complete and finished state. Everything that arrives here has some growing to do. The creative process is no exception. This story is all about growing. How we grow will be determined by many things: our environment, our capability to attain and retain knowledge, our talents, and abilities.

The mind, which is fundamental to all of this, is at first much like an empty field, and how it will develop will be determined by specific things... How fertile we keep the field and the intelligence, creativity, character, and integrity of those who we allow to plant there.

My Welsh heritage has provided a fertile field for sure, and I certainly had many intelligent and very creative characters planting there. A few even had integrity!

Some of the characters in the stories are a composite of several individuals represented as one person simply because of the cumulative affect they had on my life and also that they would appear less flawed. Many names have been changed for obvious reasons. Most of the stories are true, with the exception of a few that may have been greatly exaggerated. (If any one were to question me on any area of this it's for certain that will be the part that was greatly exaggerated. This will serve as my disclaimer.)

Herein you will find a harvest of heartfelt memories, humor, and healing that will hold for those who are able to think beneath the surface; a philosophy unfolding with each chapter. In order to accomplish this I try, in narrative and in language, to present the circumstances as they were seen through my eyes and mind as well as the eyes and mind of the characters at each particular point in time. Therefore the reader can experience firsthand the growth and development of creativity in its purest form.

I would hope that the stories go beyond just entertainment, revealing the value in ideas, and true purpose held in life's lessons. When the lines are properly connected, they reveal the secret signature of a soul.

David Holland Davies

SUBSTANCE

Chapter 1

THE EARLY YEARS

My parents were in their forties when I came along and, for about the first eight years or so, we had what might be considered a "normal" life. Both my mom and dad were of Welsh decent, both very bright and extremely talented. I can remember as a kid thinking that parents could do anything. I watched my father put an addition on our house, do the roofing, siding, electrical work, plumbing and heating. He could fix anything that went wrong with the car, draw beautiful pictures, paint signs, work out mathematical problems, and always coming up with ideas and inventions. Actually, I hadn't seen anything he could not do. I know now that he was a genius.

My mom was also talented. She wrote beautiful poetry, stories, songs, and could spell and define any word in the English language. Although my dad was basically self-taught, my mom was formally educated at a college in Vermont. I suppose I had taken for granted just how talented they were until one day after school while playing over at a friend's house. His dad was trying to replace the boards on the stairs on the back porch. He was struggling with every part of the job. When I got home I told my dad that I felt sorry that Jimmy's father was retarded. My dad quickly interrupted…

"What? Jimmy's dad is an executive at a major insurance company, what are you talking about?" I said, "Dad, the guy can't hit a nail with a hammer!" He then went on to explain in detail how people often have specific talents and abilities.

As I started hanging out with other kids I noticed something else. Their parents didn't seem to drink as much as mine did. In fact I very seldom saw any booze at the other kids' homes, at least when we were around. It was at this time that I started to realize that what was supposed to be normal might not have been normal at all. Though, being different was something I had already accepted. One day in school, probably fourth grade, the teacher was asking each kid what nationality their family descended from. As she went around the room it was: Italian, Irish, Polish, Dutch, German, Scottish, and when it came to me, "Welsh." The whole class burst into laughter! I said quickly, "My folks came from Wales!" They laughed harder. I felt like an idiot. The worst part was that the teacher never bailed me out, she just moved on to the next kid. I went home that day and told my mother what had happened and she couldn't believe it. She saw I was really down in the dumps over this thing, so she pulled out all these books and started showing me all these great people who had made history who were of Welsh decent. Many of the Pilgrims, Abe Lincoln (his mother was Welsh), Frank Lloyd Wright (one of the greatest architects), John L. Lewis, C.S Lewis, Bob Hope, Richard Burton, Andy Williams, Robin Williams, Dylan Thomas, and a host of well known greats; it seems that the world is filled with writers, producers, and actors of Welsh decent. She went on, explaining that when the real Titanic was sinking, the passengers gathered and were singing a Welsh Hymn (no mention of that in the movie.) She continued, telling me about the great Welsh Revival and about the Welsh language being one of the oldest languages on earth. After a while I began to think that maybe the teacher was the idiot.

There were other things as well that made me feel different. In the school system there seemed to be an emphasis on either studies or sports. You would follow the rules regarding studies, unless you excelled in sports, then they would bend the rules. I had no interest in sports and, though I was fascinated with ideas and inventions, there were very few studies in these areas, so you might say I was lost.

In the next few years things in our home seemed to deteriorate. I would witness alcohol bleaching the color out of my parents' lives. If there was such a thing as a devil, he had moved in with us. My sister and I dealt with it the best way we could, with the resources we had. Lynne was seven years older than me and had been teaching after school at a dance studio. She put more time into her work. I spent much time off by myself thinking. I loved thinking. I also wondered why everybody was in such a hurry. That was probably the main reason I didn't fit into the sports thing. Sports to me were all about hurry. Hurry and get your uniform on, hurry to practice, hurry home to get your homework done. Hurry, hurry, hurry. No time to just think. It was almost as if they didn't want you to think. You might come up with something that was fun or exciting. I accepted the fact that I was different and if I wanted to think, I was going to think!

There was a tree behind my house with a comfortable little spot near the top where I would go just to think. Many ideas were born in that tree. I would sit there for hours on end, drifting off into my imagination. Then all of a sudden an idea would spring into my head and out of the tree I would come and the games would begin! As I look back, if the neighbors knew where these ideas had been born, they would have cut that tree down (after

Illustration by SueAnn Summers Griessler

hanging me from it first)! From converting our old shed into a clubhouse, raiding gardens with the garden ghosts, creating UFOs, becoming motorized, turning the neighborhood upside down, and basically driving people crazy, all began as thoughts while in that tree.

Little did I know that I would enter a world where Ideas were currency and they would literally fuel the rest of my life.

As time went on my parents' drinking got worse. One day a few buddies and I were on my front porch, just hanging out. We got talking about our fathers. One kid was saying how his dad was in the war. Actually, a sailor in the US Navy, had a ship shot out from under him and spent a day and a half in the water fighting off sharks until he got picked up by another ship. Another friend, Tom Taylor, told us about how his dad came from Scotland and had done some heroic things while over there. I remember my uncle telling how my dad had saved a guy's life after he had been hit by high voltage electricity while working as a lineman, and I was just about to get into the story when the phone rang. It was a neighbor a few doors down calling. She was screaming that my father was drunk and had fallen into their hedges. The lady ordered me to immediately come and get him out of her hedges! I told my friends I had an emergency and quickly ran down the street to the neighbor's. By the time I arrived, the whole neighborhood was out watching the show. There he was, trying desperately to get to his feet and destroying the hedges in the process. My so-called buddies stood back, keeping their distance, wanting no part of this. But as I approached my dad I noticed Tom was beside me. The two of us pulled him out of the hedges and helped him up the street to our house. We brought him inside and had him lay on the couch. I breathed a sigh of relief. My other buddies were nowhere to be found. I didn't know what to say, it was so embarrassing. With my dad sleeping it off, Tom and I returned to the front porch. I told Tom I was sorry for having put him through all that, but that I really appreciated him helping. I realized that not a single neighbor offered to help. My dad had helped practically every one of those neighbors one time or another, and they just stood there shaking their heads. What would I have done if Tom wasn't there? No way could I have lifted my dad out of those hedges alone.

Tom said he understood about this stuff and went on to tell me that his dad was known to get drunk once in a while himself. He continued, saying the whole thing wasn't that big of a deal when compared to Joey Keelin's old man, showing up at a Cub Scout meeting drunk and crapped in his pants right in front of God and everybody. Poor Joey wanted to crawl in a hole. We both started laughing and it eased my pain. Then we started telling each other jokes about drunks. A few I made up myself. I was just glad it was over.

But it wasn't over. I still had to walk down that street. I still had to deal with the neighbors and what about my disappearing buddies? They'll be blabbing it all over school about what a "hero" my dad was. Well, the good thing that came of all this was that I realized what a real friend Tom was.

I kept reliving the whole scene over and over in my mind. I kept recalling the neighbors looking on, shaking their heads. I kept feeling the embarrassment over and over. I returned to the tree; I had to think about something else. Some time passed and I began thinking about the old shed that sat off in the corner of our property, how I had always wanted to fix it up into a little clubhouse. We could hang out there. I could run a line out from the house and set it up with electricity. I could dig out the old movie projector, the one with the hand crank, and we could watch old time movies. We could start a club and have members. That's it, a clubhouse! I immediately jumped down from the tree and went to find Tom. When I caught up with him and told him what I had in mind, he was all for it and said that he'd help fix it up. We headed over to check it out.

As we approached the old shed I saw what was to be a major problem. There was an enemy lurking in the building. Wasps! They were everywhere. At first I thought, this might not be a good idea after all. Tom walked up close and several wasps came out and circled his head, then they came at me. We both retreated to the house. Well, this is going to need some more thought, that's for sure. Tom agreed.

ᔕ WORLD WAR II REVISITED

The next day my Uncle Holl (Holland Williams) stopped by. He was heading up to his camp on Lake St. Catherine in Vermont. He would often pick me up and take me up for a few days. I loved it up there. He would spend the entire trip telling me war stories. He had fought in World War II as a combat engineer landing with the first American troops in Africa, fighting with Rommel "The Desert Fox." He would then go on to the battle of Anzio in Sicily, Belgium, the Battle of The Bulge, and eventually on to Germany and the end of the war.

I was born in '46 and after listening to my uncle, I knew much about the war. On this particular trip he told me all about D-Day. How our troops were ready to attack the Germans but the weather had them all on hold. They were ready and waiting to head for Normandy but couldn't launch the attack because there was so much cloud cover. The bombers didn't take off because they wouldn't be able to see their targets. The ships were in the harbor and the men were just waiting for the weather to clear. Finally the weather cleared and one of the largest assaults in military history took place.

My uncle had given me a pair of German field glasses (binoculars) he had taken from a German army officer killed in Italy. They were, from what he told me, the finest optics the world had to offer at that time. They were amazing. At a far off distance you could read the print in a newspaper. My uncle told me that somewhere in northern Italy he watched airplanes in a dogfight overhead, and through those field glasses he could see the faces of the pilots. For a kid my age to have a pair of these... you can imagine how I felt. My uncle was my hero. He was the greatest.

My uncle Holland Williams (right) in Anzio, Italy WW II 1944. The soldier standing next to him was killed shortly after this picture was taken.

❧ THE CONQUEROR

After spending a week up at the lake, and getting a good dose of WW II, I had returned home to my troubles. I still had the problem of the wasps to deal with and I knew it wasn't going to be easy. From my bedroom window I could see the shed off in the distance, and with my German field glasses, I could bring in those nasty wasps so close I could count the little hairs on their backs. I often imagined, if those field glasses could talk, what stories they could tell. I thought of how every time someone looked through them they saw an enemy. First the Germans watching our guys, then my uncle watching the Germans, and now here I am watching my enemy…the wasps. It was starting to get dark and my view of the shed was beginning to fade. I could hear thunder off in the distance and the weather guy on the radio was talking about a storm coming in. I went to bed that night thinking about my uncle and all the war stories.

After a solid night's sleep I awoke to the rain pounding the window. It was pouring down. I looked out through the field glasses to the old shed. Not a wasp moving. The weather had them pinned down. As I sat there, something popped into my head…D-Day! Would this be the time to hit those wasps? Yes! The cold rain had everything quiet on the Western Front. I jumped up, got dressed, and headed to the garage. I needed ammo and there it was, up on the shelf above my dad's tool box. Two cans of "Black Flag" wasp and hornet spray! One full and the other half full. This would do it. Now well armed and ready for action, I headed back to the bunker to figure out my strategy. Another look revealed still no movement. I would attack from the north, with no warning. I'd wipe the front lines out quickly, then I'd head inside and flank west, then toward the south, wiping out all divisions and return, taking out any small platoons left along the eastern front. When the sun comes out I will occupy all territories, which we now call "the shed."

I put on my hooded sweat shirt and pulled the draw string tight around my face, then shook both cans of hornet spray for a full two minutes, just like the directions said. I was armed and ready. With a spray can in each hand, I headed for the shed and began pumping myself up like my uncle told me combat soldiers often do. "OK, you little sons of bitches' kiss your asses' goodbye, it's D-Day and this shed is mine!" Right up to the eaves over the door I went and with no resistance, pumped those nests full of bee spray. Hundreds, maybe thousands of wasps were falling from the nests. They would hit the ground and the rain would wash them away. Within seconds I had wiped out the entire front lines and most likely the attack team that ran me and Tom off. The door to the shed was partially opened so I just gave it a kick. It flew open and slammed against the inside wall. I dove in. Once inside, I had a few surprises waiting for me. First of all, it wasn't raining inside and the door whacking the inside wall must have pissed off about ten thousand wasps. They were everywhere, flying crazily all over the place. All of a sudden I realized that what was supposed to be a ground assault was turning into a "dog fight." There were wasps coming at me from all sides. I started spinning and spraying with both hands. Many dropped and some flew away for a moment. Then… wasps at 3 o'clock! I sprayed to my right. More coming in at 9 o'clock! I turned to my left, I shoot! Got em. Down they go. Two were circling overhead at 12 o'clock! Blast em! Much of the spray came down on me. What a horrible taste and my eyes were burning. One coming in at 3 o'clock again, I raise to shoot…can is empty! Ouch! I just took a hit!. You bastards! Toss that can. Here they come again. Spray then duck!! Got em. Just as soon as the fog would clear they'd attack again. I kept spinning and blasting them till the second can was empty. I ran for the door. It was time to get out of there. I could hardly breathe. I pulled the door tight behind me so the fumes would take out the rest of them. Finally, out into the rain and fresh air. The battle was over. Wounded, soaking wet, and stinking like a chemical factory I headed for the house and a hot shower.

The next morning I awoke to birds chirping and a bright sunny day. Quickly I picked up my field glasses to take a look. A careful examination revealed nothing moving. I got dressed as fast as I could and ran toward the shed. As I closed in on it I could still smell the bee spray. I was certain that the lingering fumes must have killed everything left inside. There was a stick on the ground, part of a branch that had blown down from the storm. I picked it up. This would be my swagger stick. I hesitated for a moment, then "swaggered" in, poking around at the devastation. Truly, war is Hell. Well, for those wasps anyway. They should have known better than to mess with the general. Like my uncle had told me, you could smell the death and destruction (although this smelled mostly like bee spray.) There was nothing moving. The shed was ours! A few minutes later I heard bicycles pull into the yard. It was Tom, Danny, Jeff, Lewie, Steve, and Gary. Then I remembered, today was the day we were supposed to go fishing out to the reservoir. I proudly stood in the doorway of the shed with my swagger stick poking around. They walked over with their eyes bulging. They didn't say a word just looked around at all the dead wasps.

I broke the silence with… Well guys, we have a clubhouse.

"How did you do this?" Tom asked.

"A mixture of Black Flag and 'balls.' That's how it was done. What can I say? We need this shed. I had to do what I had to do, simple as that. The outside battle was bad enough; you remember how they came at us Tom? Well, inside they jumped me from all sides; you would not believe what I went through. Fought my way in and fought my way out. It was brutal!" (Displaying my battle scars,) "I did take a few hits but that just made me more pissed. Well, I'll tell you all about it on the way to the reservoir, let me grab my pole and tackle."

It was seven miles out to the reservoir and we had plenty of time to talk about all the things we were going to do with that clubhouse. We could get some old flower sacks from down at the bakery and make caped shirts. I could take my dad's paints and brushes and paint our logo on the door. We would paint up the old shed and get some crates to sit on. We'd put cardboard on the inside walls and paint that up, too. The ideas were coming in as fast as we could think. This was going to be great! Between fishing and talking the day flew by.

∽ CARDBOARD CRUISERS

The next day Tom came over and we started working right away. I found a couple of gallons of paint and a few brushes, so we started perking the old shed up. As the days went on, more and more kids came over to help out. I went on a mission to find some cardboard so we could fix up the walls on the inside. I had remembered seeing some cardboard out back of the TV store. Sure enough, there was cardboard alright; huge TV boxes with more cardboard inserts inside each box. It wouldn't take much to do the inside of the shed, so I went in to ask the guy if he wouldn't mind if I took a few boxes. The guy was more than happy to give me the cardboard with one condition; he said…"Kid if you want cardboard, no problem, but you've got to take it all. It's all or nothing." I thought for a moment; there were a lot of boxes out there, with more cardboard inside each box. Even if we did the walls and the ceiling we'd have so much left over. Oh well, we'll use it for something. We'll take it all!

I got all the guys together and we hauled cardboard up the street to the shed. We piled it up outside and started cutting it up for the walls inside. The boxes were huge and each one had four inserts inside each box. Something else I noticed was that everything inside the box (including the inserts) was wax coated. The inserts were two inches thick and about two feet by three feet The boxes themselves were three feet tall by almost three feet on each side. So when a box was cut open and laid out it was almost twelve feet long. If you took the bottom and the top and added them to the open length they would now be almost sixteen feet.

We were opening each of the boxes and laying them out on the lawn so we could cut them up, and an idea came to me. I started connecting the open boxes end to end and adding the tops and bottoms. They stretched out from the fence in the backyard, past the house and down the driveway and across the front lawn. It was like a long runway. I then attached the underside where the boxes connected to each other with tape. We now had one long wax coated runway. I grabbed a wax coated insert, backed up against the fence, ran toward the runway and flopped down like you would when sleigh riding. Away I went, with the wax-coated insert against the wax-coated runway, I was flying all the way to the front lawn. Wow, what a ride!

Everybody grabbed an insert and took off. We couldn't get back to the beginning fast enough. We were having such a good time that I wasn't paying attention, but after a while I noticed that I was waiting in line to make a run and the line was getting longer. At one point there were kids standing in line with inserts in their hands that I had never seen before. I had no idea who they were or where they came from. A bunch of girls were standing there watching us. One of them walked over to me.

She asked… "Are you Davie Davis?"

I said "Yep." (Many people referred to my last name as "Davis." I didn't correct them because it would work to my advantage if someone wanted to try to call my parents or turn me in for something — they would be looking for the wrong name in the phone book.)

"Is that Tom Taylor?"

"Yep."

"Is that your clubhouse back there?"

"Yep."

"We heard about you guys."

"What did you hear about us?"

"Oh, lots of stuff," she continued. "Like, you guys were fixing up a clubhouse and it was full of wasps and that you were pulling the nests out and crushing them with your bare hands. Is that true?"

"Well, sort of, I had gloves on. Who told you that?"

"It's all over school, everybody's talking about it. Did you get stung?"

"Yep. Lots."

"Didn't it hurt?"

"Sure, but look at it this way, they only *stung* me; I *killed* them."

"Is it true Tom climbed the water tower?"

"Yep. Sure did. Two hundred twelve feet."

"Is it true he's not afraid of anything?"

"Yep, I ain't seen anything that could scare him."

"Are you letting any girls in the club?"

"Nope. No girls."

"How come?"

"Cause the stuff we do ain't for girls to do."

"Why's that?"

"I can't talk about it. We're sworn to secrecy. In the club we have to take an oath."

"Really? What's an oath?"

"It's a thing where you have to follow rules and stuff. I can't say any more about it — I've told you too much already. Now, let me ask you some questions. First of all, what's your name?"

"I'm Debbie."

"Who's your friend over there?"

"Oh, that's Judy, I think she likes Tom. Would you tell him?"

"Sure, I'll tell him."

"Do you think he might like her?"

"I don't know. It depends if she's afraid of things like heights, ghosts, stuff like that."

"What?"

"Forget it. I'll tell him she likes him. Oh, and I'll let you know if we change our minds about letting girls in the club."

"Thanks. That would be great. Bye Davie."

"Bye Debbie."

It was getting dark and we started pulling up the runway and stacking it in the clubhouse for another day.

"Tom, did you see that girl I was talking with?"

"Yea, Debbie."

"You know her?"

"Yea, I seen her in school."

"Do you know her girl friend Judy?"

"No. I don't know her."

"Well, she likes you. Oh, and how did it get all over school about the clubhouse?"

"Ya got me. I can't figure that one out. I do know that ten kids want to join the club."

"What do you think about it?

I don't know — who are these guys? Can we trust them?"

"I don't know. Well, right now we've got you, me, Danny, Jeff, Gary, Lewie, and Steve. How many guys do we need? And what can these new guys do? We can't have ten guys raiding a garden, we'd be falling all over each other. How many could sneak out at night? So far just you and me Tom. And if Danny's ol' man ever caught him sneakin' out, for sure he'd get another beating."

"What should I tell these guys then?"

"I don't know Tom, let me think about this."

❧ TEST 'EM

By the time we got into school on Monday, there were more than thirty kids wanting to join our club. We really had a problem now. I had to come up with something fast. The next morning I got up early and spent a little time up in the tree before Tom came by and we would head to school. As I sat there, I thought how Tom and I could handle just about any situation. We could run really fast, climb anything, fix most stuff, and keep secrets; we had all the right things to be in the club. We could sneak out at night and get back in without anyone knowing we were gone. Then the answer came to me: whoever wanted to get into the club would have to pass tests. We would set up some tests for these guys to go through, where they would have to be able to do what me and Tom could do and, if for any reason we didn't want a kid in, like if he couldn't run fast or if he talked too much about what we were up to or if he couldn't take orders, then we would make the test even harder. Tom was afraid of nothing or no one. He had no fear, so if we wanted a kid not to make it I would just tell him he would have to climb the water tower or go into the old Myron place at midnight (it was vacant for years and haunted.) We'd do something like that.

After some careful thought I started to put together the tests that these kids would have to pass to get in. First, can these guys carry out orders? My uncle told me how important it was to be able to follow orders. I would put that test together with a running test. This test was not going to be some little test where you run against a clock, to see how fast you could run a certain distance — that reminded me to much of sports. No, in this test you would be actually running to save your ass, and it would have everything to do with following orders carefully.

Visualize a short street (one block long) — at one end an intersection where five roads came together. It's called the "five corners." There are gas stations there and a couple of stores and on the very end of this short street was a diner. On the other end of the street was the entrance to the Army Depot, now being used for warehousing. There was a guard shack at the gate. The guy in the shack was our friend. He was stuck in that little shack all day and we would go by from time to time on our bicycles and see if he needed anything, like a soda or cigarettes from the store. He really appreciated us doing this little service for him, so he allowed us to go into the depot whenever we needed to. We could ride our bikes around the warehouses and it also provided a hiding place when we were running from somebody.

Well, one day Tom and I had a water balloon fight with a few kids over at the park. We were heading home and each of us had a water balloon left over. We were just walking along, talking and kind of wondering what we could do with these two leftover water balloons. As we arrived at the five corners and came along side the diner, I noticed that there was a huge exhaust fan blowing out from the wall on the side of the building. Before we could even think about it, we lobbed both water balloons into the fan, instantly turning it into a giant water cannon! With the water also came out a big cloud of steam. I guess that some of the water swirling in the fan hit

Illustration by Bill Carney

the grill inside. About two seconds went by and the back door of the diner whipped open and out ran the cook, ready to kill us. We started running up the street toward the guard shack, the guy running after us. Lucky for us our friend in the guard shack saw us coming and opened the gate just enough to get us through. It slammed shut just as we disappeared. We hid in the bushes while we heard our friend telling the cook that no foreigners were allowed in the depot without a pass.

This little scenario would become the perfect "running test" for our "wanna-be" club members. The orders they would have to follow would be to skillfully toss the water balloons into the fan at the diner, and then you have to outrun the cook up to the gate at the depot! Make it and you pass the test. If you don't make it, your ass belongs to a very angry man and he'll probably grind you up for hamburger. The best part would be that Tom and I would be watching the show from the attic window of the old Myron place through the German field glasses.

Our first candidate was a kid from the other side of town. We'll call him Timmy Mumford (that's not his real name but close enough.) He hung out at the roller-rink where Tom and I would go roller skating on Saturday nights. Timmy bugged Tom about getting in the club and told us that he was raiding gardens in his end of town and could show us gardens that had the best stuff. He told us about super big tomatoes, watermelons, and even where there was a grape arbor filled with Concords.

We explained every detail of the running test right down to the size of the water balloons. We really wanted this kid to make it into the club but he would be the example for others. There were a few things that might help a bit though, that might give a slight advantage to a kid who we needed in the club. Like, each person is given two water balloons, but we never said that you would have to throw both of them into the fan. The other balloon was in case you dropped one on the way over. The other thing was that by now we had put the cook through this so many times his reaction time was a lot faster than it used to be. Our advice then (to the right kid) would be to toss just one balloon into the fan and do it at a "dead run" (maybe a poor choice of words). In other words, get up to speed as you pass by the launching site.

When Timmy showed up with a brand new pair of PF sneakers, we knew he was serious about running and possibly getting in the club. Tom and I both wanted Tim in and figured we would do everything we could to guarantee success. So Tom came up with a little idea that might help if anything went wrong. This time I would be at the lookout in the Myron place and Tom would be on the ground. I would give him signals as to how Timmy would be doing and whether or not he would have to use the backup plan. We also informed the guy in the guard shack that today would most definitely not be a boring day and there would be plenty of excitement. Every time we would tell him we were about to pull one of our capers he would burst into this maniacal crazed kind of laugh. I think the guy was a full- blown mental case (which actually worked out perfect for us) and he stocked up on chips and soda and got ready. Everyone in their positions... let the games begin. Timmy started out from the phone booth at the five corners and wound those PF's up to speed, swooped in on the fan where he carefully tossed in the missile. Off went the water cannon and, in what seemed like a split second, out of the side door came the angry cook. Those new PF's seemed like two white streaks under Timmy as he headed for the gate. From up at the gate you could hear the guard laughing and cheering him on. He was actually jumping up and down spilling soda and chips all over himself. Tom, hiding in the bushes below, looked up for the signal. As fast as those little sneakers were going, they weren't going fast enough. The cook was stretching himself out and gaining fast. I gave Tom a "thumbs down." He crouched into position and as soon as Timmy passed where he was hiding, Tom jumped up and tossed an empty but very large aluminum beer keg (we had borrowed from behind the Democratic Club) directly at the cook.

Instinctively, the surprised cook reached out to catch the keg and it put him flat on the ground. It took the wind right out of him. Tim ran on through the gate. Dazed and disoriented, the cook wobbled back to the diner. Tom and I disappeared.

Later we all met at the clubhouse. When Tim arrived he was still panting like a dog and was as white as his new sneakers.

"Tim, ya done great man. Well, with a little help from Tom anyway, but that's alright — we'll call it good. Now just one more test and you're in." (I think I should have waited to tell him that, he seemed to get even whiter.)

"What other tests?" he asked.

"Well, just some night time stuff to see if you are afraid of haunted houses and ghosts and stuff like that. You see, there's this haunted house, actually you ran by it, but you were concentrating on the gate and probably didn't see it. What we do is, we have these membership cards that we give to new members and we put one on a table that's in the attic of the haunted house and you just have to show up at the clubhouse the next day with the card, and then we know you were there and got it. Simple enough?" He didn't answer. "Oh, I forgot a small detail. We put the card there at midnight and take it back at three o'clock. So you have to go there and get it between midnight and three." He just stared at the wall, and then asked …

"You said the place is haunted? What do you mean haunted?"

"Well, you see that's the old Myron place and as the story goes, ol' man Myron (who was suspected to be 'Baron Von Myron') came from England, then to Boston. It was rumored that he might have been closely related to Jack the Ripper, if not maybe be Jack himself. Anyway, he decided to live here quietly in the U.S. He married Mrs. Myron and things were good for a while, that is till Mrs. Myron started foolin' around with Joe the baker. He would stop up to the house when Mr. Myron was away on business and well they would carry on. One day Myron come home unexpectedly and noticed his wife was acting pretty nervous. Then they say the Baron smelled the scent of jelly doughnuts coming from the closet. He pulled open the door and there stood Joe. They say Myron freaked out and strangled both of them. Then he run off and was never heard of again."

"They never found him?" Tim interrupted.

"Nope, never found him. But Tom's seen him. Sometimes he returns to the house once in a while."

"How's it you guys can go in there? What if he's there?"

"Well, one night Tom ran into him in there."

"What?"

"Yep, one night Tom was walking up the stairs and right at the top stood the Baron himself face to face with Tom. Tom looked right at him and said…'You mess with me and I'll strangle you!' Tom said he heard a noise and turned around and when he looked back, the Baron was gone. I think his wife and Joe's ghosts are still there. That's why the Baron keeps coming back. In fact, lots of times I've been in there I could smell jelly doughnuts myself. So if the Baron ever appears just say…'Tom sent me, I'm gettin' my card, now get out of my way!" That's all there is to it."

"Is there going to be any more tests after that?" Tim asked.

"No. You show up with the card and you're in. If you don't show up, we'll understand."

So we set the time for the test as Saturday night and a meeting for Sunday afternoon. Tim went home to change his sneakers (and probably his underwear.) Tom asked me why I was so rough on him. Didn't we want him in? I explained that sure we want him in but remember, Timmy's got a lot on the ball with his own gardens and stuff. I had to let him know we're in charge here. This is our deal, we ain't joinin' up with him, he's joinin' up with us.

Early Saturday morning after watching cartoons on TV, Tom and I went through the woods behind the Myron place, snuck in, went up to the attic and set the card on the table, but not before we sprinkled the crumbs from the box of jelly doughnuts (we ate on the way over) all over the place. We even left a half eaten one not far from his card on the table. I was glad it was daytime because I didn't especially like going into the Myron place at night myself. Tom actually spent the night there once. He wasn't exactly alone though, he had Sherry Vinovio with him. Imagine, she told her mom she was going to a "Pajama Party." (I don't think Tom brought his pajamas.)

That Sunday Tim showed up, card in hand. He didn't mention anything about the jelly doughnuts. That had us puzzled, so I asked…

"Did you see any ghosts or smell doughnuts while you were there?"

"No," he answered "but there were rats everywhere. I just ran in and ran out."

ᔪ LOSING GROUND

The tests continued for a short time and we gathered the best of the best together. But sadly the running test finally fizzled out. There were two pretty bad incidents. One kid stood there and threw both balloons in the fan then got confused and ran down Broadway instead of going toward the gate and the guard shack. He hid in a pile of tires behind Skyway Garage. The cook never found him but the guy at the tire shop pulled him out of the tires and choked him, yelling something about kids taking tires from behind the building and rolling them down the hill into cars going by.

I should have told him not to run that way. It was as if he was running from a gorilla and a tiger got him. We were very familiar with the tiger in the tire shop.

Later the cook actually caught a kid. This time it wasn't even a running test. It was just for fun. About half way up the street the kid tripped and fell. The cook grabbed him and flopped him around like a rag doll, but after he noticed the kid had pissed his pants he let him go. Then the strangest thing happened. As the cook started walking back toward the diner, I think he lost his mind. He began waving his arms in the air, skipping like a little kid and singing in Greek. All we could figure was if it was translated it would probably have gone something like… "Ha ha, I got him, I got him, I got the lit-tle bas-tard! Ha ha, I got my chance, he peed his pants, ha ha… I got him," or something like that anyway.

Some said this kid deserved it anyway. They said he was a little punk, a wise guy, a troublemaker, and the undeserving owner of a pair of German field glasses. (You really didn't think the cook would have been that happy if he hadn't gotten the top dog.) I told everyone that I didn't really piss my pants, that it was just a trick using another water balloon I had in my pocket so that I didn't get turned into hamburger. Later they put a hood over the exhaust fan that turned downward and we could no longer fire the water cannon, so that ended our little caper for good.

By now we were starting to lose ground in a few different areas. The hood on the fan dampened our running test, and it seems that some of the folks in the neighborhood were getting wise to us. One night we were raiding a pear tree behind old man Peal's house. These were the best pears in the whole town; he sprayed them for bugs and took special care of those little babies. When you bit into one of Peal's pears, the juice would run down both sides of your mouth. So one night, me, Tom, Timmy, and Gary were going to hit this pear tree. We weren't there two minutes and all of a sudden we all were soaked to the skin. Water came from everywhere, sprinklers and hoses pointing from every direction. We were so wet we could hardly run. I can remember Peal laughing in the background as we scrambled away. Peal was a clever ol' fellow and I have to admit he got us good that night.

The next day there was a bag of pears in front of the clubhouse door with a note saying, "You don't need to steal, just ask boys and you can have all you want." From that day on he had our respect. From then on it was "Mr. Peal" and he was off the raid list. Tom and I even snuck over one day and replaced the pickets we broke on his fence. It was our way of showing our respect. Amazingly, of all people Mr. Peal was the person who ended up buying the old Myron place. He tore it down and built a beautiful home there. When we heard he bought the place, we told everybody in the club that Tom went over one night and ordered the Baron out of there and told him he had to return to Boston. It wasn't a few weeks after that that we heard about a "Boston Strangler" in the papers. There was no doubt he had taken Tom's advice.

❧ THE GARDEN GHOSTS

One night we were raiding gardens over near Colonial Manor. I say *near* Colonial Manor because the Manor was off limits. It was rumored that a lot of Italian people lived in the manor and do I have to tell you what would happen if anything went wrong in there? That's all we needed was to get caught stealing tomatoes from some guy that needs them for some special sauce he makes. Besides, I remembered Mr. Happensburg (he was a genius friend of mine and an old fellow I spent many hours with) telling me that, *"Adventure must be handled with intelligence."* So I didn't think it would have been too intelligent to raid any gardens in the Manor. I never told Happensburg what kind of adventures we got involved with but I had a feeling he knew what was going on. Anyway, just outside the Manor lived Elsie Bramer. She was a widow and wacky as a bed bug. People said it was us that drove her nuts but I know for sure, she was well on her way to the mayonnaise farm before we came along. Even though she had a feeble mind, her garden was a great one for sure. There were tomatoes, carrots, and melons. I can remember they were top of the line. Well, one night we were all there and for some reason we got laughing about something. I guess we were making a lot of noise. We heard the back door open and then a spot light came on. We all ran for it, everybody scattering in different directions. She couldn't see too well, and with the capes we wore waving all around, you can imagine what it looked like through a mind that had trouble understanding things that it *could* see. It seems she thought she'd seen ghosts in her garden. She thought they were Klansmen ghosts. She told someone that her granddad had been an active member down south and moved north to get away from the Klan, and that after all these years they finally found her family and were coming after her. When we got wind of that we crossed her off the list. Strangely enough though, we started to hear about other reportings of ghost sightings. Tom said it's the "capes." When we run away they wave in the air and then, when we drop down behind hedges and bushes, they look like they disappear. I noticed it myself.

Well now, this brings into play another level of fun here. By now you might be wondering how it is we are involved with so many wacky people (I wondered that myself.) I can't say for sure but Happensburg told me once that *"Like attracts like."* That had me wondering. Just the same, the "ghosts" seemed like it could really be something we could get into, and we were always looking to get into more stuff.

Back at the clubhouse we gathered all of our capes together. We were going to change a few things. We painted one side with black and left one side white. A few we painted one side with camouflage and kept the other white. Now we could show the white on the outside but all we had to do is pull the cape over our heads and we could disappear. After a little practice we could work the capes pretty well, putting on quite a show for all who were already convinced they were seeing ghosts.

We created about two full weeks of ghost sightings and were having a good ol' time with it until we ran into some stiff opposition. A guy over on Cox Avenue decided to prove to his wife once and for all that these were not ghosts, but little humans and nothing more. When we got into his garden he was waiting, hiding behind a couple of garbage cans. He popped up, armed with a "Daisy Red Rider" BB gun (I caught a glimpse of it when I saw him jump up; I had one and knew exactly what we were up against.) Man, could that guy cock that thing fast! And shoot? Dead on! Those bb's felt like bees stinging us. The worst thing was we couldn't help "yelping" when we got hit and everybody knows... ghosts don't make noises like that! It was a terrible night for us but believe it or not, the worst was yet to come.

For the next week or so we didn't pull any capers but the season for most of the good stuff was going fast. We had to make one more run. This time we were going for the "cream." I had heard that up on Mariaville Road there was a mini-farm with every kind of vegetable you could imagine. We checked it out for dogs and geese earlier with the field glasses and were convinced he didn't have any. I think geese are meaner than dogs and I don't know what they like to eat. A couple of hot dogs worked to get you enough time to run away from a dog, but geese... they just wanted to bite you. Anyway, this guy was far enough out that he hadn't heard about us or the ghosts, so we figured we were home free. Me and Tom snuck out about midnight and rode our

Illustration by Bill Carney

bikes till we got close to the farm, then hid them in the bushes and walked in the woods the rest of the way. We had our sacks over our shoulders, ready to get our bounty. It was really dark and the mosquitoes were brutal. That didn't matter; it was going to be so worth it. We had trouble finding it in the dark at first but finally we could smell the veggies. We started crawling in and then it nailed me! An electric fence! The kind they use for cows. Wow, did that hurt! Tom was already inside the garden and never got hit. I said "Watch out Tom, electric fence!" He tried to get out but he got nailed. He kept trying to get out but couldn't find the way he got in and kept running into it. I backed away in the bushes and kept hearing Tom getting hit by that damned fence, until finally he found a place to crawl under it. This wasn't fair! How are hard working garden raiders supposed to operate like this? That night we went home empty hearted and empty handed. We had had enough. It was time to move on, but to what? To where? I needed time to think. The next morning I climbed into the tree and sat there. I thought about how much fun we had this summer and the things we had done. Clearly the gardens were done but I did not want to admit defeat. We were on top for a while. Now we got outsmarted by all these people. We need what my uncle called "Fresh Fire." We were always ahead because we were always thinking. What we did was always new — we caught everyone sleeping. Once they figured us out then things changed. We need something new!

ᔰ "DOWN-UPPANCE"

Some of the kids from down in the city were starting to hang out at the park. These guys were pretty tough and they were just looking for trouble. They had heard about our raiding gardens and the ghosts. I figured it was best to be friendly to them, and I would let them have some fun too. I gave them maps of the gardens to raid and, just because they were very special friends, my secret map of the best gardens of all. These included Mr. Ryder's on Cox Ave. and all the ones in Colonial Manor (Happensburg always said respect was to be earned.)

One of the kids from the city who was usually trouble for everybody was "Mousie" Mastrianni. He was a real wise guy and loved to intimidate other kids. He had this thing that he was known for where he played "chicken" with his bike. Mousie would ride right at you and just before he got to you, he'd "veer" away at the last second. This would scare the hell out of most of the kids. Some kids didn't know what to do and jumped off their bikes. Well, as luck would have it, here was Mousie coming down the street and guess who was coming in the opposite direction? None other than Terrible Tom Taylor! Mousie crouched down in his attack position and started for him. Tom just kept on coming, never breaking his stride. Closer and closer they came. Then at the very last second Mousie veered! Then Tom veered! Right at Mousie! They hit head on! Both bikes went straight up in the air! When the dust cleared, both Mousie and Tom crawled out from a pile of twisted wheels and handlebars. Mousie, holding his ribs, fell to his knees, moaning. Then a few feet away we saw Tom, bleeding from his lip and holding his arm. The strange thing was Tom was laughing! Mousie saw him laughing and as soon as he could catch his breath, blurted out… "Are you nuts?" Tom, trying to stop laughing said… "Hey… you like to play chicken. I like crashin'! We both had fun today!"

We never saw Mousie in Rotterdam again after that. Once again, "Adventure handled with intelligence" How about…"If you don't use your head, your whole body suffers."

Three weeks had gone by and we started hearing horror stories about kids getting caught raiding gardens in the Manor. It seems that a Mr. Velcastro and his workers caught some kids in his garden. Nobody would say exactly what happened but we heard they were taken into his garage and he explained in detail what would happen if they were ever to be in his garden again. The thing that got to me was that my "water balloon in the pocket trick" was becoming so popular.

There was something about the Garden Ghosts that I couldn't quite let go of. Maybe it was that the thing sort of took on a life of its own. We would get the thing going and then people would help it along. We'd pull a caper on one side of town and three people on the other side of town would swear they had seen ghosts too. I think people just want to be involved in things or maybe they want to be noticed or something. I'll have to ask Happensburg for his thoughts on this matter. I knew one thing for sure; I really liked things that, once started, ran by themselves for a while. I knew that something was right at my fingertips, something big. I just needed to think about it.

For now anyway, I had more important work to do.

Chapter 2:

FINDING MY NICHE

I had been practicing my freehand lettering on just about anything that paint would stick to. The door on the clubhouse, the walls inside, everything that I thought needed some lettering. My dad showed me a few tricks and I was doing pretty well, though most of the stuff I had been doing wasn't all that important. That was about to change. I was about to create my first real job. This would be the first lettering job for customers.

I had five sets of roller skates to letter for buddies. On the side of the heel of the right skate, I was to put the kid's favorite stock car racer's number. Mine included. I was getting the yellow #3 Pete Corey. Tom wanted #75 Erv Taylor and Lewie, #24 Kenny Shoemaker. Jeff wanted #37 Jeep Herbert and Gary, #5 Dutch Reed. How cool it would be to have our favorite car number on our skates. I had been practicing with a brush and paints, getting the exact style and colors of the lettered numbers so they would be just like the ones on the car. It took me a while but they came out pretty good and we all showed up at the roller rink Saturday night, ready to race around and show off our skates. What a hit it turned out to be. We raced around the rink pretending we were the drivers. We had heat races and a main event. Jeff crashed and wrecked his numbers up a little but even that was cool. I left there that night with three more sets of skates to paint. Two sets for numbers and one for a name to be in script with shadowing on it, and a repair job on Jeff's skates.

Both my dad and Mr. Happensburg got the biggest kick out of my lettering stuff. My dad told me that as soon as I reached a certain level of skill he'd show me how to do "gold leaf" with real gold. When I told Happensburg about all of this, he quickly mentioned he needed initials on his leather briefcase.

It seemed like the week flew by and there we were, walking into the rink again and I had all the kid's skates done and ready as promised. They were waiting at the door when we got there. I can remember how good it felt to have done those skates for those guys. They were flippin' out over the lettering, especially the kid that had his name in light gray script with a maroon shadow around it. His dad came up to me and said he was nervous about his son giving his skates to some kid to letter them, but that his son had assured him this isn't just some kid, it was Davie Davies, who had a reputation for this stuff. He shook my hand and said "You did a fine job, son."

Wow! I was flying' high. That felt so good. Kids were hanging out with us and telling me how nice the lettering was; I hadn't ever felt anything quite like it. The owner of the rink came over and introduced me to a professional dance skater. He suggested that the guy have me do a set of initials on his skates. He stood there thinking about it but didn't say anything. So I said… "It's funny you mention initials, I got a set of initials to do on a briefcase for this business executive in 'Gold Leaf,' and because I'll have the gold out and all, maybe I can fix you up." Hearing that, he wrote his initials on a card, put the most expensive set of skates I had ever seen in his case, and handed them over to me.

✺ YOU CAN'T MIX BOOZE WITH GOLD

I figured it this way: either I was going to reach the gold level this week or I'd just get my dad to do it as an example to show me how it was done. No worries. I left that night with his skates and two more sets for lettering and numbers.

It turned out to be a very nerve wracking week. The days flew by and my dad got home late every night. I hadn't even had a chance to mention the job to him until Friday night.

There we were at the kitchen table with gold leaf, paint, brushes, beer bottles, and a very expensive pair of roller skates. Now, my dad explained, you must let the sizing (a varnish like material) dry to a perfect "tack" before you can lay the gold. If you go too soon, the sizing melts into the gold and you have no shine. If you wait too long, the gold doesn't stick and it looks terrible. I managed to letter the sizing on just fine. Now I asked my dad, "How do you know when it's ready?"

He explained…when it is "just dry," but not too dry. If you touch it with your finger it seems dry yet you'll feel a slight tick as you pull away. That's the right time.

"Well, how long will that be?" I asked.

"It could be forty minutes or four hours. It will depend on moisture, temperature, lots of things.

I had the other skates done, so we sat there watching paint (or in this case sizing) dry. Forty minutes went by. My dad touched the sizing, shook his head.

"No."

He had a couple more beers (actually many more beers) then one hour and twenty minutes went by. He touched it again.

"No, this is stubborn sizing; it's got oil in it we just have to wait."

More waiting, (more beers.) I asked "Can we heat it with something or put them by the electric heater?

"No!" he said loudly. "You never rush sizing! You'll ruin it!"

Finally, at about two and a half hours my dad nods off. Snoring away, he's out like a light. Now what do I do?

Dad? Dad? I can't wake him. Mom, can you wake dad? She tries but no luck. She says something. "What Mom? He's what? Coma-toast?" Oh boy, what now? I touch the sizing. My finger sticks to it. "No" not yet. We wait (did I say we?) Every ten minutes I touch it. "No" not yet; then another half hour passes. I'm really nervous, if this fails what do I tell the guy? I don't even know him. The owner recommended me. I thought about what my dad said. "It must be dry but your finger feels a very slight "tick" when you pull away." I reach over and touched the sizing... dry! I could rub my finger across it, but as I pulled away I felt the slight "tick." She's ready. I carefully pulled the leaf of gold from the book and laid it on the lettering, carefully rubbing the back of it, pushing it into the letters. Now take the soft piece of velvet and use it to remove the excess gold (the gold will only stick where there is sizing) and finally burnish it to a high gloss. Yes! I got it. Perfection! The technique was mine — I owned it (and I earned it.) The gold sparkled on the black skates. I then added a burgundy shadow to each of the letters. They quickly became three dimensional.

My mom, clearing the beer bottles from the table said, "I have never in my life heard of anyone putting gold leaf on a pair of roller skates."

I thought for a moment. Wow, these could be the only pair of skates with gold leaf initials in the entire world!

I went to bed that night but couldn't sleep. My mind kept going over the events that took place in the last few weeks. How Mr. Happensburg had pushed me and my dad together so that I might keep developing this craft. He had told me that there was an embryo there of something very good. He was all about "Good." I thought how wonderful it felt to be recognized and praised for what I had done. I was amazed how many adults were commenting on the work.

In school I always felt so low, but outside was a different world, where I felt strong, important, valuable, and in control. I owed Happensburg much. When I get home I'll get his briefcase and "size up" the initials. I couldn't wait for my finger to feel that little "tick" and I could lay down the gold. The lettering was becoming an important part of my life. Every day in school I'd be sketching out a layout for a set of numbers or a name for someone. I remember one day in social studies class I was sketching something, when Joe Johnson passed his notebook over to me. He said "Dave, give me a fancy '32' on that, would ya?" That was his dad "Rollie" Johnson's race car number. Without hesitating, I started a script "Johnson's" and under that a "32" with full shadowing and an outline. Before the bell rang at the end of the period I handed it back completed. (Little did I know where that was going to take me) That little name and number on that notebook would open up a whole new world for me. In the meantime, the parents of the kids I had done skates for were getting lettering done. I was lettering bowling bags, and golf bags, and even a steamer trunk for a kid's older brother who was going off to college. I was putting names on bicycles, and lettering number plates for motorcycle racers, registration numbers on boats and signs for people's camps. To the delight of my dad and Mr. Happensburg, the clubhouse was turning into a little sign shop.

UFO'S

Tom came over Saturday and we sat around figuring the whole thing out. We decided we would still all go fishing as much as we could but we'd let everything else go. No more capers? We sat quietly for a little while and then I said ...

"You know Tom; these neighbors have been brutal to my family, with my dad's drinking and all. They smile at me in the store then as I walk away I hear stuff come out of them that really gets to me. "That's the Davies kid. His dad's always drunk, falls in people's hedges, awful, awful, just awful I

A show card sign for a local band "The Fabulous Chessmen."
Freehand lettering by the author age 13.

tell you." Tom, nothing would do me better than to teach them a lesson. When we had the ghosts going on we had their heads spinning. They were seeing ghosts when they weren't even there. They were scaring themselves with their own fears. That's what we need, another ghost deal but not ghosts this time. Give me a little time to come up with something that will scare the hell out of them."

Tom smiled. "I know for sure you'll come up with something. Let me know what, when, and where. Talk to ya later."

I couldn't help thinking how happy it made Happensburg to see me doing (as he put it) **"more constructive things"** with my life, and that he was pleased that I was **"leaving childish things behind."** But in my mind I had one more mission. A mission that needed to be done and it would be no childish thing. Oh, I was ready to move on alright, but how nice it would be if I could come up with something that they would remember for some time long after I had left this stuff behind? Wouldn't that be great? It would be what my mother once referred to in a play as the "coup de grace." She said it meant the "final stroke," the finishing touch.

It seemed as though I was approaching a fork in the road. I was being forced to make choices I had never had to make before. One day on the way home from school while going by the park, I saw some kids flying kites. For some reason the image of the kites flying in the air stuck in my mind. Later, on TV, there was a news flash on something going on having to do with UFO's and aliens from outer space. For the next few days everywhere I went it seemed like that's all everyone was talking about; aliens, UFO's, and flying saucers. The TV reports went on for about a week and one morning, one of my neighbors said the magic words as I walked by her house on the way to school. I heard her tell another neighbor that she thought for sure she had seen a flying saucer in the sky the night before.

There it was. The break I had been waiting for! So she thinks she saw a flying saucer? OK, I'll give them flying saucers! This is better than ghosts. This will be the coup de whatever! "The final stroke."

Now how to put this together… That day in school I tried to figure how I could launch something into the night sky that would scare the hell out of those idiots. Bottle rockets? No, too familiar. What could I launch into the sky? How about a kite painted like a flying saucer! No, that would look fake. I sat in school drawing saucers and kites and aliens. As I drew the kite I added three flying saucers to the tail. There it was! We could take a kite, spray it flat black and then, instead of rags for a tail, take some fishing line and run it out fifteen feet or so behind the kite. Attach a large ball of aluminum foil with a flat rim around it, then after a few feet, another one, etc. On just the right night the flat black kite against a dark sky, the saucers would appear to fly alone, we might be able to pull this off.

⮑ ENGINEERING

They had been throwing out leftover foil and large aluminum cake plates over at the bakery; we could get everything we needed from over there. After we got everything together, we'd pick a night with heavy clouds and no stars out and launch the kite over the neighborhood. The flat black kite would be far away from the saucers and hopefully go unnoticed. Anyone looking nervously to the sky would see the saucers flying around up there and it would set the stage for all the wacky kooks to start "kookin' out."

Right after school Tom and I got a kite and quickly painted it black. Then we got a bunch of foil and started making the saucers. After dark, we'd go in the field behind the Democratic Club and see if she'd fly. Under the cover of darkness we brought the whole rig over to the field and got ready to launch it. Tom ran with the kite several times but it couldn't lift the saucers up. Our first attempt was a failure. We needed a much larger kite. So it was back to the clubhouse. Over the next couple of days we gathered up some pieces of balsa wood and light pine. We used wide paper from a roll of banner paper my dad had, and by using the original kite for a pattern, duplicated the kite in a much larger scale, painted it flat black, and then out into the night for a second try. This kite was really hard to get to fly. We couldn't run fast enough to get it to stay up. It would start to come up but when we stopped, it went back down. Tom even tried riding his bike and pulling it up but no go. We would need a night with forty mile an hour winds to lift this baby up. I was beginning to think this was a stupid idea. Back to the clubhouse. That night I lay in bed thinking how I could get that kite up. I thought maybe I could call "Scooter John" and have him tow it up with his scooter, but that would cause way too much attention.

Besides "Scooter" was probably still mad at me for the time I had him bring that big snapping turtle home that we caught at the reservoir. We tied it to the seat behind him and we thought it would be alright. How were we to know it would bite him in the ass while he was riding down the road?

Illustration by Bill Carney

Anyway, we needed to catch some wind somehow. Happensburg told me *"the true inventor is a problem solver."* I said to myself "come on… you can figure this out. We have to solve this problem. It's 'lift,' we need lift. We— need—lift." I dozed off to sleep.

On the way home from school the next day I ran into Debbie. We walked along together and she asked me if I had thought about letting girls into the club yet. I told her that it was funny she asked because I had been thinking about letting maybe just one girl in, to see how it worked out, and that Tom and me had a big project we were working on and that it was taking all our time and energy right now.

Then I asked her if she could get out any nights. She said, "Maybe, if I stayed at my cousin's house I could get out, she don't care."

"Well, the reason I'm asking is that if you were willing to do a little scouting work with me some nights, I may be able to get you past the tests to get in. You've heard about the tests, haven't you?"

"Yes" she said "I heard about the tests, but are they for girls, too?"

"Sure, they're for anybody getting in the club but like I say, if you could help me at night once in a while, I would waive the running test, the haunted house test and you wouldn't have to climb that dammed water tower. And because you will be doing night work with me, I will make you a secret member, just so there's no jealousy with other girls wanting to get in. How about that ?"

"Thanks Davie, I really appreciate it."

"I'll see you later Debbie." (I thought to myself … her having to climb the water tower? I think I might have been laying it on a little thick.)

Then it came to me… THE WATER TOWER! That's it! We could launch the kite from the water tower! The wind is always blowing up there!

What was about to take place over the next couple of weeks was to be nothing short of amazing. It would involve not just imagination and ideas but engineering and coordination, choreography, and some very serious skills. We were barely teenagers and had already experienced more than some people though their adult lives. We had taken notions turned them into thoughts, then into ideas and used them to our benefit. We had overcome fears, learned skills, manipulated people and circumstances (not to mention dealing with the ramifications of alcohol), creating our own world and functioning within it. We had been stung by bees, shot with bb guns, electrified by cow fences, and chased by humans, dogs, geese, and even a bull. Yet we survived and became stronger. When an enemy would threaten us, either Tom would give them a beating or I would create a hell for them that, in comparison, a beating would have been the far better choice. We were actually quite dangerous armed with intelligence, courage, and creativity. We were cunning and careful in doing everything right, (while doing the wrong things.)

I had to run the whole water tower thing through my mind first. Then sort out all problems and solve them one by one to get the results we needed. This took time and concentration. I knew there wasn't enough room inside the girded ladder to haul the kite up. Tom will have to climb up carrying just the twine. Then put a set of keys or something on the twine and unroll it down so I can hook up the kite. Then he could haul it up from over the rail and, once it gets halfway up, it'll catch some wind and off she'll go, directly over our neighborhood! The wind has to be from the west. I quickly visualized the whole thing happening. It seemed simple enough. As soon as I could find him I told Tom I had the answer to our problem. When we got together we went over everything like a general would before a battle. We got everything ready and waited for a cloudy night. A week or so went by and I had been so busy lettering things that I hadn't thought about the kite at all. The phone rang and it was Tom.

"It's pretty cloudy out there tonight, Dave. No moon or stars showing. What do you think? Why not give it a try; come on, this is the last big one and the night is perfect for it."

Tom loved the capers and we had so much fun, his boring job at the market didn't do anything for him. It was different for me, my lettering things was a lot of fun and providing plenty of excitement.

I thought for a moment … I owe this to him and what about the idiots in the neighborhood? I ran outside. The wind was from the west. "Let's do it!"

We met at the shed and began getting everything together for the trip over to the tower. Tom would handle the kite and all the string. Just before we were about to leave we heard a gentle knock on the door of the shed. It startled both of us.

❧ DEBBIE SHOWS HER STUFF

When I went to the door I was surprised to see it was Debbie. She began…

"Hi, I just stopped by to see if you might need me for anything tonight. My mom and dad are out of town and I'm staying with my cousin all weekend. She has her boyfriend over, so she said I could stay out till midnight if I wanted to."

Surprised, I told her… "Debbie, Tom and I are involved in a very important thing right now so maybe this would not be the best time." Then she interrupted me saying…

"I understand, but do you need help with anything? I really don't have any place to go tonight. I can follow orders and I can keep secrets. You told me how important that is. Please Davie, I promise I'll do whatever you need me to do. I'll keep quiet and I'll help with whatever you need. Please Davie, give me a chance."

I asked her to wait outside for just a minute while Tom and I have a talk. Then I told Tom how she wanted to be in the club and I sort of told her she could do some night stuff with me and kind of be a secret member and all, but I didn't expect her to show up tonight of all nights. He asked if I thought she could be quiet about what we were doing, and if I thought she could, and then let her come along. We might need some help. I was ok with her but I was amazed that Tom was so good about it. OK, then we'll bring her along.

I called her in and we took a few minutes to explain everything that was going on. I also told her this was a top secret mission and even the other members didn't know about this. So, if we hear anyone saying anything about this we'll know right away that it was her who told someone and there would be serious consequences.

As we headed for the tower Debbie came up with an idea.

She said… "Tom is going up on the tower and we'll be on the ground right? Then how can he tell us if he needs us to do something? Listen, my dad has a very expensive set of walkie-talkies that he uses for hunting. No one is home; I'm going to go get them." She took off running.

Walkie-talkies! What an idea Tom, that'll make things easier. Hey, she's already working out better than I expected.

Debbie returned in about twenty minutes with the walkie- talkies. She also brought a huge deep sea-type fishing reel loaded with line. She said her dad had used it before for flying kites; it made it easier to release line and reel it in, rather than trying to roll up all that twine on a stick. She continued…"That kite will pull hard way up there Tom; you had better clamp the reel to the rail." (She also brought a couple of c-clamps and rope.)

Wow, having her along was looking better and better. Tom put the reel, the clamps, and the one walkie-talkie in his satchel, then threw the strap over his shoulder. We grabbed the ladder that we always kept in the woods next to the tower and used it to climb up to the steel girded ladder attached to the tower. I held the bottom of the fence up while we slid our ladder under the fence. Then Tom went under. Debbie held the fence while I went under with the kite and the flying saucers. Once inside the fenced area, Tom would put our ladder up, climb up to the tower ladder, and then climb that ladder all the way to the top. Once he reached the top he would release the line with a heavy fish line sinker on it for weight, to get it down to me. I would hook up the kite and then he would haul it up. Hopefully, part way up it would catch the wind and launch out into the open sky. We waited patiently for Tom to climb to the top, talking back and forth on the walkie-talkies. It took a while; he had to rest a few times on the way up. That is a scary climb. The wind was from the west and would put our saucers right over the depot and in clear view for anyone in the neighborhood.

After what seemed like a very long time, Tom was up to the top. He lowered the line down to us and we hooked up the kite. I held the saucers away from the metal rigging under the tower as long as I could, hoping they wouldn't get tangled on the way up. It wanted to go under the tower, where it was sure to get tangled. Tom kept pulling up and finally, about one third of the way up it started to catch the wind and pulled out away from all the rigging in the tower. Now it was going out as it went up, the three saucers hanging straight down. About the halfway mark it started to really fly. The saucers came up and they were catching enough wind now to carry it up. What a sight! Tom's voice over the walkie-talkie came…"I'm releasing line. She's flyin' Dave!" I returned with… "Let her go Tom, let it out!" Tom told us to hang on a minute while he clamped the reel to the rail. Now securely in place, he let more and more line out until those saucers were really up there. You couldn't see the kite at all. The line was almost all the way out so he locked the drag on the reel. The saucers looked like they were miles out in the sky and we could see them clearly, but they looked fake because they were wiggling back and forth as though they were on a flag pole. Then sometimes they would spin from the wind. They looked anything but real. I thought "how could we have a failure at this level — all this planning and work for no good." I told Tom what we saw. He reeled it in toward the tower and began toying around reeling it in and then releasing it. We noticed that when he reeled it in, it would wiggle and spin, but when he released it for a moment it would free-fall and, for just those few seconds, it looked real. The three saucers would follow each other across the sky just like they were supposed to. Then I decided we had one shot here. Maybe, if everyone were looking up at just the right time, Tom could cut the line and the saucers would free fall across the sky, and as they fell, (being they are so high up) would give the appearance that they were flying away. They would fall into the depot and we had a place in the fence to get in and retrieve the evidence.

Now, how can we get people to look up in the sky at the right time? And how about old lady Willis, the town mouth and her kookie friends? Debbie quickly asks… "Where does Willis live?" I told her the location of her house, about half way up the street. Then Debbie did something that was totally unbelievable. She said "You watch me from the end of the street. Tell Tom to get ready to cut the line, I'll take care of the rest." I asked, "What are you going to do?" "I'm going to get people to look in the sky, you tell Tom to get ready."

Illustration by Bill Carney

She ran over to the street where Willis lived, stopping directly in front of her house. Then she started looking toward the sky. She just stood there in the middle of the street looking into the sky. A man came out on his porch and asked if she was alright. She said, "I saw something in the sky that frightened me." He came down off of his porch and stood in the road with her. "What was it and where did you see it? I don't see anything." She said "I saw it above those trees. It was three shiny things in the sky following each other." They both stood there, then a neighbor came out, then another. Now four people stood in the road looking up and she repeated over and over what she saw. Then old lady Willis came out from her house and down into the road. Quickly, I called over the walkie-talkie… "Get ready Tom!"

They're all there looking up and right after Debbie points to the sky, I'll tell Tom to get ready to cut the line.

Debbie yells out "There they are! They came back!" Then Debbie starts screaming! I immediately tell Tom to "cut the line!"

The three saucers shoot across the sky and disappear off in the distance behind the trees by the warehouses in the depot. They looked like they went miles away in the sky. Debbie turned and ran down the street. Everybody was buzzing. They all saw it. No one could deny it; they had seen a U F O (Unidentified… Flying… Object!) And that's exactly what they saw. There were no Martians and it wasn't from Mars, but it was *unidentified* and it was an *object* and it was *flying*. We waited for Tom to get down from the tower and then went into the depot to find the saucers. They were in a tree toward the back end of the depot. We retrieved all the evidence. We busted up the kite, crunched up the foil saucers, and wound up all the line. We put all the stuff in separate garbage barrels behind a warehouse and headed back to the shed.

✎ FULL OF IT

What a night it was, and Debbie, wow what a girl. She had brains and talent and ideas. She was amazing. We could never have pulled that off without her. I had misread her. I just wanted to impress her and show her a good time. She showed us a good time. This was the first time a girl had ever been involved in any of our capers and she really helped us. That night it was after midnight when I walked her to her cousin's house. We talked all the way. When we got there I asked her if she wanted me to explain to her cousin that we were watching a movie and lost track of time or whatever. She said no, she would handle it. Then she told me that tonight was the most fun of all. She said she loved adventure and somehow she knew I was full of it.

She continued… "You are full of it Davie, but that's what I like about you."

I told her that I would call her the next night because Tom and I were going fishing in the morning. It's the only day he has off.

She asked "Where do you guys fish around here?"

"Well mostly the reservoir, out toward Altamont and sometimes Frenchie's Hollow, the backwater of the reservoir."

"Oh, yea I know where that is. What do you catch?"

"Mostly sunnies but sometimes a bass or two."

What, Deb likes fishin'?

"Sure do! Go with my dad all the time. What do you and Tom use for bait?"

"Worms mostly but sometimes a spinner" and,

(She interrupts)…"No, no, you want bass? Then what you need out there is… ah…umm… never mind. If you bring me sometime I'll tell ya! In fact I'll show you how to catch more bass than you ever caught. Well, you just think about that Davie and give me a call when you can. Goodnight."

She leaned over and gave me a kiss on the cheek, then disappeared through the doorway.

Wow, all the way home I kept thinking I've been outflanked, outfoxed, outtalked, outsmarted, and the craziest thing was, I wanted more of it! Debbie… What a girl! What a night!

"Oh Davie, give me a chance, please Davie, please."

I've been hoodwinked! Why that little… She took advantage of me. But she's so cool. We're going fishing too, bet your boots we are, but not with the guys, oh no, she'll out-fish me too probably, so if I 'm going to be a fool we'll be alone when it happens. I can't wait. What, to be a fool? What's happening to me? What the hell am I saying? Debbie, Debbie, Debbie, Debbie, Debbie, Debbie, Debbie…

The next day Mr. "Hap" stopped over. He asked if I would come over to his place, he wanted to chat with me about something. He seemed very serious. I finished what I was doing and practically followed him home. As I approached his house he opened the door to his porch, invited me in, and asked me to sit down at this small table there on the porch. He went into the house and a moment later he returned with several books and he put four of them over on a shelf nearby. Then he sat down at the other side of the table.

He began… "David, you seem so calm. Don't you realize we are being invaded by aliens from outer space? Why my goodness, there have been sightings of flying saucers. I don't understand why you are not frightened out of your wits like the rest of the folks in the neighborhood."

(I sat there with my head down trying to figure a way out of this.)

"Wait, maybe you don't know anything about this. You've been so busy, you probably haven't heard a word about any aliens or saucers or ghosts. How about kites? Heard anything about kites?"

Ah…kites? Let me think…

He quickly interrupted. "Never mind! You're going to try to defend yourself? You're unarmed, son."

He sat in the chair across from me. He was silent, his head back looking at the ceiling, trying to calm down. A few moments pass, then…

"Do you remember when we first met?"

I thought for a moment, "Yes, it was at the grocery store. You were carrying bags of groceries and having a tough time. I helped you with them. It was four years ago, right?"

"Yes David, that's right, it was four years ago and you were with several other kids in the parking lot. Outside the store I realized that I had walked over there and the three bags were going to be a problem. They were heavy and just too much for me to carry all the way home. I was just about to go back in and leave them there and come back with the car, when you came over and offered to help. I know it seemed like no 'big thing' as you said, but it was a big thing to me. Not just the carrying of a couple of bags a few blocks but the whole picture. Especially looking back and the friendship that developed from that day until now. Let me give you my view of what transpired…"

"Here I was with a problem and there were at least six maybe eight kids in that parking lot. Now let's be realistic, I am an ugly decrepit old man, and here I am having a problem. Most kids don't even look at me. Yet one kid with a great big smile on his face came over and offered to help. You impressed me that moment David, and have continued to impress me ever since. I have gotten to know you quite well over the years and watching you has brought joy to my life. I made up my mind back then that I would help you as much as I could, as long as you would listen. If you were to stop listening then I would stop talking. You have never stopped listening to me, so here we are."

❧ THE LEMONADE STAND

"Do you remember the lemonade stand?"

"Yes! The lemonade stand! Wow, how could I ever forget the lemonade stand?" (He started to smile) I immediately started telling how much the lemonade stand meant to me and how much I had learned. He put his head back, relaxed in the chair, closed his eyes, and asked me to tell him in detail what had taken place with the lemonade stand.

I saw him relaxing, so I began recalling how I was complaining to him that I was too young to have a paper route, not old enough to work any place, and wanted a job and didn't know what to do.

"Then you told me I should go into business. I remember laughing because I thought you were joking with me" (He started to smile.) "Actually, I thought you were nuts!" (That got a chuckle — he was enjoying this and he looked more relaxed, so I kept on going, trying not to leave out any details.) "Then you told me that there is no age limit for a person or kid to make money in a business. Then you kept dropping hints left and right until the spectacular idea of a 'lemonade stand' came up. You agreed to help me design and build it. I also remember you had me make drawings with measurements and a material list. You suggested putting wheels and a hitch to attach it to my bike (which I didn't think was necessary), but turned out to be a great idea. Building it was fun. I remember my dad laying out the lettering 'Lemonade' and letting me fill in the letters with his sign brushes. I remember you got a kick out of that. Then came the business part, that wasn't fun. By the way… did you know what was going to happen to me at the corner store?" (Mr. Hap was smiling from ear to ear.)

"I can't remember that part David, you'll have to refresh me. Go ahead tell me what happened at the store."

"Alright, you told me that you had, let's see, what words you used… Oh, you had "exhausted all of your finances" in materials and hardware building the thing, and that now we were going to need product. We made a list for that, too. I told you that I would get the money from my dad. You said that was not a good idea because I didn't need a partner and it wasn't necessary to bring in outside financing when maybe the people at the corner store would be willing to float me for a week or so. That would be a much simpler deal. Then, if I can remember exactly, you instructed me to hook up the stand to my bike and bring it to the store, then show the guy at the store that we had a stand all ready to go and just needed product to sell, if he could let me charge the stuff for a week, till I could pay him. So I did exactly what you told me to do, but it didn't go too good. I introduced myself and asked him if I could show him something. He stuck his head out of the door, looked at the stand but didn't say anything, then asked me what I wanted. I told him I had a list of stuff but I explained that I couldn't pay him for a week, and before I could say anything more he told me to get out. He called me a wise guy and some other names. You must remember that Mr. Hap, I was really upset." (He still has his head back, his eyes closed and continues to smile,) then…

"Yes, now that you mentioned that, it seems to me I remember that part. You wanted to quit and forget about the whole thing. What happened next?"

"Well, come on Mr. Hap, you know what happened. You gave me one of your pep talks about how businessmen have set backs from time to time, but they don't give up at the first little bump in the road. I remember thinking you were nuts again and that if this was a little bump in the road, then what does a businessman have to go through? I thought, well now I'll ask my dad for the money and it'll be alright. What you said next, I didn't want to hear, in fact at first I pretended not to hear you at all."

He interrupts. "I remember that! It's all coming back now, go ahead, continue."

"Well, like I said, I couldn't believe it but you wanted me to go to another store and you made me rehearse the whole thing all over again."

He interrupts again. "What made you stick it out David? Why did you continue?"

"I don't know. I think maybe because we had so much into the stand. Our time and all the wood and everything. You were taking the time to do something for me — I guess I thought I could handle another bump. But this time was different; you knew the people and you told me that I could say that you sent me. With that I knew I wouldn't feel like some jerk coming in off of the street. By the way, you didn't answer my question; did you know what would happen to me at the first store?"

He answers, "Are you asking me if I 'set you up'?"

"Yes, that's what I'm asking," (he continues with a chuckle in his voice)

"Now David, how could one predict such an outcome? Why, I thought for sure once he'd seen that beautiful, handcrafted mobile stand with the hand lettering on it, all hitched up to your bike, I would have thought he would have given you the store. Obviously the man was a fool. Now, with the new store, did my recommendation manage to smooth out a few bumps? Please continue."

"Yes, this was a lot different, the people were very nice. I pulled up in front, just like the other store and went in. I introduced myself, told him you had sent me and told him I would like to show him something. His name was Mr. Cohen. He came right outside. I told him you and I had built it and that I had done the lettering. I didn't tell him my dad laid out the letters for me. Then he went to the door and called out to his wife. I remember him calling 'Deirdre, (dee-dra) come and see this.' She came out and they walked around the stand, looking at every part. Then Mr. Cohen said 'Dee, is this not the nicest lemonade stand you have ever seen?' She answered… 'Indeed it is! Young man, you must be proud of that!'"

"Yes. Mr. Happensburg and I built it together."

"Mr. Cohen then said 'Ah yes, Happensburg, the genius.'"

Hearing that Mr. Hap sat right up in the chair and said…"Did Cohen really say that? Or are you kidding?"

"That's exactly what he said!"

"Why didn't you tell me that before?"

"I probably did tell you. Aren't you having problems remembering all this? Isn't this why you are having me go over this whole thing?" He settled back into his chair and continued to smile.

I continued, "Then Mr. Cohen went on to say, 'You must be quite a fellow yourself, to be an associate of such a learned scholar as Happensburg.' Then he asked about the lettering. I told him my dad laid out all the letters first for me, then he let me use his brushes to fill them in. Mrs. Cohen said, 'You are very gifted to be able to follow the layout as you did. Nice job!'"

"I thanked them for everything that they said and almost forgot why I went there. Then Mr. Cohen asked 'What can we do for you, son?'

Oh, yes, well we need stuff, I mean 'product' for the stand. Lemonade mix, sugar, cups (I pulled out the list) right here, this is the list. Mrs. Cohen reached over and took it from my hand. Quickly I said, 'Wait! I have to explain. You see we have excused, I mean exhausted all of our financials... ah, we have... a... we don't have any money to pay for the stuff right now but if you could let me pay you next week?

"I really messed up what I was supposed to say. I remember Mrs. Cohen holding back a laugh and saying she would start gathering stuff together, so I figured we were ok. Mr. Cohen then said that if I was an associate of Happensburg, he would certainly set something up for me. I remember Mrs. Cohen telling me she did not want me selling a lemonade 'mix' from such a masterpiece, as she put real lemons in the bag and handing me a metal squeezer. Her own. She told me it was on loan and that I must promise never to let it out of my sight. Then Mr. Cohen had me sign a paper with all the stuff listed and he said he'd give me a couple of weeks to pay. He also said that he appreciated my allowing him to do business with me. I thought that was cool."

"Well, Mr. Hap, how am I doing? Can you recall all the rest of our business adventure? Or are you going to make me go through that whole deal? I think I know what this is all about. You love hearing about all the times you've come to my rescue. All those times you've bailed me out. That's it!"

"Now David, I have never come to your rescue, nor have I ever bailed you out. I have merely given you some advice from time to time, which I assume you had used wisely! Now you understand that I'm getting old and sometimes I need to have some help recalling things. Now, why don't you continue; I can vaguely remember the lemonade stand venture having a few 'twists?' So now you go ahead, I'll try to remember."

Happensburg had no problem remembering anything; he was sharp as a tack.

I still didn't know what he was up to so I continued, reminding him how I sat there day after day with the lemonade stand with little or no business, deeply in debt. Wondering what I would tell the Cohen's, those nice people who helped me and trusted me. I kept thinking how Mr. Cohen told me he appreciated me doing business with him. What business? A week had gone by and I had taken in $1.25, 25 cents of which I'd used for a bag of chips. So I had one dollar in the drawer. "Then you stopped by. Do you remember stopping by?" He nodded yes. "You asked how things were going, but I think you could tell how things were going. Then the four-thirty whistle blew and you asked what that sound was. Once again I thought you were nuts, because everybody knew what the whistle was. Then do you remember what you said?"

"No, tell me, what did I say?"

"You said, 'Oh yes, the four-thirty whistle, that's right, everyone gets out of work at the depot and they head down to the bus stop. All those sweaty, thirsty people head for the bus stop. If a lemonade stand was to be set up down by the bus stop, it might do a little business.' Then you said what a great idea somebody had of putting wheels and a hitch on a stand, had to be very clever, whoever thought of that."

"I was about to learn something else. It was about Location. A very important lesson you taught me Mr. Hap. We went from no business, to running out of lemons, ice, and cups. I can remember going over and paying my bill at the Cohens' and getting more stuff and this time paying up front. I told Mr. Cohen I appreciated him helping me get started and I was going to return the favor by bringing him some serious business. Not only mine; I told my dad what the Cohen's had done for me and he started buying his beer there."

❧ WHERE DID HE GO WRONG?

"David, I think you could have gotten another season out of that lemonade venture but you wanted to move on. You didn't seem to be a 'retail' person, at least when compared to your artistic ability. I really see potential in that lettering. That could really be something. I'm trying to figure out where I went wrong with you. You were heading up the ladder and then somehow you started this vendetta against the neighborhood. I want to continue helping you but… I just can't keep loading a loose cannon. You come to me for advice, I give you advice, and then crazy things start happening. I feel responsible. I'm sure you have what you believe to be a valid reason for your resentment against the people in this neighborhood, but I personally want no part of it. People are just people. Some, I realize, are very shallow in their understanding of other people's problems. They take up a tiny little space in their tiny little world."

"Should you choose the correct path, you will have access to a much larger world, unbounded and limitless. Your world is already growing every day. I don't see you as a bully, so why would you pick on someone smaller and weaker than you? These people you dislike will never leave their little world, they'll never go where you will go, and they'll never see the things you'll see. The gossip, the things they say, it's just a form of entertainment and it's all they have. Where you are going there will be enemies more powerful than mere gossip and a few words thrown around. Talented people have to deal with other people's many forms of malicious envy and the difficult task of keeping a reputation intact. You must learn certain disciplines and be tougher on yourself than anyone would be on you. And by tough I don't mean being 'hard.' Many people think they're tough but what they really are is hard. Let me put it this way…you see David, leather is tough, glass is hard. Leather can take a beating, but one sharp object and glass is gone.

Regarding people, when you hear… "It's my way or the highway." That's not tough, that's just hard. When you hear…"I'm sorry, I was wrong," ' now that's tough.

There is a distinct difference between "superficial hardness" and an "inner strength.""

"In your world you will need to cultivate three traits. They are humility, compassion, and understanding. I ask that you search deep in your heart and retrieve them David, and I know they're there, because if they weren't there, we would never have met."

Chapter 3:

THE ULTIMATUM

"**Y**ou are going to have to make a decision regarding our friendship. I must know clearly where *you* stand, so I can determine where I stand. When a person has to make a decision, they need 'information' so that they can make a well 'informed' decision. Do you understand and does this make sense?"

"Yes. I understand."

"Alright David, let me get the information." Mr. Hap walked over to the shelf where he put the books he carried in earlier. He brought the books over to a table where the titles were just beyond my view. He then put two of the books on one side and two on the other.

"This is the information we can work from. You'll find the information in these books quite valuable. However there is supreme conflict regarding the information in each of the sets of books. You will have to choose only one set and basically disregard the other. The reason for this is, no matter what you may think, a person cannot serve two masters. Let me be clear that in this case the 'masters' would be only the thinking process, not the individuals outlined in the books. To serve a human master would constitute slavery, and that is not what I am talking about here, because you have the benefit of 'choice.' For example, how much progress did you make with your lettering during the time you were engineering your little outer space project? Are we on the same page David?"

"Yes Sir."

"OK, now if you choose to continue your vendetta toward the neighbors, and want to satisfy your hunger for revenge, then you will need to work from these two books. These men are experts in causing pain and suffering. They were very creative in the ways they went about their business and used power to their full advantage. They would frighten and intimidate people into conforming to their way of thinking. They controlled countries and the millions of people living in them."

"Now over here, the books on the other side of the table are reference and information of another kind. These people are also very creative. They represent a very different philosophy. They preferred working in a free society. They did not have the kind of power the other men had, but a different kind of power and a tremendous amount of influence over countries and the people in them as well. I'm sure you will recognize the authors in both sets of books so before I reveal them, what are your feelings so far?"

"Well, I understand the thing about two masters. I remember setting everything up for the kite caper and not having any time to get any lettering done. Then we had to wait for cloudy weather and I got back into lettering stuff, and then two weeks went by and Tom reminded me the weather was right for it. Then I had to drop everything and switch my thinking to get back into that."

"Good David, very good. I feel that you're getting it. Now, be honest with me. It must have felt pretty good when you pulled the kite 'caper' off. But, on the other hand, it also felt good when you delivered the skates. So, because these are at opposite poles, I have a couple of questions… Which felt better? And which holds within it a better and more promising future? You may think that is a loaded question but think for a moment how good it might feel to square up with not just the neighborhood, but how about a couple of those teachers in school. How about the teacher that has been trying to force you into a sports program? You told me he even pressured you, trying to get you to, as you said… 'Bounce a ball and put it in a basket.' (Join the basketball team) With the kind of magic you've been handling, you could bounce him into a basket. How would that feel?"

"Of course, if you go the other route employing your artistic ability, I can see you moving up to sign and vehicle lettering and probably making more money in a few hours than kids your age make in a week, not to mention doing what you love. Many people make good money but few are lucky enough to make money doing what they love. Isn't that interesting… one thing involves Love the other involves Hate. Oh well, I guess that's the way it is."

"Anyway, remember that when you choose one you **must** give up the other. It is much like when two opposite weather fronts come together, where hot air meets cold air, things start spinning. It's called a tornado. In this case we're talking about experiencing a mental tornado. The spinning will be inside your head. We have discussed many things, most of which have been on the intellectual level. There is a spiritual component to this as well. I had plans to discuss that with you but right now I need to know where you are going first. For now you will just have to take my word for the fact that you must choose just one and completely give up the other. Now let me reveal the authors and give a brief outline of their accomplishments. Here we have a book on the life of Ben Franklin, an inventor among other things. I'm sure you have heard of him. Ironically he used a kite to prove something also. Then the other book is the life of Henry Ford, an industrialist. Now over here on the other side of the table we have a book on the life of Adolf Hitler, Chancellor of Germany. The other book is about the life of Josef Stalin, also a powerful leader. All of the men represented here were extremely creative and had a profound effect on the world as we know it. I think it is safe to say that at this point in your life, relatively speaking; you may have something in common with each of them. As I said, they were all very creative. Also, they were very good at organizing people and convincing them to do what 'they' (the men mentioned) wanted done. However, we are talking about different mentalities, all starting out with the best of intentions. All appeared (in the beginning) to have constructive objectives and goals. Hitler and Stalin were focused on and were seriously affected by 'political power.' Franklin was not so concerned about political power in and of itself, more so the scientific or mechanical. Ford was interested in political power but mainly using it to elevate his agendas as an industrialist. Franklin and Ford, over time directly or indirectly had much to do with providing employment for millions of people. What went on in the minds of Hitler and Stalin caused the death and destruction of millions of people, the emphasis being on end results. Do you see where I'm going with this David? I believe that just as you can catch a cold by standing close to someone who has the germs, a person can be affected spiritually and mentally by another person, as well. Have I not affected you David? Is there anything you do not understand thus far?"

"I understand everything so far."

"Can you see how stressful it would be to try to mix two different mindsets? Yet many people do. There are people who work for the mob, yet they attend church on a regular basis. This kind of behavior splits the mind in half. I happen to believe that it's one of the causes of certain mental disorders."

"David, I've always talked to you like I would talk to an adult. There are reasons for this. First of all, I believe young people your age have the capacity to retain a lot more than they are currently receiving. For example, in the seventeen hundreds when this country was being formed, they were sending delegates to France and Spain to set up trade deals for the sale of sugar cane, tobacco, etc. Some of these young men were in their teens. They spoke the King's English and had a vocabulary equivalent to that of a Harvard graduate, of which many might have been. We are currently experiencing America seriously "dumb'd down." There is no doubt that the information you have grasped from our relationship has given you an 'edge.' It's what you are going to do with that edge that concerns me. So before we go any further, it's decision time David. Which side of the table are you going to reference?"

❧ THE EDGE

"Well Mr. Hap, let me say this, it means a lot to me that you talk to me as an adult. You are always giving me new words for my vocabulary. I feel very different when I'm around you. I feel smarter and like I could do anything. So let me talk to you like an adult, or at least I'll try. You said a lot of things to me that affected me since I've known you. But one thing you said stuck so hard in my head that I kept hearing it over and over again. You said, *"If I was your age and knew what I know now, I would have the world in the palm of my hand,"* do you remember that?"

"Yes."

"After about a day of that ringing in my head, I thought… he could never go back and become my age, but what if I could learn what he knows *now* while I'm still young. I have learned only a small amount of what you have in your head Mr. Hap, but look what we have done! 'We' meaning me and Tom, Mr. Hap. I know you were sort of involved but it's not your fault that we, I mean "I" misused what you gave me. Everything you have just told me makes sense. So, that book over there with the Nazi sign on it, that isn't going to fly. And that goes for the one with it. If my Uncle Holl ever saw that thing in my clubhouse, he'd level the place and kick my ass into next week. So there is no hard decision here. I sure would appreciate you letting me borrow those books on Franklin and Ford for a while though."

"Now, I have an adult question for you Mr. Hap. My Uncle Holl and I have talked about the situation in Germany. My dad told me you're Jewish and that you had lost members of your family over there. So, what are *you* doing with those books?"

"I tried to make sense of it David. I tried to somehow understand the insanity of it all. Everything on this planet must be fed in order to survive. I wanted to know what 'fed' this. What was it conceived of, that sort of thing. I was looking for the embryo."

"Did you find the answer?"

I stopped looking David. That was then and this is now. You have made the right decision and I congratulate you. It's not going to be easy old habits die hard, but I'm sure if your heart and mind continue to have constructive thoughts, they will produce much in the area of happiness, wealth, and even health. Just for the record David, I thought the kite that 'I' was flying might have gotten away from me, but I can see now it's still hooked up and about to fly higher than ever."

He handed me the books on Franklin and Ford.

"Thanks Mr. Hap, and just for the record, let me also say this…

"I'm sorry. I was wrong."

❧ FUNDAMENTALS

Fun was always a very important part of my life. I was also learning that fun would not be possible without "*da-mentals.*" I had been a wise guy, a punk, and a host of other things but I absolutely refused to be stupid. I enjoyed the company of intelligent people.

I always felt great after talking with Happensburg. It was like filling my tank with fuel. He told me if I was to learn what he "knows" now, we are going to have to bump things up a bit. He instructed me to add one new word to my vocabulary every day. That would be 365 new words every year. He suggested today starting with **"Ultimatum"** (A final statement of terms.) He also told me that "cursing" was a sign of a person having a minimal vocabulary. Also, that he wanted me to think of cursing as being "cursed," the opposite of being "blessed." Remember… we can't serve two masters.

I told him I'd work on it. That night I started reading about Ford. My dad had talked about Ford many times. I remember him tricking me with a question about Ford. He asked me, "Who invented the automobile?" I said Henry Ford. He laughed and said, "Nope, he came up with the 'Assembly Line.' The first working concept of a manufactured automobile was the brainchild of Daimler Benz and he named it after his daughter 'Mercedes.'" My father was always coming up with little brain teasers.

Ford's engineers developed the first V-block engine. Ford was quite a guy, at age forty he was flat broke, then went on to become a billionaire.

My dad told me every Model "A" Ford off the line was "pinstriped." The color on the stripe matched the color on the wheels. My dad did some pinstriping himself. Now *that* was something I'd like to learn. The brush he used was like a knife. They called them "dagger stripers."

Happensburg made me report to him once a week on my reading and we would talk about these great men. I was finally learning about inventors. To me there were no higher people than inventors; my dad said they moved the stock market and Mr. Hap agreed, so it must have been so. I wasn't an inventor yet but I could work ideas pretty well, so I felt it wouldn't be long before I got "hooked up."

Interestingly, as I read more and more about Ford, I discovered that he was an "Anti-Semitic" (prejudiced against Jewish people.) When I asked Happensburg why he hadn't told me about this, he said…

"I thought it best if you told me David."

Chapter 4:

EXPANDING MY HORIZONS

The kids at school were talking about a "soap box derby" that was coming up and there were different businesses that were sponsors. You go there and pick up the rule book and sign up and they would supply you with regulation wheels. You could build the car any way you wanted to but it had to be within guidelines of length, width, weight, etc. I thought maybe I could build a derby car. It sounded like a cool thing to do. I could paint it and letter it up just like a stock car.

There was a dealership on Broadway that was listed as one of the sponsors, Al Mangin's Auto Sales. I rode my bike down there and went in to sign up. There wasn't anyone in the office, so I wandered into the service department. One of the mechanics asked me if he could help me out. The name on his shirt said "Jack." I told him I came to sign up for the derby and needed to get my wheels so I could get started. He went on to tell me that you are supposed to have your parents sign the papers and that the wheels were (if I remember correctly) ten bucks. I told him I'd better come back then, I didn't have ten bucks on me. Then I thought ... hey, it don't hurt to ask, Uh, sir do you think Mr. Mangin would trade me the wheels for some advertising on my car. I do lettering and it's going to look just like a stock car when it's done. Stock cars have advertising on them, you know." He said he didn't think Mangin would go for that. Then he asked me what kind of lettering I did. I showed him my bike; I had a yellow #3 on the chain guard and Pete Corey written in script next to it. I told him my dad was really good at sign painting and he taught me freehand lettering. He thought that was pretty good and asked if I ever lettered a tool box. I said no, but let me take a look at it.

When I saw this guy's tool box, I couldn't believe they made tool boxes that big. He said he would like his name right on the front, and that if I could do that, he would guarantee me a set of wheels and if it came out real nice, a few bucks to boot. I told him I'd be down tomorrow right after school and take care of that for him. Wow, this is going to be the most expensive thing I ever lettered.

I returned the next day and lettered "Jack Muldowney" across the front of that box. Jack got me the wheels and gave me five bucks on top of it. We became great friends and I added another "genius" to my list of friends. A year later he had me letter his wife's new Corvette. The lettering read... "Cha-Cha" in one-inch letters next to the door handles. Shirley "Cha-Cha" Muldowney went on to become famous in drag racing circles. She held national records in 1977, 1980 and 1982. A movie about her life, "Heart like a Wheel" was produced in 1983. (More about Jack and Shirley later.)

✍ DAVIE-MOTORIZED

I brought the wheels home and started making plans for the soap box car. Somehow building a soap box car and reading about Henry Ford was a bit of a rub for me. Ford was about engines, power, and steel. The plans for the derby car were too... **"Restrictive"** (To hold down to keep within limits,) my new word for today. So I decided to "invent" my own car and it will be "motorized." So I **"immediately"** (Without delay) started looking for the "embryo." The stock car guys always started with a frame first. I would have to build a frame.

At this point I realized I hadn't been in the "thinking tree" in a long time. I had kind of out grown it I guess, but I thought just for the heck of it I'd go there and think. As I sat in the tree I realized I had out grown it. I actually felt stupid sitting there. I thought that if Debbie ever came over and saw me in the tree she'd probably laugh at me. It's really strange, the affect a girl can have on you. I better get out of here before someone sees me. Just as I climbed down from the tree I noticed the old ladder that we used over at the tower. The one we hid in the woods. Tom and I brought it back to the clubhouse after the kite caper. It was actually half of an extension ladder. As I reached the ground, an idea dawned on me. That ladder could be my frame! The side rails, cross members, everything I needed. All I have to do is put some plywood on it and axles under it, then figure out steering and motor mounts. This was a Hel- I mean "heck" of a start. I stood there for just a moment and realized that the old tree had done it again. Another idea was about to unfold. I measured what I thought would be a good length for the car. "Wheelbase" would be the proper term. Then I took a handsaw and cut the ladder. I almost felt Tom should have been there because this meant the trip up the tower was officially over. Later, while telling Happensburg about the ladder, he said the act of cutting the ladder was "**Ceremonial**" (A formal act or ritual) and a very important moment in time.

The old ladder must have enjoyed the excitement as much as we did, because its role in our lives was far from being over and it was about to enjoy one last "burst" of excitement.

ꙅ INSIDE THEIR HEADS

My dad explained to me that with any kind of invention there should first be developed a "prototype" (a model or early example, first form.) Mr. Hap told me to *"just begin."* That in and of itself draws much into the creative mind. So I began the designing of a working automobile. I'll admit it didn't look like much at this point but I was on my way. While in detention after school, I started making a parts list.

- Motor (from lawn mower, horizontal shaft type)
- Axles (must fit holes in the derby wheels so I can use them)
- Steering, Plywood, V-belt pulleys (one the axle size, one the motor shaft size)
- Fan belts and screws

Now let's see... Bob Mott had an old reel type lawnmower with a horizontal shaft behind his garage. It sat there for a long time, I wonder if it runs. I'll use pipe for axles. Plywood, I have some pieces my dad had left over from a job...

Just then I was interrupted by a deep voice. "Davies, how much do you weigh?"

I looked up to see one of the senior members of the school wrestling team, standing over me.

"I don't know, why?"

"Come on with me, I want to get you on the scale, I'm hoping you're going to be 97 lbs. We've got a spot open on the team."

I didn't move.

"Come on, come on, I haven't got all day! Let's go!"

I said "I'm not interested in being on the wrestling team; I'm not interested in sports at all."

He stood there staring at me for a few moments, then left the room. He was very angry.

You would have thought that I had spit in his face. He was insulted. I had already gone through all of this with the basketball coach. I thought everyone knew where I stood. Little did I know the chain reaction this would cause. They needed another person on the team. Two of my friends were already on the team and were unbeatable. I had great respect for them but I didn't fit in anywhere near that team. It was as if I had let my country down. One by one the teachers turned against me. Many dropped subtle hints about lack of school spirit, etc. I became an "outcast." Sitting in detention after school became a way of life for me. Here I was, stuck there until almost 4:00 every day and I had jobs to do. At first it wasn't so bad because I would use that time to layout a lettering job on paper or make lists of things I needed, etc., but then the teachers would take my pencils and paper away and force me to study things I had no interest in. Ironically, it seemed to me in a small way I was suffering from the same type of thing my Uncle Holl had fought a war against. The same things Happensburg and his family had dealt with. Where was my freedom to think and create?

I didn't mean to hurt the guy from the team or the school in any way, but I was busy doing other things. I was getting inside the head of Henry Ford and was about to build my own working concept of an automobile — didn't anyone understand? I had my lettering and pinstriping going on. To go off in some other direction that had no future for me would be foolish. I knew somewhere deep inside that I was living in my own world. I did not fit in the school system. Up until now I had been in and out of trouble most of the time, but since Mr. Hap and I had our little talk, I had changed direction. Studying Ford and Franklin was a good thing. Not just to write some essay or a report, but to really get into their heads. I had always wanted to know what was in Happensburg's head and now I had other great minds to draw from as well. Ford himself said…"I don't pretend to be the smartest person, but I surround myself with the most intelligent people in the world." My dad always said, "I don't know everything, but I do know everybody!" So, if he needed an answer, all he had to do to was to ask someone he knew (I personally thought he knew everything and everybody.)

I could see now that everything was starting to connect. Everything was starting to make sense. My lettering was valuable to me because it was putting me in touch with the people that could help me. The lettering got me my wheels.

There is a sign on the front of Bob Mott's building and it's all faded out — I'll bet I could trade him a repaint on the sign for that motor I need. Besides, if I was lettering his sign on the front of the building, there's no telling how many other jobs I might pick up. I felt like I had a tiger by the tail.

When I gave my weekly report to Mr. Hap I explained all this to him. He reminded me what he told me before, about it not being easy and that I was going places where others cannot go and will not understand. He explained that I was a "non-conformist." (One who refuses to be bound by the accepted rules, beliefs, or practices of a group.) And that may not be so bad or it may be very bad, depending on certain things. In life, it's most often "majority rules" and it makes it uncomfortable for those who don't conform. He explained that history shows that it's been the "non-conformist" that seems to move progress along. What they call "breakout thinking" that brings the world to the next level. He went on to explain that we must be careful, that many non-conformists often end up confined in one way or another as in my case, detention. Only *you* can determine if it's worth the suffering. This is a good way to find out how much something really means to you.

When I told my dad about all this, he had an interesting response, "Being a non-conformist will separate you from the masses, remember Crows fly in flocks, the Eagle flies alone."

He said, "Other people don't necessarily know what is right for you, only you can determine that. So, set some goals and then **do what you have to do**, **when you have to do it, whatever that is,** and before long you'll know whether or not you took the right road."

This all made perfect sense to me. I decided not to get upset with school. I would just let the teachers teach and the wrestlers wrestle, and I would go about my business. They could live in their world and I was going to live in mine. I immediately went back to making plans. Not only for my motorized car but also, that when I became sixteen I would be out of the school system.

Chapter 5:

THE MAGIC IS STILL AROUND

Everything seemed to fall into place pretty much as planned. Mott went for the sign deal and even got the mower motor running and "tuned" it up for me. While I was at Motts' I lettered another tool box. It was for one of the guys there, his name was Ed Pieniazek. I told him I didn't want any money, that I would trade him for some welding I might need done (he gave me money anyway and told me that if I needed some welding he'd take care of it.)

Within a few days I had all the parts gathered for the car, except for the steering, one of the things I hadn't quite figured out yet. When we were younger, we had put together a few "downhill" cars and the steering was just a 2x4 with an axle going under it. A bolt in the center provided the "pivot" point and you would steer it with your feet or a rope tied to each side. The new car would have a body on it, so the steering would be inside. You wouldn't be able to steer with your feet and trying to control a rope with both hands outside the car wouldn't be too cool. So I set a goal to "invent" the steering in this car.

I quickly learned that setting a goal to invent something can be frustrating. Setting a goal usually means to begin with an end in mind. When you are inventing something, you may be going toward an end but you may not know exactly what that particular end is. What I learned was that when you are in "undeveloped territory," which was where I was most of the time, the best thing to do was to *"go as far as you can see; from that point, you'll be able to see further."* This always worked for me in my "capers." You are still working toward an end result, but that specific "end" may change from what you had originally "**envisioned**" (To picture in the mind, foresee.) My new word for that day.

Happensburg and my dad were eating this up. My dad was thrilled that I was studying Ford and inventors. Mr. Hap could see that I was way ahead of my one new word each day and that I was reading more, as well as putting it to "**practical**" (Capable of being used or put into effect) use.

"My world" was getting larger by the day. Getting in trouble was the furthest thing from my mind.

Interestingly, as I look back I remember with my "capers" I was getting a bit "cocky," or we'll say over confident, but now being surrounded by all of these "thinkers" I remember feeling humbled. *"The more I learned, the more I realized I didn't know."* It seemed that one door after another kept opening for me. There were always problems that had to be solved. As I solved a problem, I grew much more in knowledge and skill.

I knew my dad really wanted me to build this car when he said… "You realize *'Until it's actually built, it's just bullshit. Only you can make this a reality."*

He agreed to help me with the steering but it would be my own design. I was to do the work and all **"fabrication"** (To construct, assemble.) Fair enough. I told my dad that it was a big task because I knew very little about steering and how it should be. He said, "Let's not think of the whole project let's take it one step at a time. We'll break it down into increments." He continued, "Sometimes *'by the yard it's hard but by the inch it's a cinch.'* Let's make the spindles first. These are mini-axles that can turn independent of each other. Then we have to connect them with a 'tie-rod' and, as the name implies, it ties the two spindles together. Then the steering arm will have to somehow grab the tie-rod. Moving it would move the spindles and control the steering. So for now, think *'spindles.'*

We put the ladder frame up on a couple of saw horses and located a place where the front wheels should be. He took two pieces of angle iron and allowed me cut them. They had to be the same height as the frame. We drilled holes in them and bolted them to the frame, one on each side. These were to mount the spindles to and would provide the strength to hold the spindles in place.

At this point my dad said "You have to design something that has an axle to hold the wheel and is attached to the frame mount, and it must be able to move back and forth so we can attach that to the tie-rod. Now think about how this can be accomplished. Make a few drawings, toss around some ideas." He continued…"I realize Ford is gone, but the 'magic' he tapped into is still around. Try to tap into his thinking. If Ford was your age and faced with this task, how would he approach this?"

After school I sat in detention with a book open, pretending to be studying. In my mind I knew the axle must be able to "swing" back and forth freely but yet somehow be fastened to the angle iron my dad put on the frame.

Every now and then the teacher would get up and leave the room to bring paper work to the office or whatever. While she was gone I would pull out a pencil and try to come up with something. I always liked to "think on paper." It was easy to know when she returned because the door would squeak when she opened it. I thought if someone ever oils the hinges on the door, my warning device would be gone. As I sat there with the school book open, I kept hearing the door squeaking. But it wasn't opening or being used. This was almost to the point of being annoying. I looked up and stared at the door just to see if it was swinging a little from the wind, or if someone had opened the outside door down the hall or something. It didn't move. Then I realized that something inside my mind was causing me to focus on the hinges of that door.

There was the answer to my steering. "Door hinges!" Door hinges would give me the "swing." I could have Eddie weld the axle to one side of the hinge, and then I would bolt the other half to the angle iron my dad bolted to the frame (ladder.) This would allow the wheel to turn and swing free but still be held in place. Then somehow I needed to hook the tie-rod to both hinges and go to the next step, which was how to grasp the tie-rod with a steering rod called a "tiller." The early automobiles had "tiller steering." The idea of the steering wheel was originally taken from a boat. Ford was one of the first to use the "wheel" for steering. I guess I had my first invention in the making (this is excluding U.F.O's or anything of that nature.)

After getting out of school I picked up a piece of pipe that would fit in the hole in the wheels and cut two pieces long enough to go through each wheel. Then I took the pipe and the hinges over to Ed to have them welded. When I told him what I was doing he suggested welding "tabs" on the inside part of the hinges to bolt the tie-rod to. He suggested making a simple tie-rod out of a piece of angle iron and drilling three holes in it, one on each end and one in the center. Then just drop bolts down through the ends and don't pinch them tight but leave them free to move. Then drop your tiller steering rod down into the center hole and you would have your steering. The tiller rod would be shaped like an "S." The steering handle would be directly in front of you as you sat in place and then would extend along the frame held in place with the u-clamps that hold electrical conduit on walls, then the other part of the S-shape would drop down through the frame into the tie-rod hole. Move your handle to the right and the steering rod would push the tie-rod (connected to the spindles) to the left causing the wheels to turn right and the opposite direction would have the wheels turn left.

Mott himself got a kick out of my steering idea. He asked me if I had put any "caster" in it. I didn't have a clue what he was talking about. He asked if the angle iron I had already attached to the frame was straight up and down. I said it was. He said you need to give it some "caster" which is "tilt" or "angle" to the spindles or you'll have a tough time getting it to go straight down the road. With zero or negative caster the steering will be real quick and the thing will wander from side to side going down the road. He said just take the bottom bolt out of the angle iron and move the bottom of the iron forward and drill another hole so that it is tilted back or angled slightly. If you have enough "caster" you can take your hands off of the steering and it will still go straight. Also measure the "toe-in" before you cut the length of your tie-rod. With the spindles in place and the wheels on the car, measure across the front of the wheels, inside edge of tread to inside edge of tread, then measure across the back, in the same position. Have the front be a quarter of an inch shorter, toeing the wheels in slightly. Then measure the length you'll need for your tie-rod. This will also help it go straight as well as help in turning.

Bob Mott had built champion race cars and to have him take time to help me with my rinky-dink homemade car was quite an honor. I couldn't believe he was interested in what I was doing.

✎ ONE BOY-HALF A MAN
TWO BOYS-NO MAN

By Saturday I had the spindles assembled and in working order. I put the wheels on and measured for the length of the tie-rod and had bolted it in place. Now I had to mount the motor and the rear axle and line up the pulleys. For now it would have to be "direct drive." The belt would connect the engine to the rear axle and you would just push start it and go. I didn't know what else would work. Cars have clutches so the engine and drive line can be separated. There was a centrifugal clutch you could get that was also a pulley that went on the engine but they were expensive, so direct drive will have to work for now. I kept reminding myself this was just a prototype and all I wanted to do was get this thing up and running with me piloting it down the street so that I could say "I built an automobile." I could get the "bugs out of it" later, perfecting all the little stuff, like brakes, clutch, and all that.

(Direct drive without brakes? What happened to "Adventure being handled with intelligence"?)

That afternoon a couple of friends stopped over. I thought, "This is great, I'll have help figuring out the motor mounts and where I'll put the rear axle." Well, they hung around for a while but didn't offer much help. One of them was playing with the drill, making holes in the sawhorses. The other one was scribbling all over the paper that I had measurements on. Then they started cracking jokes about the project, saying it was the "stupidest" thing they had ever seen. One of them said that you can buy a go-cart from Sears that has steering and a motor all set to go, just pull the cord and you're running. They finally left. I could hear them laughing all the way down the driveway.

I stood there looking at the ladder with door hinge steering and thought to myself, "Maybe they're right, this is a stupid project." Then I thought for a moment; if I didn't start this project I would have not met Jack Muldowney. Bob Mott didn't think it was stupid. Eddie would never have welded stuff for me if he thought it was stupid.

Mr. Hap explained to me that it isn't the "thing" that matters anyway; it's the "spirit" of the thing. It's the people involved in the "thing," and it's what you can learn from the thing that really matters. Besides, this was "My" thing.

That night I had a long talk with my dad about the whole project. He told me something I never forgot. He advised me that, *"Sometimes things that count aren't always counted;* **and** *things that are counted don't always count."* He went on to say that, "Some people are 'object driven' and others are 'purpose driven.' Objects being circumstances, situations, and things. When those so-called friends of yours 'put down' your project they became an 'object,' and you allowed that object to change your feelings about something that meant a great deal to you. Not to mention how much it did for you regarding your relationship with other inventors and creative friends. How could you even let that happen? Those kids haven't built a goddamned thing! If you are to become an inventor or artist or whatever you decide to be, you must become "purpose driven."

It's been said...

"To disregard your goals and dreams to "fit in" with or gain favor of others is a violation of your own self worth."

I knew in a small way I was part of something big. At this point I readjusted my goal slightly. I will finish this project to the point that it will be able to cart me down the road, powered by the mower engine, and I will steer it with my steering. I'm not going to go so far as to build a body for it and all of that. Then I could say I built a working concept of an automobile. Even though it might be crude, I would have accomplished what I set out to do.

Within a week I had mounted the rear axle and positioned the motor. There were many trips to "Baldie's" junkyard but it was finally coming together. Gas tank, fuel lines, throttle linkage — all hooked up and a "kill switch" in place. At this point it would have been nice to have brakes, but that would take some serious engineering with such a small axle and the thin little soap box derby wheels. I had a design on paper for the brakes, using two V-belt pulleys with belts fastened on one end to the frame and the other end clamped and pulled by a cable. I also had an idea for a clutch using another door hinge under the motor, with a handle welded to it so you could adjust the tension on the belt

So here it was, still very much in the "rough," just a small piece of plywood over the rear axle to support the motor and gas tank, and another small piece for me to sit on. The entire ladder was still exposed. I wanted everything open so I could see it all working, the steering especially.

Considering the "looks" of this thing, a night launch would probably be best, so I set Wednesday night for the best time to fire it up. It was going to be a little hairy starting because I would have to push start it, then jump on and take it from there. Tom said he would help but he had to work till 10:00 every night. It sure would be easier if I had someone pushing to start it. After the episode with my buddies, I wasn't about to ask any of them. If I ask my dad to help he'd see that I didn't have brakes and make me hold off until I engineer a brake system.

There was one person I could call that I know would show up.... I was very anxious to see what Debbie thought of the whole thing. She was usually open to new things and understanding about ideas. How would she react to this? Well, I think it's the adventure involved with the idea that she likes. This is an invention — nothing more, nothing less — but somehow inside I really wanted her to appreciate what I had done. I knew I was taking a big chance getting her involved, because if she thought it was stupid...Well, I didn't want to think about how I would feel.

I heard the familiar gentle knock on the clubhouse door and opened it to let her in.

"So, what's the big secret thing you've been so involved with?" she asked.

(I pointed to my automobile.) "It's a home built automobile. Just a proto-type now, it needs to be finished but tonight I was just going to see if it runs down the road straight and all."

She slowly walked over taking it all in, not saying a word. She looked underneath and checked out the motor, then grabbed the steering bar and moved it back and forth. "You built this yourself?"

"Yep."

"Pretty cool. You haven't run it down the road yet?"

"Nope. Not yet. That's what tonight is all about."

She kept looking all around it. She pointed to the pedal, then asked..."Is this the gas?"

"Yep."

"Where's the brake?"

"I haven't got that far yet. I just want to make a run with it around the block. Then I can finish the body and the brakes later."

"How do you start it?"

"It's going to be 'push start.' It's direct drive, so when the wheels turn, it turns the motor. So tell me, what do you think? Am I crazy or what?"

"This is a real surprise to me. When you called I had no idea what you were up to. I think it is really cool that you are building something like this. It's really clever, the ladder and all. I rode my brother's bike one time without brakes and I never forgot how it felt, not being able to stop. This thing has a motor, that's scary."

"Well, it has a kill switch to shut the motor off, and then the compression slows you right down. That won't stop it quickly but like I said, I'm only giving it a test run. I've got an idea for brakes but it would take a while. I just want to be able to say I built a car that actually took me for a ride under its own power. I thought it might be nice if you were there for this very special occasion."

"Oh. Wow, Davie… that's so nice. You don't know what that means to me. So it's just you and me?"

"Yep."

"So that means I would be the one pushing, right? You need me to push you down the road to get this thing going. I get it."

"Ah, well, yes I wanted you to be part of this. How would you feel if you had your hands on the plane when the Wright Brothers first took off? I'm offering you a piece of history here girl. I could have had ten of my friends show up for this, no problem at all, but I chose you. I just hope you appreciate it."

She just stared at me for a moment. Then, "Start this thing up, I want to hear it run."

I went over and opened the gas line, and gave the wheel a spin, the motor turned over and it started right up. It had a "straight pipe" and no muffler, so it was really loud. Then I pushed down on the gas pedal to rev it up and the pedal stuck wide open — the motor was screaming! I reached over and hit the kill switch and nothing happened. Then I pulled off the spark plug wire and the engine shut down. Our ears were ringing.

She's standing there staring at me again.

I checked out the throttle linkage, which was a car hood release cable I got from the junk yard. It had a "kink" in it and it didn't release when I let off of the pedal. I felt like a jerk.

I really didn't want to scrub the launch but I would have to have a working throttle to operate this car. I thought about controlling the throttle right off of the motor with one hand and steer with the other, but I would have had to reach over the hot exhaust pipe to do that. I unhooked the cable and started the motor again, this time controlling the throttle by hand, right on the motor. I rev'd it up and backed it down. "There, all fixed, minor problem." Then I got an Idea…

❧ HURRY IS NOT OF THE DEVIL, HURRY IS THE DEVIL

"How are you going to manage that while driving this thing?" She asked.

"I'm glad that you asked that because there is no one else I would trust for what we need to do."

She interrupts with… "Why do I have the feeling I should be leaving right now before you say another word?"

"I can't believe that is coming from you, a person who loves adventure and excitement. Do you have any idea what I'm about to offer you? I am offering you to be the first human being to pilot my new invention while I ride on the back controlling the throttle. We will make history together tonight! But if you want to turn me down and let this opportunity slip through your fingers, go ahead. Must I remind you, I have friends that would give anything for a chance to be part of this?"

Debbie walked over and stood in front of my automobile. She asked me to grab the back so we could get it off of the saw horses and put it on the floor. As soon as it was on the floor, she climbed on it and grabbed the steering and then sat quietly for a moment.

❧ DEBBIE TAKES CONTROL

"Alright, I'll do it; I do want to be part of this. You work that throttle thing and I'll steer. Let's go right now before I change my mind."

Just then the reality of the whole thing kicked in. What am I doing here? What if something goes wrong? This may not be such a good idea after all. It's just too dangerous. I don't want her to get hurt. On second thought I better hook up the brakes. If it were just me I wouldn't care, but I'm not putting her in danger. We'll do this later.

I told her we should wait and maybe do this another time when I have brakes and it's safer. She answered with…

"Aw, Davie… You are so sweet. Now let's cut the bullshit and get this thing rolling. I'm steering and you're gassing. Let's go! This sounds like excitement to me and I'm ready. When you called me I knew you were up to something and it meant excitement. With you it's always excitement! I told you that's what I like about you. Now fire this baby up!"

I hesitated, thinking I'm losing control here. What do I do now? Well, a quick trip around the block, no problem. I guess it'll work (I think.)

I took the belt off the engine pulley so we could roll it out of the shed and get it into the road. Then put the belt back on as Debbie nestled into the seat. For just a split second the thought ran through my mind… "How does she always end up in the driver's seat?" and what am I doing pushing?

No time to think about it now, just push and let's go. I gave it a shove and the motor fired up. It was really loud with the straight pipe. Within seconds we were rolling down the road. For a moment it felt good. Then I realized I was having a problem controlling the throttle; the thing kept jerking back and forth like a carnival ride and it almost tossed me off. Once I got the hang of it, we really started to enjoy the ride. The wind started blowing in our faces and at one point my eyes started watering. We were motoring! Then, as we picked up speed the thing started to wander all over the road. I remembered I never changed the angle of the spindles like Mott had told me to do. The faster we went the worse it got. Debbie was enjoying it and kept asking to go faster. I'm trying to explain what was going on but with the noise and wind it was no use.

We were coming to the end of the street. I yelled out… "Take a right!" She went left! I screamed…"What are you doing!" She yells back …

"I want to go by my house my brothers are playing in the street. They've got to see this"!

"No! No! There's a problem with the steering|! We have no brakes! Watch out! We're coming to a stop sign!" I let off of the throttle and it backfired so loud it deafened me for a second and a foot long flame shot out of the pipe. I reached for the spark plug wire and got jolted. I tried to reach the spark plug again, and right through the intersection we went.

She yells out…"Davie! Do that when we get to my house, that's cool. Make it backfire! Do that again!"

House lights were coming on as we ran down the side streets. Turn right! We've got to get back; we're waking up the whole town! Straight through another stop sign and then left onto her street, right past her house. Her brothers were sitting on the front porch; one had a football in his hand.

I let it backfire! We watched the ball fall right out of his hands and his jaw opened wide. Obviously they couldn't believe what they saw.

Nothing that unusual, just their sister steering a motorized ladder with some nut riding on the back firing flames out into the night sky, that's all. How would they explain that to mom?

In a flash, we disappeared quickly down the street. I found myself pleading with her, please Deb, take a left now, and please head back.

As we finally headed back down the side street a police car passed through the intersection ahead of us. We saw him glance over in our direction. A few seconds went by and we approached the intersection. I was hoping he didn't see us. It must have taken a moment to register what he saw but finally the brake lights came on. I saw him backing up as we went through the intersection.

What now? No choice, run for it! "Ok Debbie, you wanted excitement? You got it, gal." I throttled her up and away we went wandering all over the road, she could hardly hold it at high speed. We slowed down, turned and went between two garages, coming out onto the next street. We could see the lights from the police car one block over. He was facing up the street. We pulled between a hedgerow and some trees and stopped. We walked out from behind the hedges and looked between the houses; we could see the police car on the next street. It was stopped. The officer opened the car door and stood there.

"He's listening for us," Debbie whispered. We thought we were safe behind the hedges for the time being until the porch light came on. "We have to leave now!" I pushed it off and we were gone. But where are we going? "We have to get to the woods by the water tower, it's our only shot. We can run the car into the woods and hide there." The tower was about six blocks away from where we were. The police car was facing down the street, so we headed up the street we were on and then around the block and down the other side.

The motor seemed even louder than it was before, and for some reason it was "backfiring" twice as much, even though I was trying to keep it quiet. A thousand things were going through my mind; the worse thing was that I only put a little gas in the tank that I robbed from my dad's lawnmower, so I knew we had very little time to work with. We had to get this thing over real quick but not too quick, as we had to make it to our destination. We had to go four blocks down Westcott and then left onto Bernard, then two blocks to the tower. We made it to Westcott with the police car one block over on the next street; now if we can go the length of four blocks we could hide once again. I had to get full speed out of it but the steering was so rough, wandering worse with more speed.

I give Debbie credit though she was managing really well under the circumstances. Even with the wandering we had reached some serious speed by the time we reached Bernard Street. So much speed that when Debbie turned,

Illustration by Bill Carney

the front wheels skidded and the rubber came right off of those skinny little soap box derby wheels. Now we're running down Bernard St. on bare rims with sparks shooting off of the front wheels, fire coming from the exhaust, and sweat running from both of us. As I looked back I saw lights coming down Westcott; it had to be the police car. If we could only get to the corner at Wallace and turn before he looks down Bernard St., we'd have enough lead on him to make it to the woods behind the tower. I cranked it for everything it had; Debbie tried her best to keep it in the center. I knew if I let off the throttle it would backfire so I just kept it wide open as we rounded the corner. On the turn, sparks were shooting five feet in the air off the front wheels. I looked back and saw the lights of a car approaching just as we rounded the corner.

Illustration by Bill Carney

We made it! Now down to the end of Wallace, a left through the alley road and into the woods. As soon as we hit the ally road I pulled the spark plug wire off and when the thing rolled to a stop, I yanked off the belt and we both pushed it up to the tower and into the woods. We crouched down beside the car and waited, listening for cars. There were cars going up and down the streets, police cars were everywhere; we just stayed out of sight. We both lay there panting. A police car came up the road to the tower. We crouched down as low as we could. A light shined over our heads for a second and then the car pulled away. Debbie reached over and put her hand on my chest.

"Is your heart pounding? Oh yes, I can feel it."

Then she put my hand on her chest.

"Can you feel mine pounding?"

I just nodded; I couldn't believe she had my hand over her breasts. Now my heart was really pounding! I started to pull it away, but she held it there. She was staring right into my eyes.

Instinctively I leaned over and kissed her. Everything became quiet. I didn't hear anything. After that kiss I kissed her again. Then, we just held each other for what seemed like a very long time, neither of us speaking a word. The worry of the police looking for us and what might happen was far off in the distance now. Nothing outside of her and I seemed to matter.

Amazingly, we were parked ten feet from where we kept the ladder hidden when we climbed the tower. The old ladder had found its way back home.

✎ LITTLE LIARS

After a while we came out of the woods and walked over to the five corners.

Just as we arrived at the parking lot of the drug store, a police car pulled up. The window went down and I saw it was Bud Whitney and George Bangard, two of Rotterdam's finest who I knew well.

"Hey Davie, how are you?" Bud asked. "And who's the cute gal with ya?"

"Oh, this is Debbie."

He continued…"You know, maybe you guys can help us out. We had an incident earlier that put one of our officers in a very precarious situation. It seems that he saw a couple of kids just about your age running around on some kind of a contraption, that… well, according to the officer, resembled a ladder with a motor on it. He supposedly chased the dammed thing for quite a while but it disappeared. He's been taking a lot of ribbing back at the station from some of the guys; you can imagine when he radio'd in that he was chasing kids on a motorized ladder. Normally I would think that maybe the guy was a candidate for the rubber gun squad but it seems some folks in the neighborhood saw a contraption also. A couple over on Paul Ave. said something 'landed' by their hedge row and when they turned the porch light on it 'took off.' Then a lady on Bernard St. said she saw some weird thing go by her house, and there were sparks shooting straight up from the front and fire was shooting out of the back end of the thing and two kids were riding on it.

You wouldn't know of anything like that taking place, would ya Davie? We'd really like to find this contraption!"

"Gee Bud, you say it was a contraption? I ain't seen nothing like that around here? You seen anything Deb?"

"Nope. Nothing like a contraption around here."

Bud began again…"I should inform you that a couple of kids we just talked to down at the park said that you happened to be building something that looked like a ladder and were putting a motor on it, and being that the both of you are covered with grease and smell like gasoline, might make me think that we're closer to this contraption than we think. Now, what can you tell us Davie?"

"Well Bud, if you see those kids again, you tell them I said that was the stupidest thing I ever heard. Why, you can go right down to Sears and buy a go-cart. It would be pretty stupid to try and build a contraption. And if Debbie's chain didn't come off her bike so many times tonight, we'd still be ridin' it and we wouldn't be all grease. As far as the gas smell, well I thought we could clean the grease up with the gas but Debbie wanted no part of it, so we were going home to clean up. How's that?"

"You know, every time something crazy happens in this town they want to blame me. Last I heard they blamed me for ghosts and flyin' saucers they saw in the night sky. Now this contraption thing, man, what's next?"

Just then Officer Bangard got out from the other side of the car and walked over to me.

"Come here Davie, I want to talk to you alone for a minute."

We walked away from the car where no one could hear us.

"Now Davie, forget that I'm a policeman and just see me as a friend for a moment, ok? We want to clear this thing up and you don't have to be involved other than directing us to that contraption, which I think you might know where it is. Whoever built this thing must have a few bucks tied up so what do you think that the guy who made this thing …not you, but that guy would take for the thing? Say ten bucks? Maybe you could take the money and see that it gets to the right person. You know these guys who build things like this, I know you do. What do ya say, deal? He sure ain't going to be riding it in this town again. Davie, the thing is trouble. Well? Ten bucks to get rid of trouble and clear this thing up and get those guys off my, I mean that officer's back? What do you think? For a friend …"

George stuck the ten in my pocket.

"I'll go home and make a couple of calls, George and I'll get that information for ya. I'll call the station in an hour, ok? But remember, I ain't involved, right?"

"Right. Now get home and stay out of trouble, hear me? I'll be at the station the rest of the afternoon. You call me!"

"Yes George. Thanks."

MOTO-ROMANTICS

I began walking Debbie home.

"Some night huh?"

"For sure."

"You ok?"

"Yea. Sorry you lost your car."

"Oh, that's ok."

"You can build another one Davie, this time with brakes and better stuff. I know you can. I'll help you if you want me to. I think I pushed things tonight and probably caused most of the trouble."

"No. It was fun! How about the sparks off those front wheels!"

"And the backfire! Or whatever you called it! How about my brothers! Did you see their faces?"

We both started laughing.

"Hey, I even got ten bucks out of the deal. How's that? All that fun and ten bucks to boot. No regrets Deb. Not for me. You?"

"None at all! Davie…What about the little thing back in the woods?"

"What thing was that?"

"You kissed me."

"I did?"

"Twice!"

"Twice?"

"Oh, like you can't remember. I bet you remember my heart beating though! Huh?"

"Oh, that. Yea, I remember that." (Smiling)

"Am I to think you're just like all the other guys? Maybe just crazier? That kiss meant something to me. If it didn't mean anything to you then you're just like every other guy."

"I'm kidding. It meant a lot to me, too."

"Really?"

"Yes. It just caught me by surprise, that's all."

"Me too. That was the best part."

"The best part? Come on Deb, you like the excitement, the crazy stuff. You said so yourself."

"I know, but that was exciting in a different way."

She stopped walking, then grabbed my arm and turned me toward her. She looked right into my eyes...

"I really mean it that was the best part."

We continued walking.

"You mean you would want to hang out with me even if there wasn't excitement?"

"David, with us there will always be excitement, I'm just thinking of a different kind."

(Did she say "David?" What happened to Davie?)

One hour later...

"Hello, Rotterdam Police dispatch, how can I help you?"

"Patrolman Bangard please."

"Hello, Bangard, how can I help you?"

"George? Davie here. I got that information for you. The contraption is over behind the Democratic Club in the woods, right near the water tower. Can I ask what are you going to do with it?"

"We need to show the guys that there was a… whatever the thing is, and then we want it out of commission. It's been an embarrassment… On the radio and every police scanner heard me, I mean the officer, chasing a motorized ladder with two kids on it around town and it lost him twice, he's takin' quite a ribbing for it."

"George, who is it that tows vehicles for the Police Department?"

"We'll have Mott's pick it up. They'll take it to their impound yard."

"Ok, George, glad I could help out."

Later… I had been trying to come up with a name for my automobile and that night it finally came to me… I'll call it the "Boomerang."

Chapter 6:

kNOw MORE !

It wasn't long before my dad found out about my little excursion. He was furious! He told me that for a time he thought I might have a brain, with once in a while maybe even a spark of intelligence in it. But now he was totally confused.

He began with…"David, do you remember years ago when you asked me … 'When does a person begin to become intelligent?' Can you possibly remember what I told you?"

"Yea, you said 'That process begins the moment we realize how stupid we are.'"

"Well, when are you going to start the process?"

He was pissed.

Happensburg joined in with one of his little phrases …

"Foolish repetition is the trademark of a tiny mind." They reminded me that we (Debbie and me) could have been hurt or killed. I had no argument for that.

Later Mr. Hap and I had one of our serious talks. He had a way of analyzing things and clearing them up. "**Analyze**" (to separate into parts or basic principles.) My new word for the day.

"You have fallen into a very old pit David," he explained. "You have been distracted. The key warning that you missed was '*hurry.*' I never saw you hurry with your art work. Though while working on your car, you were cutting corners, either forgetting or omitting important things, etc. in an attempt to get it done. It was clear to me that although your mind was there, your heart was not. You were hungry for results and not enjoying the process. When you are working with your paint it is evident that you do not want to put the brush away. You enjoy the process as well as the results. You have lost your car David, but you may have found your heart. I suggest you follow your heart."

"Whatever we focus on will get larger in our lives. Whatever we put energy into will grow."

"This also is 'double-edged,' as you can imagine. I told you back when you had made your choice that it would not be easy. Now that you have a girl involved in your life, things are going to take on yet another dimension. Your world is certainly not getting smaller, that's for sure."

ᔰ A TURNING POINT

The strangest thing happened to me in school that would realign me and set me on the right track. I don't think I was aware of this at first but as I look back, it was clear that what took place definitely changed things regarding my direction in life.

There was this kid named Kenny and for some reason, we had become enemies. Not really of our own choosing but other kids had somehow pitted us against each other. Every time we'd see each other we would end up in a fight. The other kids would edge us on and be entertained while Kenny and I rolled around in the dirt. Well, on this particular day in school, I was walking up the stairs and on the landing between the floors, I met Kenny coming down the stairs. We were both alone. I was coming from the principal's office. I don't know where Kenny was coming from but there we were, facing each other on the stairs. He looked at me and I looked at him.

Then he said…"I don't want to fight with you" and I said, "I don't want to fight with you either." "Then why are we fighting with each other?" he asked. "I don't know," I answered. Kenny extended his hand. I shook hands with him. "Friends?" he said. "Friends." I concluded.

It felt like a huge weight had been lifted off of me. I can remember even to this day that "feeling." We turned to go our separate ways and then Kenny called out to me. "Hey Dave, everybody says you do lettering or sign painting. I have a boat my dad and I built, it's one of those 'Hydra-plane' types we built from plans out of a Popular Science magazine. It needs registration numbers and some lettering. I never thought I could ask you before, but I guess I can now, would you letter it for us?"

"Sure. I never lettered a…what did you call it?"

"Hydra-Plane. Wait till you see it, this thing came out beautiful. All it needs now is some of your handy work to be complete." Then he took out a pen and jotted down his phone number and address. "Whenever you can do it Dave, just let me know."

Kenny was a really nice kid. I had made a friend and picked up a new job. But it was more than that; we had been enemies and through a small miracle, all that had changed.

That week I met with him at his home and began lettering his Hydra-Plane. I spent many nights working on the project and Kenny and I became good friends. I would have to say this was a clear example of good triumphing over evil.

◈ GETTING SERIOUS

It was clearly time to get down to business. I looked over a lengthy list of names and phone numbers of people who wanted lettering done. Again, Happensburg was right, I had been distracted. It was just that the world I was living in had so many roads. There were so many exciting things going on in my life. My choices were many. Every now and then I would hear one of my friends complaining that he had nothing to do. Nothing to do? I found that difficult to understand. This was confirming once again that I was living in a different world.

Over at Jim Young's garage, Ray Vines was finishing a stock car and he said he'd give me a shot at lettering it. This would be my first complete; my very own design, stock car lettering job. I had already drawn out several versions of the #75. A copy of the "5" on the five dollar bill looked interesting and provided me with an idea, and then I designed a "7" that would work with that.

Rollie Johnson had called and talked with my dad about several possible lettering jobs. Rollie was Joe Johnson's dad. It seems that Joe had shown his dad the notebook that I penciled the #32 on, and told him that I was doing lettering around town. Rollie ran a body shop in Rotterdam and was well known. He also had a reputation as a race car builder and driver. I remember hearing his name mentioned many times over at Mott's and other garages around the area. My dad explained that the call from Mr. Johnson was very important and he wanted me to stop over and see him right away.

I rode my bike up the driveway to the front door of "Johnson's Garage." Just as I got off my bike, the door opened and out came a person I recognized immediately — it was "Jeep Herbert," one of the top race car drivers at Fonda Speedway. I had done lettering on his race car but never met him personally. Wow, I didn't know what to say. He smiled and said, "How ya doin' kid?" as he walked by. I can't remember if I said anything to him or not. I think I just nodded or something. Now I was getting nervous. This was serious. Would I be able to do the kind of work these guys would want?

I opened the door and walked into the garage. Two men were standing by the front end of a truck, talking. They gave me a quick glance and then continued talking. I felt awkward interrupting them; they seemed to be focused on something important. One of them was clearly Joe's dad, as he looked just like him.

"Can I help ya, are you lookin' for Joe?" he asked.

I explained who I was and that I had come over to talk about some lettering that needed to be done. Both of them seemed to perk up and the guy I thought must have been Rollie said…"This is the kid I was telling you about." The other guy was Will Courtney. Rollie introduced himself and Will and said that he had heard about my lettering things around town and had seen the notebook I did for Joe. He went on to explain how he had many lettering jobs if I could do them, and they were having a terrible time trying to get sign painters to do truck lettering. Some didn't want to leave their shops and others were drunks and not dependable. "This truck right here needs lettering," he continued, "and I could have dozens more if you thought you could do them."

I looked over at the shiny paint on the truck and all I could think was, if I made a mistake could I get it off before my paint stuck to that fresh paint. I started to tell him I never lettered a freshly painted truck before, but hesitated. Trying to act somewhat professional, I asked what he used for paint on the truck. He said "'enamel' but sometimes we use 'lacquer,' any problem with that?"

I knew if I was working on fresh enamel that it might be dangerous because the paint I was using would "bite" into it and that would leave little room for mistakes. It would have been better if it were lacquer because my paint could be removed before it dries. Oh well, no mistakes. I explained this to Rollie. He told me that if I wanted to remove fresh lettering from fresh enamel, some motor oil on a rag would dissolve the lettering off without harming the enamel. Then wipe the oil clean with a quick wipe of mineral spirits. He had seen one of the sign painters do that before.

I had a really good feeling about Rollie and there was a very special spirit in that garage. I hadn't been there ten minutes and already learning. I felt very comfortable there. Will Courtney asked if I did any pinstriping.

"Funny you should ask," I answered. "My dad and I have been just recently working on pinstriping."

"Good, I got a motorcycle for you to do."

I thought to myself, oh boy, here comes a quick course on pinstriping. Hope the ol'man ain't drunk.

Many things were about to change in my life and career with my new friendship with Rollie Johnson. He was connected with so many people. I noticed that the whole family was into go-cart racing. Between the truck lettering and numbers on go-carts, helmets, and trailers, I could see there was enough work right here to keep me busy for a long time.

That summer, between Young's garage and Rollie Johnson's I was a busy kid. Another major hurdle I had to overcome was having to work with people watching. It was difficult enough getting the brush to do what you wanted it to do when nobody was around, but try it when five or six people are watching your every move. This was tough, but I knew I had to overcome any nervousness if I were to continue on. It was a tradeoff, I guess. Giving up comfort for money and a bit of fame. The more people watching the better for business but the harder for me. It was interesting though, how people would react to my lettering. Many were fascinated by watching free hand lettering being formed with a paint brush, others seemed to be jealous and would come out with rude comments like "I think you should have used a different color" or "That's an expensive truck you're working on son, you better not screw it up." As I look back, I can't imagine someone saying something like that to a kid, trying with all his heart to work at a very difficult skill. Especially when they were only watching and were not the customer and had nothing to do with the job. I'm not talking about somebody just kidding around, I didn't mind that. All in all, the garage people seemed to be the best people to work for, so I leaned in that direction with my work.

The pinstriping started to come into play as an accessory to the lettering on cars and trucks and really started to take off.

I had been practicing designs in anticipation of pinstriping Will Courtney's motorcycle but this guy that hung around Young's garage said he had a buddy that wanted striping done on his bike. It turned out that the first real motorcycle that I ever striped belonged to "Indian John," a well-known biker of that day. John hooked me up with a slew of other bikers… Arnie Peek, "One Eyed Willy," "Crazy Otto" Hosier, "Blackie" Van Vorst, to name a few. The biker world was fascinating. These guys knew how to have fun. I kind of became their mascot. They dragged me to hill climbs and rallies and I got to hang out at such famous establishments as "Berrys Inn," "The Lost Valley Grill," "Harvey's Inn," and a few more not worth mentioning.

After striping the Indian's bike, he said he was going to take me up to Laconia, N.H. the biggest bike rally in the northeast. I didn't know what or where Laconia was but I was about to find out.

Picture me riding on the back of Indian John's motorcycle, my paints and brushes spread out in five different guy's saddlebags, heading through the mountains of New Hampshire. Oh, and everybody is drunk except me. Every time these guys would see a neon bar sign they would pull in.

Later it became a hundred miles of gut wrenching twists and turns. On the other side of "Hogback Mountain" all you could smell were brakes. After a while though, the smell went away, along with the brakes! I can remember the Indian, all drunked up, trying to gear down for a turn. He had a tank shifter, with a suicide clutch (foot operated clutch) and he got it stuck between gears and couldn't slow down. We went off the shoulder of the road through some bushes, between a couple of trees, and then back on the road again. I'll never forget it. He went off the road drunk as a skunk and came back onto the road sober as a judge. The rest of the way he was as steady as a rock.

I just let the wind dry my pants out. There's no way those guys would believe I was carrying a water balloon in my pocket.

We finally did make it to Laconia. A friend of Indian's owned a bar there. We set up out front. In those days, Laconia was a wild place and it was about to be true to its reputation. It seemed some overzealous law enforcement pissed off a few Hells' Angels and the whole town erupted. We were just outside of town and there was a lot of crazy stuff going on but I tried to focus on my work.

I saw this huge guy wiping his bike down (he was a member of some motorcycle gang.) I thought …He needs some pinstriping on that. So I said how about some striping, buddy? Just then I noticed Indian and the guys trying to get my attention. They were waving their hands and shaking their heads indicating "no, no, not that guy Davie, wrong guy!" The guy just shrugged his shoulders and said sure, go for it kid, let's see what you can do. I put a design on the front fender, then another design on the back fender. Then he said… write "Screw You" just above that design for me, too. I followed his orders and even shadowed it with another color. I thought it looked great. He gave me a nod of approval and so I said, "twenty should cover that." He laughed like I told him a joke, then he stomped my paint can into the ground. I looked over at the guys, but all they had to say was "better let that one go Davie."

Before I could regroup my thoughts I had my next customer, another big guy, bald, except for a lock of hair coming from the back of his head running down his back. He had chrome arm bands and German war metals pinned to his chest, but he didn't have a shirt on. I was just finishing the back fender of his bike when we saw National Guard vehicles go by heading for town. The guy handed me ten bucks for the work I had done. I stuck it in my pocket and started packing things up. People told us there was a full scale riot going on at Weir's Beach and everything was moving our way. We had just enough time to get packed up and head out. Cops were everywhere; one wrong move and you were locked up.

I would return to Laconia many years later, with a much different approach to working up there.

(*More about Laconia in chapters to come.*)

These guys knew how to have fun but it wasn't the best environment for me to work in. The garages and the race car people provided a much safer place to work, and there were no guys with German war metals pinned to a bare chest.

Finally, I got to pinstripe Will Courtney's bike — designs on tank and fenders, and "Slo-Poke" in script on the bottom of the rear fender. Courtney and Rollie Johnson were two really clever guys. They could build just about anything. Someone would come in the garage with a problem and these guys would solve it. They were actually inventors in their own right. Hanging around these guys was like going to college. Every day I would learn new things. The best thing was that I brought something in that they didn't do. Many times I was involved in some of their projects, mostly on the tail end with some embellishment.

As great as the lettering was for me, the pinstriping seemed to have even more value. I can remember well-meaning friends and even relatives saying "that stuff is pretty neat but I can't see how someone could make a living making lines and squiggles on cars."

I saw this in a completely different light. I felt as though I was working with one of the most diverse forms of art known to man. Literally, any object could be pinstriped. Trucks, pickups, tractors, cars, antique, custom hot rods, vans, motorcycles, furniture, farm equipment, you name it. Just about anything but wind and water can be pinstriped. The great thing was that I could create my own designs and styles of striping.

Most stripers were from California and at this time, there were few people around doing any pinstriping. My dad had dabbled with it, mostly lines and some design work on fire trucks, but no real "custom stuff." This was something I could call my own. The designs they were using on the West Coast were an inter-twining of lines all the same thickness, now known as "Old School." I could duplicate that style easy enough, but I wanted my own style. I remember my dad teaching me calligraphy and telling me that the beauty was in the combination of "thick and thin" strokes in the letters. The down stroke was thick and the up stroke was thin. The contrast between the two gave beauty to the lettering. I started using that theory with pinstriping. One stroke thick, the next stroke thin, so forth and so on throughout the entire design. This was very different when compared to the single line strokes the California guys were using. Later I would add another color but only in the thick stroke. I also noticed that the West Coast stripers were always using contrasting colors. I started using soft shades composed partially of the background color. The striping looked as though it was born with the car. Something else I discovered back then; pinstriping if done correctly, brings out the object, not itself. This gave this form of art tremendous value. A few carefully placed lines and designs and you were looking at a different vehicle. Pinstriping was a creative person's dream. I had another "Tiger by the Tail."

The lettering and pinstriping would carry me through my teenage years like a genie riding on a magic carpet.

I found myself going places I had never dreamed. Constantly surrounded by race car people, custom car buffs, and geniuses of every kind. These were, for the most part, people with very little, if any formal education. Happensburg once told me that, *"Creativity is contagious, and that Genius teaches itself."* There was proof of this all around me, and also the presence of a spirit that seemed to choreograph everything.

❧ THE HOOD

I had been so busy with my work that I hadn't seen any of the guys that were in the club except in school. Tom was working at the grocery store and the rest of the time with his dad. I walked home from school with Danny and Tom but after that we went our separate ways. I have to admit we did kind of miss the capers we pulled but we had grown and had to leave the childish things behind. Well, one winter day on the way home from school we were walking past Poutre Hill. What we saw looked like a Norman Rockwell picture. The kids were sleigh riding down the hill and their little scarves were blowing in the wind as they scurried down the hill. They all had these new sleds, the biggest craze; they called them "Flexible Flyers." Every kid seemed to have one. As we stood there watching, I asked… "Danny, why don't you ask your ol' man to buy you one of them "Flexible Flyers?" (That was kind of a private joke. Danny's family moved here from Communist Poland and his old man was the meanest person I've ever seen.) He chuckled and said sure I ask my ol' man for a "flexible flyer" and first he'll show me "flexible," and then he'll show me "flyer." We all laughed and continued on our way. Then I got an idea.

"Hey guy's follow me." I took them over to Baldies junk yard. It was right across from Johnson's. Baldie was right out front when we arrived.

"Hey Baldie!" I yelled out (he didn't hear so well,) "You still got that '51 Buick hood out back? The one with dents in it?"

"Yep, it's out there. Who wants it, you?"

"Yea, what would ya take for it?"

"What in hell ya going to do with that, Davie?"

"We're going to use it for a toboggan."

"Go ahead, take it Davie; you can paint me another 'keep out' sign for the back gate when ya get a chance."

"You got it Baldie, thanks." We carried the Buick hood over to the clubhouse. I got a couple of candles and we waxed the underside. We ripped out the insulation and stuffed the inside with cardboard.

The next day during school we told some of the guys that were in the club to meet us at the top of Poutre Hill right after school. Tom and I brought the hood to the top of the hill. Five of our guys showed up.

Illustration by SueAnn Summers Griessler

There was the Norman Rockwell picture, the kids and their little scarves waving down the hill. Well, that was about to change. All the guys climbed into the hood. I shoved her off and jumped in myself. We probably should have balanced the load better, but what did we know — we never rode this thing before. The big steel hood weighed a ton and with all of us in it, the thing really started to roll down that hill. One of the guys shifted his weight and the thing veered to the left going across the hill, then he tried correcting and the thing swung to the right; kids were jumping out of the way and running to get away from it. One kid let go of the rope on his sled as he jumped out of the way and we crushed his little Flexible Flyer like a pancake. We picked up so much speed that we went past the run off at the bottom and went half way up the hill on the other side. What a ride!

After a short time, Mr. Rockwell would have had to paint a very different picture. There were Flexible Flyers leaning against all of the trees and kids waiting in line to ride the "Hood." They were all yelling … "Hood! Hood! Hood!" as they waited in line.

It was good to have some fun with the guys. I know they had a good time but I couldn't wait to get a brush in my hand and get back over to Johnson's — that was where the action was. I liked working there. The work was challenging but it kept me on my toes, or should I say Rollie kept me on my toes. He was really strict about my being on time for jobs and anything I agreed to do, I had to do it. No ifs, ands, or buts. This was my first real experience with *discipline* regarding my work and my talents.

I always wondered how my friends who were involved in sports stuck it out through all the practice and training, especially the guys on the football team. I would watch them after school running in the heat with full uniforms and all the gear. How do they stay with it without quitting? But later at the big game, when one of them caught the winning pass and carried it through the end zone with everybody cheering, I could see it was all worth it. For me, many jobs were really difficult. Often, halfway through I would take what lettering I had on it off and start all over again. But when I finished and the owner picked up his truck or car or whatever, he was happy and that is what was important.

Discipline, once my enemy was now becoming my friend.

Chapter 7:

CREATING VALUE

"**V**alue" (Worth or importance of something.) The very reason I was allowed to be around people in the garages was that I had brought in something of value. The better I became at my craft the more valuable I became. I thought back to my little lemonade stand. It wasn't nearly as valuable on the side street near my house as it was down by the bus stop. The ideas I had, when properly developed, had value. Maybe not so much in school, but in the right arena…

The teachers in school often used the term "pie in the sky" regarding my thoughts and ideas.

I am approaching my sixty-eighth birthday while writing this book and I can honestly say that I have had prayers answered, had dreams come true, and experienced the "pie in the sky" with such reality that I enjoyed it with ice cream. I will also tell you that none of this would have happened had it not been for a large measure of God's grace. Don't ever give up on your dreams or let anyone tell you they can't come true!

If you wish to do what you love to do and make a living at it, then "what you do" must have **value** to those who will be purchasing it or supporting it. The secret here is in "what you can **give**, not what you can get." It all has to do with a mindset and a *spirit of contribution*. I'll discuss this later in the book.

I was realizing that in the environment I was working, ideas would flourish, especially around race cars. Many skills were involved in order to maintain a race car. It was a haven for ideas and inventions. I also experienced the value of "problem solving," the core of the true inventor.

If you can solve some of your own problems, you can be very happy. However, if you can possibly solve some of other people's problems… you can be rich.

The inventor is a problem solver.

Think of it this way… if an invention solves a problem in the kitchen, it could have some value. But if an invention solves a safety problem on the job, or if an invention solves a medical problem, then the value increases immensely. And the decimal and comma will spread apart accordingly.

It seemed that every day there were problems to be solved. The exciting thing was that they got solved! My experiences with my neighborhood capers came in handy. I was no stranger to problem solving, this time on the positive side.

There was no doubt I was on the correct path because everything in my past seemed to hold value regarding the present and often the future. At this point I was so thankful that I had taken the RIGHT path. If I had continued with the destructive mentality, who knows where I would have ended up. But with a constructive mentality, the opportunities were as Happensburg said… "Limitless."

There was something else that held value during these times. Things were not going well at home and my work provided a refuge, and often an escape for me. I need not go into details about what went on at our home — that would have little value. It was for certain though that it was not getting better. The whole alcohol thing really bothered me. I liked the biker crowd but working at bars and around drunks really bugged me. There wasn't any drinking around the race car people or at least the ones I was involved with, so I just stayed the course and in the direction I was heading.

❧ THE VALUE OF COMMON SENSE

"Common sense" has tremendous value. Wisdom is rooted in common sense. Let me give you an example of wisdom rooted in common sense.

We have all heard the term "starving artist." When we hear that, we envision an artist trying to sell paintings on a street corner or in a gallery somewhere. Whenever someone would ask me what I did for a living and I said that I was an artist, there would be sympathy on their faces and then they'd say something like "Oh, I see, well good luck with that."

But common sense revealed something to me. The money I could make as an artist would be directly *proportional* to the **VALUE** of the object I was putting my artwork on.

I attached my art to things that already had value.

This is where as artists we must be very careful. It is so important that once our talents are developed, we then take them to the highest possible level.

The concept is simple. Let's say for instance that I hand paint a name on the back of a boat for someone at a local marina. I would charge X dollars. Now envision lettering the back of a boat at a marina in Ft. Lauderdale that has a helicopter on the deck. Same money? Not on your life! I actually had that exact experience.

How about lettering race cars? There would be a huge difference between lettering a "hobby car" with plain lettering, to applying Gold Leaf to a car driven by "Pete Corey." I knew that I had to develop my skills to the point that I could position myself accordingly.

Working around Johnson's, Mott's, and Jim Young's garages gave me the leverage I needed.

It was time to change my title to "Commercial Artist." That had a much better ring to it.

At this point in time I was realizing the true effect and influence my Dad, Happensburg and other adults had on my life. I was very fortunate to be surrounded by such wonderful people. Being around adults became quite comfortable for me. Although I had fun with kids my age, there wasn't much to draw from them. I loved knowledge and learning new things. The kind of education I was receiving on the "outside," seemed to have value in that what I learned could be immediately applied to something. If I learned a new letter style or pinstriping design, I would apply it to some car, truck or object within days. I fully understood *application* and its relationship to *education*. With an understanding that this was only the beginning, it was clear that I was on the right path.

"Education attains its true value when associated with Application"

✍ "THE WHIZZER"

I got a call from an excavating contractor who wanted lettering on a pickup truck. He asked if I might be able to do the work in his garage, as he was building a bumper and ladder racks for the truck and needed to take measurements as he went along. He assured me that no one would bother me and the garage was well lighted. This sounded great, to get a break from all the activity at Johnson's. I loved lettering but with people constantly watching and asking questions, it was starting to wear on me. He said he'd pick me up and accommodate me any way he could if I could do it. It worked out perfectly. A few days later there I was lettering the truck, with the guy in the other part of the garage welding away on the bumper and racks.

As I lettered the truck, I noticed over in the corner of the garage a bicycle that had a motor on it. It was covered with an inch of dust. When the guy came over to take another measurement off of the truck I asked him about it. "It's a "Whizzer" he said. "The thing has been there in that corner for ten years. They were popular for a while — I think Sears handled them. You could buy the complete bike or there was a kit you could buy and put it on a bike. This was the complete bike. The motor doesn't turn over; it's stuck from sitting there so long. It did run when we put it there years ago. My brother ran it for years. He's living out in California now. Are you interested in that thing? You'll probably have to take the motor apart to get it running."

"What would you take for it?" I asked.

"Tell you what, give me some of that 'fancy work' what is it... pinstriping? On the hood, tailgate, and a little around the door handles and it's yours. I'll trade the pinstriping for the bike. Fair enough?"

I finished the lettering and put the striping on the truck where he asked. We loaded everything in his other truck and he brought me and the Whizzer home. It was after dark when I rolled her into the shed. I told my dad what had taken place and he came out to take a look.

"It's just stuck from sitting so long," he said. "The rings on the piston attach themselves to the cylinder wall. Pull the spark plug out, I want to try an old trick."

I got the plug wrench and removed the spark plug. My dad left for a moment and returned with a bottle of Coca-Cola. He poured some down into the spark plug hole into the cylinder.

"There, let her set overnight and tomorrow I'll bet she'll turn over. The Coke will eat the corrosion off of the rings. Then, with the spark plug out push the bike down the driveway turning it over. Let it 'puke' all of the Coke out of it then put a little motor oil in the cylinder and turn that over. Not too much oil though, or it will foul the plug when you go to start it. While the plug is out, hook it to the plug wire and lay it against the head on the motor, turn it over and see if you have spark across the electrodes. If you have spark and compression and fresh fuel to the carburetor, she should run."

The next morning I wasn't even hardly awake, I got dressed and ran out to the shed. I grabbed the pulley on the side of the motor and gave it a twist. She turned over! Quickly I put the belt on the pulleys, rolled it down the driveway and "puked" the Coke out of the cylinder. I followed my dad's instructions to the letter. A little oil in the spark plug hole, then I carefully put the spark plug against the head and as I turned it over saw the bright spark shoot across the electrodes. Next, I put the plug in and gassed her up.

To start the Whizzer you would pedal it while holding down a compression release, then when the engine fired let up on the release, twist the throttle, and away you go. Well, I did exactly that and there I was taking a ride on my Whizzer. Quickly though I returned and put it back in the shed. I couldn't wait to clean and polish it up and tell all my friends what I had here. But then I thought for a moment…wait, why not make this spectacular? I had a plan.

Debbie had called several times and I hadn't gotten back to her because I had been so busy lettering stuff over at Johnson's. I promised her we would go fishing but I wasn't looking forward to pedaling my bike (with her riding on the handlebars) all the way out to Frenchie's. My bike was so slow and hard to pedal, I had trouble keeping up to the guys when I was riding alone. But now that had changed. Once again I was "motorized."

As always there were a few minor problems. Not the least of which was that this was a motorized vehicle and illegal to run on the road without licenses, etc. But as I looked at it sitting there, it was just a basic bicycle except it had a motor and a shiny chrome gas tank sitting there for everyone to notice. The motor was small and tucked neatly in the frame but the tank was the problem. I thought of removing it and attaching a small can someplace hidden out of sight. Then an idea came to me.

I would strap my jacket over the tank, put the tackle box over it in such a way that when needed, I could drop the sides of the jacket down and cover the motor, and with fishing poles attached we would have a very practical disguise. Would it work? We were about to find out.

I had been pushing the brush pretty hard and a day off to go fishing, especially with Debbie, would be great. That alone would have been wonderful but I thought I might have a little fun and "bump" things up a bit. I'd invite the guys to go fishing, too.

This is the way it unfolded. Everyone met at my place and we got ready to go. The Whizzer and Debbie were hidden away behind the shed, all ready also. I told the guys I had to wait for Debbie and convinced them to go ahead and we'd meet them up at Frenchie's later. They took off. We would give them about a ten minute head start. Debbie and I climbed onto the Whizzer. I pedaled down the driveway, let out the compression release and we were off.

How nice it felt to feel the wind in my face. Debbie held on tight. The motor was quiet and ran smooth. We would travel mostly back roads except for a stretch of Guilderland Ave. out to Rt. 20. We kept watching for police cars along the way. No problem on the back roads, everything was going fine, but as soon as we hit Guilderland Ave. we saw a police car coming. I immediately dropped the sides of my jacket down, stood up and began pedaling. He went right by and never gave us a second look. Perfect! I love it when a plan works out. Now if we can catch up to the boys. I throttled it up and we looked ahead. We went over a railroad bridge and the motor strained with both of us on the bike, but we made it. I knew we had flat road ahead, so no worries. What happened next I will never forget. There they were about a quarter of a mile ahead, pedaling away. We got closer and closer, both excited knowing what was about to happen. Finally, we crept up behind them and then... we pulled out and passed them! Their mouths dropped, eyes popping out, totally in shock at what they were seeing. They tried to keep up but couldn't. Debbie waved as we drove off. We headed on to Frenchie's Hollow. When we got there Debbie quickly ran around, turning over rocks to find a couple of large "grubs" to use as bait (her secret for catching bass), and we had already caught two large bass and got a little "necking" in by the time the guys arrived — that added a little frosting to the cake. Then everybody took turns riding the Whizzer. Debbie and I traveled many miles that summer and no one ever detected our little disguise.

A year or so later I traded the Whizzer and a few bucks for an Indian motorcycle. It was all apart in several boxes and baskets. When I picked it up I asked the guy if he was sure that everything was there. He assured me everything was there.

"Not for nothing," I said, "but I have a buddy who is going to put this thing together for me and he's a member of a seriously bad ass biker gang. He said he'd really be pissed if all the parts ain't there, so if there's a problem I'm giving' him your address and phone number — you can deal with him." With that the guy went into his back room and brought out another box with extra parts.

Will Courtney actually put the bike together for me and he did it in less than a week. He lived right near Larned's sand and gravel pit and I would leave the bike at Will's garage. From there I could take it behind the gravel pit onto the road along the railroad tracks and ride. Actually, I could go all the way to Frenchie's and the reservoir by following the tracks behind Larned's.

You know I had to take Debbie for a ride on the Indian. As I said, a year or so had gone by. I called her up and told her we should go fishing on my new ride for old times' sake.

What I hadn't realized was that Debbie had changed.

She showed up in a tank top and tight shorts and took me by surprise. Let's just say she had "filled out" some. She reminded me of the scar she got on her leg from the hot exhaust pipe on the Whizzer; it was completely gone. I looked at those legs and thought... "Those aren't even the same legs she had back then."

We jumped on the Indian and went down through the gravel pit and up onto the road alongside the tracks and headed for Frenchie's.

Illustration by Bill Carney

This rig carried us much better than the little Whizzer. It felt good, shifting gears and having a V-twin engine with some power between my legs and her arms around me. I remember thinking ... "It don't get any better than this." . Then about a mile and a half out Debbie leans over and giggles in my ear... "Davie... we forgot the fishin' poles."

Would you believe... it just got better! The fish will have to wait.

Chapter 8:

PETE COREY

The list by the phone was getting longer and jobs were building up at Johnson's. It was hard to keep up. Everyone seemed to be in a hurry. Stock cars got damaged every week and getting a sign painter to do them was a real problem. I was solving that problem.

Although Pete Corey had gained much fame while driving Bob Mott's yellow #3, he was now driving the #37 out of AC Body Works. He had been involved in a bad accident at Fonda Speedway and ended up losing a leg as a result. He was determined to keep driving and the guys at AC's were building a new car for him while he was recuperating. I was to letter it. AC Body Works became a new hangout for me. Pete spent much time there himself and we became

good friends. Pete was very intelligent and creative. The better I got to know him the more I admired him. We had much in common. Pete would come up with an idea and immediately put it into practical use. It seemed while everyone was copying everyone else, Pete was always on the cutting edge, always thinking ahead. He would read the rule book on what was allowed at certain tracks and then figure how he could stretch things to the max, or many times come up with something that the rules did not include, often catching them sleeping. For a time I believe they were rewriting the rules around Corey's thinking. Pete had talent as a race car driver but unlike many other drivers of that era, he didn't "man handle" the car. Although Corey was fearless, he was smooth; he would finesse the car, using every trick in the book in order to win. And Corey won many races.

I spent over a week lettering the #37, along with the truck that hauled it. Pete was really pleased with the job. I told Pete someday I want to be a professional at this. He stood there for a moment then handed me a hundred dollar bill and said, "Let that be today, you are professional David. This is one of the best looking cars I've ever driven."

A hundred bucks was a lot of money in those days — I didn't know what to say. He went on to say "You've got all these a-holes chasing you down for your work; if you adjusted your prices you would eliminate half of them, and make twice as much money."

Pete was all about money. I had heard stories about Pete in his younger years when he raced at the old B and K speedway. They would pay twenty five bucks to the winner of the main event and give a contingency prize of ten dollars if you crashed real bad or rolled your car over, as the fans loved that stuff. Corey would win the race and, just as he passed the checkered flag, he'd crank the wheel and deliberately roll the car over to collect another ten bucks. His style of driving drew large crowds everywhere he went.

By the time Pete and I met he was a highly polished and very successful driver. Having really nice lettering on the car fit the mode. At this time most of the stock cars running local tracks were not that great looking. To have a really sharp car was a tremendous boost to a driver's ego, not to mention the morale of the crew. Also, sponsors were more apt to get involved when the car looked good. I could clearly see I had another tiger by the tail. I enjoyed hanging out with Pete Corey, not just because he was a celebrity, but he was intelligent and often talked about ideas and even philosophy. He was impressed with what I knew about life and ideas, and I was impressed with what he knew.

Pete was pretty straightforward and to him, most people were idiots or a-holes. Although Pete and I connected on many things, this was where we disagreed. I really liked the people I worked for. Some had a lot of money, some had little, but I truly enjoyed working with most of them.

Stock car lettering turned out to be a very good thing for me. For the most part I could have free reign at layout and design. Sometimes there would be some company logo that would have to be put on a car but generally I could do whatever I wanted to do. I could experiment with colors and letter styles.

Pete Corey hooked me up with dozens of owners and drivers. All Pete had to say was, "This is the kid that does the lettering on my cars" and I was "in." Most of the car owners were businessmen, so I would spin off lots of truck lettering, signs, and pinstriping from them. Once again my world was getting larger. Pete Corey was fueling my rocket to the moon.

"Leveraging" (Mechanical advantage.) My new word for the day. In this case, "positional" advantage.

It may seem like everything was coming my way easily and that every stroke of the brush was like waving a magic wand. Not true. In those days every job was a challenge, with its own difficulties. It was difficult enough developing my craft, but dealing with different people every day was a craft within itself. Many people took advantage of me. I was wide open for trouble in certain areas, simply because at that point in time I had talent that was quite well developed, but little education regarding business or understanding people and what they were capable of. It's a combination of things that make it all work. I see no point in going over the details of every problem I had or every job that someone screwed me out of, and after all, some of the people that I had problems with are my good friends today. Times change and people change.

There was however one incident that I feel is worth discussing in that the lesson learned had tremendous value to me.

☙ AGAINST THE LAW

There was a man that owned several businesses. Somehow he got my name and called me about doing signs for one of his businesses. I looked the job over and gave him a price. He said OK, go head, do the job. It took me a week or so to cut the material, paint the backgrounds and letter the signs (keep in mind; I was only fifteen years old.) When I finished I delivered the signs to the location. Within a day or so he had someone put them up. When I went to get paid he asked me if I had a registered business. I told him no, I just do this stuff and that I didn't know I had to be registered for anything. He informed me that there was no way his accounting department could pay me. He said that if he knew I didn't have a registered business going in, he would not have had me do the job. When I suggested taking the signs back he said he had paid someone to install them and that it would be against the law for me to remove them from his property. He had all the answers including threatening turning me into the IRS for operating an unregistered business.

At first I didn't know what to do. Many things crossed my mind. Why would he do this? I felt powerless. Then I thought... mostly negative things, like striping a few motorcycles for a few people who specialize in taking care of problems like this, but clearly that wasn't the way to go.

I started to realize that "bullies" weren't just the kind we experience in school, but they were out there in life as well. I handled the bullies in school by using "leverage" with friends or a little "creativity." But what I learned back then was that I usually won the battle but often started a war. I had no time to put energy into this, let alone start a war with this guy. I remember Happensburg's little discussion about trying to serve two masters. The path I had chosen had no options for revenge against anyone.

My Uncle Holl, when talking about war told me ...

"Always choose Good over Evil. Good has but one enemy, Evil. On the other hand, Evil has two enemies, "good" and "itself."

My dad reminded me once again... *"If you don't use your head, your whole body suffers."*

So the great lesson I learned would serve as payment and I simply moved on.

❧ TREMENDOUS CONFIDENCE

Being around adults most of the time and actually being involved with the things they were doing gave me tremendous confidence. I was willing and most of the time able to do many things.

Chapter 9:

THE BACKYARD BODYMAN

A round this time I had been in and out of so many body shops and witnessed enough paint work on cars that I thought I might give it a shot myself. I had picked up a '41 Plymouth coup that was in real great shape. It hadn't run in many years but the fellow I bought it from assured me "It ran when he parked it."

My dad did his usual thing. He'd coach me, but always allowed me to do the actual tasks myself. "That's how you learn" he'd say. I never complained. I was 14 years old and had already owned several motorcycles and now my own car. I often wondered if my dad wasn't a heavy drinker and such a "happy go lucky guy" if all this could have ever happened. Other kids' parents would never have allowed these things. The tremendous amount of freedom and countless opportunities I had for a kid my age were amazing.

The paint job I created on the '41 left much to be desired but it provided a wonderful learning experience. There were some pinstriping designs added later but regrettably there are pictures of them.

My dad, my dog "Teddy", me, and the '41 Plymouth coupe.

My first complete paint job. I added a fair amount of pinstriping later but regret having no pictures of the '41 pinstriped.

Chapter 10:

IDENTITY

As I was developing my craft I was also getting quite a reputation, a reputation that was working for me. I did not want to disrupt that in any way. With this "reputation" many things were changing including my "identity." My new friends didn't know me as a little punk or conniver; all they knew about me was that I was the kid doing all this lettering and pinstriping for everybody. I was now known as a creative "Commercial Artist." I was going through a kind of transformation and it felt good.

There was something else that came with my new identity, I now had *something to protect*. I remember a couple of characters that I was once involved with, approaching me asking for help with some caper they had planned. I won't go into details but what they had in mind was very much against the law. I wanted no part of this, simply because I had *too much to lose*. They had no reputation or identity to worry about, but I did. When I told them how I felt, they did everything they could to insult me and hurt my feelings, even telling me that we were no longer friends. I think they call this "peer pressure." Instead of feeling bad, I felt like I had body armor on, what they said meant nothing to me. They went their way, I went mine.

I could feel something watching, guiding my life. (More about this later.) It was evident that what had happened to me during my childhood proved extremely valuable. My craft would not only feed me but it kept me safe during the events that took place regarding the development of my talent, the people that came into my life at the precise time, the circumstances and the sequencing of events that changed my attitude were not happening by chance or mere luck. There was the obvious presence of a higher power. When Happensburg told me that the choices I would make would have "spiritual ramifications," I had no idea what that meant. At this point it was starting to make sense. I continued to make mistakes but as soon as I realized a mistake was made, I would try to get back on track as soon as possible. I remember not wanting to disappoint whoever or whatever was watching over me.

An identity proved so valuable to me that long after I was married, when our children's abilities became evident, we cultivated their talents and tried as quickly as possible to establish their identity so that they too would have self-esteem and something to protect. Most importantly regarding decisions, they would have something to lose.

It is obvious in today's world many of those who get involved in major crimes, hurting others as well as themselves, have *no identity and little or nothing to lose.*

✎ ATTITUDE

Not only do I believe that attitude is important, I believe that attitude *controls everything.* When I changed my attitude my life changed. Changing your attitude is not just changing the way you act toward people or things, that's only part of it, and in many cases, it's just an "act." I'm talking about changing the way you actually *see* and even *feel* about things. Changing the way you perceive things.

I started to realize that there was a kind of "magnetic field" around human beings. This field seemed to be controlled by our attitude. Did you ever notice how some people just seem to attract problems into their lives, while others seem to have all the luck. Well, I've been on both sides of that fence and you would be amazed just how much you can control circumstances in your life by harnessing the power of "attitude." It's much more than just thinking positive, although that's a good start. It's actually *living* positive.

As a young artist I was often attracting people who would take advantage of me (like the man mentioned earlier.) I started to develop an "attitude" that was not very positive. So I once again resorted to "creativity." Whenever I would see or feel that someone was going to take advantage of me, I would try to get "crystal clear" on all aspects of what we were doing. If they were trying to deliberately make things confusing or create "grey" areas, I would minimize everything that I could and get out of the situation as fast as possible. As a kid that's all I could do. On the other hand, when I ran into good people who were kind, considerate, and appreciated what I was doing for them, I gave them my all, actually giving them much more than they paid for. Before long it seemed like I was surrounded by good people. I was beginning to understand *"like attracts like."* However, I had to hold up my end as well. This was all supported by creative thinking and quality work.

Mutual respect reigns when both parties have something to lose.

Another slant on this would be... A bad attitude combined with the wrong set of circumstances and a person ends up in prison. The right attitude with the right set of circumstances and a person can enjoy an abundant life. It's that simple.

However, *ignorance* can make simple things complicated.

Speaking of ignorance, I started to realize that I was caught up in a certain form of ignorance myself, a sort of

S.N.A.R.E. Stubborn Negative Attitude Regarding Education (formal education)

As I met more educated people representing genuine "substance," this attitude would eventually change.

Let me put it poetically...

"I've been up, I've been down;
I guess you could say... I've been around.
And now I feel I have something to share;
Who really knows where anyone goes;
Though wherever that is, it's your Attitude that will be taking you there."

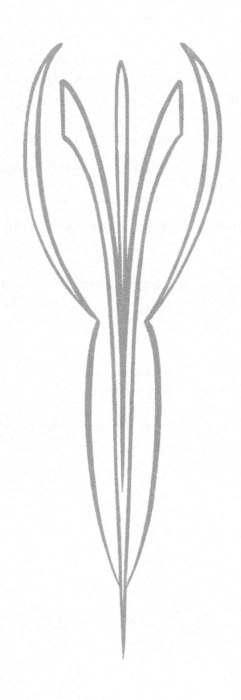

Chapter 11:

A STRONG SENSE OF PURPOSE

Something else that was very important in "guiding" me in my younger years was a strong sense of purpose. Once again my craft played the important role. I knew very little if anything about "setting goals" yet I was unconsciously setting and achieving goals. My craft was the nucleus for all of this. Everything in my life revolved around my art, my friends, my income, my joy, and as I mentioned before, my refuge. I was aware of what was happening and thankful every day. This had brought a new dimension to the word *"gift."*

I was developing a "Belief System," something that truly worked for me. An example would be… Happensburg telling me, *"If I was your age and knew what I know now . . ."* and how I wanted to know what he knew **now.** It was coming true. *"Ask and you shall receive"* was actually happening. This is not to say that every foolish thing I asked for came my way, that's not true, but the important "life changing" things did come true.

All of this sparked an interest in *philosophy* (An examination of basic concepts such as truth, existence, reality, causality, and freedom), my new word for the day.

I wanted to know "literally" what was happening in my life, and also "what" or "who" was watching over me. A study of philosophy proved to be very *"valuable."* Not so much regarding who or what was helping me though, that turned out to be *"spiritual,"* but a philosophy regarding my work and the people I had been dealing with.

I can remember pinstriping a man's motorcycle, imagining myself not as an artist but rather a "tailor" making a suit for this guy. The motorcycle would represent "who he was," much like the clothes a person wears. He was very conservative in mannerism and well dressed. This set the stage for very thin lines, tight designs, very soft colors related to the background color, etc. I "knew" this would work for this man and it did. Another person might be flamboyant, loud, aggressive, and egotistical. The lines would change drastically. A much heavier stroke with more sharp spikes in the design work would work well for him. To prove this theory (or philosophy) as I called it back then, just imagine turning these jobs around and doing the conservative job for the egotistical guy; he would feel "short changed" or the other man would feel that I had gone way too far. These are extreme examples and this concept had to be seriously "fine tuned," so matching the lines with the individual became a game with me. The unique thing was that it separated me from other artists that were merely "decorating." I was using a "conceptual" approach in my work. As the years went by, I became very good at matching the job to the customer.

I am surprised to this day that although our styles are so often imitated, other artist's never caught on to my concept. They imitate our work but often put the wrong style with the person. Although, if either the customer (or the artist) are not aware of this, then I guess it wouldn't matter, although it's the misplaced purpose that reduces their work to mere "decoration."

∾ CREATING… A MONSTER

At fifteen I was trying to handle something much larger than I had bargained for. It took a considerable amount of time to do each lettering job. The jobs kept on coming faster than I could produce them. This created quite a dilemma, especially with race cars. They would get damaged or even destroyed, and as soon as they were repaired they would need to be lettered for the race on the weekend. This presented a lot of work to be done in a short amount of time. The other problem was that I was the last person in line. The lettering was last, after the body, the tires, the motor, etc. It was often… "Davie, I'll pay you next week, ok?" Pete Corey would keep telling me to get rid of half of these guys, but somehow I just kept trying to get them all done. I would skip school sometimes two or three days a week to get jobs done. Then when I went back I would have more detention, which meant falling behind and then having to skip school again to get caught up. It was a vicious circle. The very thing that provided my refuge was now consuming me.

It became impossible to do all the work and take care of everyone. I couldn't just call up someone to help me with the work. I was the only one that could do the lettering and pinstriping. The burden on me was tremendous. If I only had more time, I could get more done. Finally, summer vacation came and provided me with more time to get work completed.

It was 1962 and that summer I turned sixteen. I could legally quit school. I could get a driver's license. These were major milestones in my life. It seemed I was finally about to gain some leverage over some of the authority that had ruled over me for so long. It was time to plan my escape. Escape from the "confines of institutional learning." The major stumbling block was my parents having to sign the proper papers for this to happen. All I had to do was convince them that leaving school would be the right thing for me to do. I would be able to advance my career now, when I'm on a roll or at least giving it a try. I thought, it would be a kind of "leave of absence." Yes, that's it! I would tell them I would just leave for this year and if it doesn't work out, I would go back next year and continue my high school education. Just give me this year to try to expand my career. That'll work. That's exactly how I'll present it to them. They could see that I had a good thing going and I wasn't just trying to "get out" to "hang out" or anything like that. (Of course once I was out I had no intentions of ever going back.)

In September of that year when I returned to school I put my plan to work. The first thing was to get the proper paper work from the office without anyone of power knowing what I was up to. There was a girl that worked in the office that I could trust to get me the paper work. She knew that I was rolling with my career and also believed the leave of absence story. This way, no one would be able to talk to my parents and convince them not to sign.

It took a little time to put everything in place, so I ended up being in school longer than I anticipated. During that time, if there were any doubt in my mind about my going in the wrong direction, it was erased when I ended up in detention once again, this time for talking in class. I made myself a promise that once I left the halls of detention, they would never see me again.

The very next week I had the papers in hand, now to convince my parents to sign them.

Chapter 12:

CREATING FREEDOM

It was actually easier than I thought. My presentation was flawless. It went over without a hitch. Of course, the part where I told them that the teachers and the administration at school thought that because it was such an unusual set of circumstances (my being talented in areas that they could not offer any training), that it was a good idea and that "they would hold my 'paper work,' anticipating my return next year," was most convincing. With that, I got the signatures.

I thought about a grand exit, telling them exactly what I thought of them, but that could be dangerous and besides, I was getting what I wanted, why be foolish? If I told them about the world I was living in they wouldn't even know what I was talking about. The important thing was, they no longer had hold of me. I had the freedom documents in my hand. I even had them notarized to make sure no one could change anything.

When I presented the papers to the principal you would think a bomb went off. It was as if I put a stick into a bee's nest. He was freaking out and telling me I couldn't do this and couldn't do that. I just explained that the paper work was in order and I turned and walked away. By the time I reached my locker, other teachers were approaching me and telling me what a mistake I was making. I was surprised how fast the word spread. My only concern was getting to the door. One of the male teachers grabbed my arm. I informed him my paper work was in order and I HAD DONE MY HOMEWORK, and that if he didn't let go of me he'd be hearing from my attorney. This time it was I who was in control. He released his grip and I headed down the hall and out the door.

I have to admit, there was a "tinge" of regret, but the anger and resentment was so deep that any doubt I had about leaving quickly disappeared. I also knew that I had better make a success of my life or I would be the biggest fool this school had ever known. High school dropouts traditionally pay the price for not getting an education. I was aware of this and made myself a promise that by the time my class graduated, I would be recognized as "successful" in my field. I honestly didn't think I was going backward but *forward,* actually getting a "head start" on those who were "stuck" back there in school. It was my thinking that while "they" were trying for the "Honor Roll" I was already "On A Roll" and the best thing to do would be to keep on going in the direction I had chosen.

ꕥ REALITY CHECK

This had proved to be quite a summer, after getting my driver's license, exiting from school, and having lettered some of the top running race cars in our area, you might say I was riding on a pretty high horse. My confidence level was through the roof.

I had heard that Happensburg had returned from Europe and I just couldn't wait to tell him about the successful life I was living.

I pulled up to his house in my gun metal grey '55 Merc (a car I picked up from a friend of Rollie Johnson's.) On the lower part of the front fender was written "Steel Lady" in "Old English." (Names lettered on cars became another tiger I had by the tail; more about that later.)

I was so glad to see the old fellow and Happensburg was very glad to see me. I started right in telling him how much my life had changed while he was in Europe. I went on and on patting myself on the back, bragging about how well I was doing. When I explained in detail how I pulled off my escape from school, he became visibly upset. In reaction to that, I quickly told him how many of my friends were looking up to me and in the circles I was traveling I was well respected. What he said to me brought me down a few pegs. It went something like this…

"In a land of Idiots — half a brain is King."

"I strongly suggest 'King David' that you use the other half of your brain to come down off your high horse and realize what you are doing. If you think that I could rejoice in your arrogance after you manipulated everyone, including your very ill parents, you're wrong. Once again you've done everything *right* while doing *the wrong thing.* How can you be proud of that? Haven't you learned anything from me?" (He remained quiet for a few moments to regain his composure.) Then… "Do you know what a paradigm is?"

"No."

"Well let's just say it's 'your view' of something. Your "Window of understanding." The teachers in school don't hate you, they aren't happy when you are in detention. They may not be aware of your talents and know very little if anything about your personal life. They're doing the best they can with what they have and what they know about you. I'll admit their 'paradigm' may not be accurate, but neither is yours. The teacher that grabbed you by the arm probably thought you were making a terrible mistake and reacted accordingly. What you did was sneaky and one sided and the fact that you are so proud of what you did disturbs me."

"If you had debated the issue of quitting school and presented all the facts, I could respect that. More than likely, you could have done quite well in a debate and gained tremendous respect from them in presenting who you really are. But to pull what you did deserves no respect. It was pure manipulation, nothing more. Let me give you one of the secrets of life David. Here we are discussing an issue; although the circumstances are different, the fundamentals are much the same as when you manipulated some of your neighbors. In life this happens often, but the point being that you should have learned something the first trip around so that this time, when a circumstance presents itself again, you should have the 'tools' in place to handle it in a more intelligent manner than when you were less experienced. Do you understand? This is precisely why some people suffer their entire lives, simply by ignoring that principle. The train stops several times but they fail to board. What stops them? Usually Pride. And while we are on the subject, let me say this…"

"In your little pond you may appear to be a big fish, but if you were to work alongside some of the real masters of your craft, you may come to the realization that you have some growing to do. You are calling all of your own shots. I strongly suggest that you search out the real 'players' in your field and see how you compare to them, then and only then would you know for sure where you stand regarding your status as an artist."

Wow, the wind had gone from my sails. As usual, Happensburg presented his case with precision and accuracy. I was on a high horse and now been thrown to the ground. What truly amazed me about my discussions with Happensburg was that every time he would pull me back, or *cut me down* with corrective criticism, I always had the feeling that somehow I was moving ahead.

The next day while still healing from Happensburg's slicing, I witnessed something that confirmed everything that had occurred. As I pulled into a friend's driveway, his neighbor was just a few feet away and what she was doing caught my eye. She was "pruning" or "cutting back" a berry bush. I stopped for a moment, fixed on her clipping away. She happened to be very friendly and immediately started explaining that she cuts the plants down in the fall for their good health and when they come back in the spring, they'll produce much more fruit. I told her that made perfect sense.

I understood clearly the teaching in Happensburg's wisdom. The pruning or cutting of bushes to produce a better crop is a natural principle. Once again, in the world I was living, everything was related in some way to everything else. Was this a guidance system for me? I took it as confirmation. I could move on now, better "pruned."

These little incidents that kept happening in my life, I called "road signs;" they became "indicators" that I was at the right place at the right time in my journey. They renewed my faith in whatever was guiding me.

The study of philosophy was becoming even more interesting to me. **I also learned to keep a close eye out for repeat circumstances and kept the tools handy to deal with them.** In doing this, I feel I avoided many a crisis in my life.

"Crisis Demands Change"

ॐ *ON TOP OF MY GAME*

Having wheels under me and free from school, it seemed like the world was mine to explore. I began to search for the "Masters" in my craft. The next year or so, in addition to my own work, I would spend much time meeting and often working with many of the well known sign painters in our area. Admittedly, I learned something from every one of them, but noticed that many of them had taught apprentices over the years and that the apprentices had become a "copy" of themselves. This was not for me, and ironically I came upon an idea, later realizing it was actually an old philosophy…

"He, who uses everyone's ideas, can become most original." (Confucius)

I would combine the styles of many to work out an original.

I don't think it hurt me at all having worked alone for so long, because I had developed my own style and that had given me a definite edge. I don't think any of the so-called "Masters" would have respected me had I represented someone else's style.

None of the so-called sign masters knew anything about pinstriping. Most of the major pinstripers were in California, with a few in New Jersey. I was surprised that the sign crafters hadn't picked up on it. Everyone looked at it as a totally different skill. Sign lettering and truck lettering, went with pinstriping "hand and glove" as far as I was concerned, and one definitely complimented the other.

Many of the old sign painters were taught their skills at Pratt Institute in New York City. Pinstriping was considered a novelty and not recognized as a "trade skill." Here, once again, we see the "imposed limitations" of institutional learning. It always amazed me to see how many limitations people put on themselves. People in groups often become "**cattle-ized**," they do what they're told and grow old. They just follow along and never step out of bounds. Throughout history it has been the "non-conformist" that has moved things forward. They were the ones that stepped out of bounds and created new pathways.

I never regretted not having a roadmap to follow; it only helped me become better with a compass. It seemed I was in undeveloped territory most of the time anyway and was becoming comfortable there. I'll prove my point...

My dad told me once that Henry Ford would return. Not him in person but the concept that Ford represented. Ford created an industry that had a *life of its own, a language of its own,* and He single-handedly *moved the stock market.* Years later, along came Bill Gates creating an industry that took on *a life of its own, a language of its own, and moved the stock market.* Both Ford and Gates qualify as "non-conformists." Both men stepped out of bounds. They certainly were not average "do as you are told" Joes.

By this time I had met many people in the sign industry. Freehand painters were always in demand so I had no problem hooking up with any of them. These men were artists and by nature, artists are "different." Some were very easy to work with but most were very difficult. Not a single one of them used philosophy regarding their work. Nor did they know anything about pinstriping. They were, for the most part "conventional."

There was one craftsman who I always admired and, after seeing and working with so many others, I came to admire him even more. He painted signs and race cars mostly as a hobby or side line. This man was very different from any of the other painters I knew. He didn't drink or smoke; he had a wonderful personality with people and was the most "stable" artist I had met.

From what I had seen in my life and the people in my trade, this was the man I would most want to emulate. His name, *Carl Borst*. He worked with his family running the Borst Oil Corp. He was multi-talented and extremely creative. Besides being an artist, he had become an accomplished "gunsmith," restored antique cars, and numerous other things. Not once did I ever hear him boast or brag about his work or his talents, yet he was as accomplished as anyone I have ever known. Let me make it clear that it wasn't only his craftsmanship that was so impressive, but "the man" himself. You have to realize that although I had a lot going on and had accomplished much for my age at that time, my life was filled with chaos. I used manipulation and talent to extract what I needed in a very chaotic existence. Many of the craftsmen I had known and learned from thus far where seriously flawed. It was obvious that Borst displayed as much talent as a person could possibly possess, but he also represented *stability*, and above all, *integrity*. The men I had always admired were considered successful, but their "home lives," the time spent with their wives and children, often didn't reflect it. Borst was clearly different. Borst was always very kind and gracious toward me, though I had the feeling nothing that I represented would even remotely impress him. He was out of my league. I had been involved with hawks, vultures, parrots, and probably a few magpies, but for the first time in my life had clear view of an *Eagle*. I'm sure he was never aware of the influence he had on my life in those early years. I was watching at a distance, a very talented and truly great human being.

It had been many years since I'd seen him, so one day I stopped to say hello and to see how he was doing. I have to admit I wasn't surprised to see that the Borst Genius had continued to unfold. He is now involved in wood carving. His work is phenomenal. The best I have ever seen. Not surprisingly, Borst is considered by his peers to be among the best.

He told me he had recently returned from England where he had attended symposiums and lectures on wood carving. He was only too happy to share many of his own techniques with the folks over there. His work has been displayed in many wood carving magazines and his name is known in wood carving circles throughout the world. Once again, I am totally amazed at the genius of Carl Borst.

118   DAVE DAVIES, SR.

Chapter 13

THE "NAME" CRAZE

I thought it was so cool that Jack Muldowney had given me the job of lettering "Cha-Cha" on Shirley's Corvette, but actually I recall the first name I
ever lettered on a car was *"Miss Pauline"* on the # 77 stock car. I had no
idea at the time I was doing the original lettering that Miss Pauline was
much more than just a name on a car, but actually a "Grand Lady" and the
owner of the 77 car. After lettering her car she had me letter the window
of her beauty shop (my first window lettering job). I was fourteen years
old. Not surprisingly Miss Pauline was well connected with many business
people in the area and my friendship with the Grand Lady moved me up
the socio-economic ladder a bit. I went from riding to the races in trucks
with the guys to riding with her in her new Cadillac.

I had seen names on the show cars in magazines and it really appealed to
me. I wasn't surprised when my friends wanted names in their cars, but I
had no idea how that fad would take off. I think it was an identity thing at
first, but quickly turned into a fad. Some of the hotter cars actually gained
a "reputation" and were identified by their names. Most were named after
current hit songs; "The Wanderer," "Loco-Motion," "Blue Velvet," "Ramblin'
Rose," and "Runaround Sue," to name a few. Then came "Nut Buster," "Wild

One," " Bear and A Half," "Who's sorry now," "Street Fighter", "Mid-Nighter," "Powder Puff," and "Tuff-a-Nuff." You name it and I lettered it on somebody's car. Girls often just had their name on the car. Once I lettered a name on the fender of a girl's car – no big deal, except it was actually her dad's car! I can remember him driving all over town with "Suzy-Q" on the front fender (he was probably looking for me!)

But by far the best names were the ones on race cars and drag cars, and one of the most clever names ever applied to a race car was coined by Ronnie Abbott on his national record holding dragster "HELL'S A POPPIN." When he pulled that car up on the line, visualize everyone holding their hands over their ears, flames shooting out of the pipes, and reading the bold letters displaying clearly what was going on. The name said it all.

Lettering names on boats was also very popular and often very clever and unique. Some that stick in my mind were… "Aqua-holic" and "Mino-pause," to name a couple, and let us not forget the guy who had me letter "Jan's Patio" on the sides of his bass boat. I asked if that was the name of a tavern or a bar; he said, "no, my wife was saving to put a new patio on the house and when I found out where she kept the money, I took it and bought the boat."

I remember thinking "good luck with that buddy. I wonder what it'll be like sleeping on that thing."

How about the words "Absolutely Not!" in large script letters across the back of a new boat that probably had more motor in it than most cars? I'll let you draw your own conclusion on that one.

Chapter 14

PICTURE THIS

R olling from one job to another had become a way of life for me. Now with wheels and more freedom, the extra time was filled in quickly with more work. The race cars I had done were "standing out" among the others and had become the subject matter of *John Grady* the track photographer at Fonda Speedway. John was another multi-talented guy. Not only was he a photographer, but a school teacher and also wrote a column for the local

newspaper. Photography seemed to be the nucleus for everything in John's life. He would always strive to get in a place or position where he could get the best shot, often putting himself in serious danger. Pete Corey once told me that he got tangled with a guy while coming out of the second turn and started flipping down the back stretch. As he was rolling over and over, there was Grady (just a few feet away,) clicking pictures. Sure enough, that week John stops over with a series of pictures in perfect sequence. He had caught on film every individual roll that car made down the back straight-a-way. It was no surprise that publications like "Speedway News" and the likes were using John's pictures. As I said, John was multi-talented. In his weekly column we would experience another picture of Grady's creation, this time with words. John told me once that, "the stories that follow my work were carrying me and making me so popular." Then he went on to say… "If you ask someone… who lettered your car? They might say Joe so and so from Troy. That is the end of the story. But if they say Dave Davies, then there would be the story. Bob Mott would start telling everyone how the police chased you and your girlfriend around Rotterdam on a motorized ladder contraption, or Corey would tell the story about the first time you gold leafed the numbers on the side of his new car and at the first race he wrecked it. I asked him in an interview if he regretted having the gold leaf job done. He pointed to the mangled car with the roof crushed down and front wheel missing, and brought to my attention that there wasn't a scratch in any of the gold leaf numbers. He said my only regret was that I didn't have Davie gold leaf the whole damned car!"

I was very fortunate to be the subject of some of those articles and many pictures over the years, and I seriously thank John Grady for helping make those years so special. One of John's favorite stories… (I know this because he reminds me of it every time I see him) was when Joe Leto "kidnapped" me.

Joe Leto was a major player in the racing game. He owned a trucking company in Albany and they ran a car (sometimes two cars) at Lebanon Valley Speedway, the #50's. These were winning cars and he always had top drivers. Some people said Joe was involved with a big organization and the name began with an "M," (let's just say it wasn't the Mickey Mouse Club.) I asked him once about it and he assured me that these were only rumors and that the organization was non-existent.

I had lettered cars and several trucks for Joe. He always treated me very good. In fact, whenever I needed a few bucks, I could always see Joe and he would "bankroll" me. I liked Joe; we were good friends. Joe had a problem with his blood pressure; he had a portable machine with him and he was always measuring it. He claimed waiting on me to letter the cars was a major cause of it. He was not accustomed to waiting for anything. Well, this particular time I was running behind and had told Joe that I would be there the next day. Before I realized it, two days had gone by. I was lettering another race car and the guy kept adding stuff and it was taking much more time than I thought and I tried explaining this all to Joe. Somehow though, Joe found out where I was doing this car. So there I was, working on this race car and I noticed a black Lincoln pull up outside the garage. I heard somebody say "Who are these guys? They look pretty official." Then two men came in and stood there watching me. The man that owned the garage asked if he could help them with anything. They just shook their heads "no" and continued to watch me. To say there was some serious tension in that garage was an understatement. At one point one of the guys said… "This car is done, let's go." Then he walked over, closed up my paint box, and took it out and put in the trunk of the Lincoln. The other guy picked up the rest of my stuff and put all that stuff in the trunk. The first guy walked over and held the rear door of the car open for me. Everyone just stood there, no one said a word. Then the first guy got on the phone in the car (few people had phones in their car back then.) He said something to someone and then stretched the cord and receiver out to me. I said… "Leto?" The guy nodded in the affirmative. As I put the phone to my ear, all I could hear was… "Davie! Do you have any idea how high my blood pressure is right now?" He rattled off some numbers, something over something. Then continued… "Those gentlemen are going to bring you here. Now, they have instructions to get you anything you need. So if you want food, or a woman, or anything else, you just tell them because you are not going anywhere until my car is done."

If I were to record every story about my experiences around race cars, this book would be over a thousand pages.

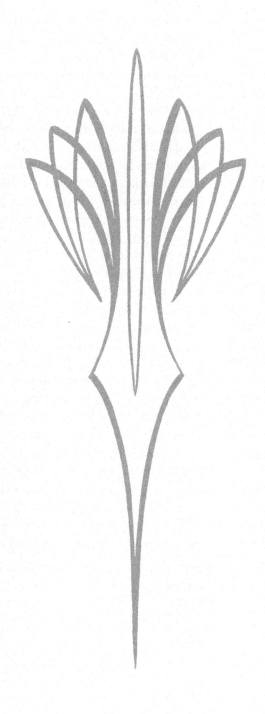

124   DAVE DAVIES, SR.

Chapter 15:

THE PLAYING FIELD

Whenever I felt like experimenting with custom paint and wanted to try out a new pearl, candy color, or metal flake, all I had to do was mention my idea to the car owners and they would hand me a wad of cash and say "go for it kid, get whatever you need." The chemistry involved was extensive and certain paints and clear coats were not compatible. Stock cars weren't show cars (back then), so if there were problems we could cover them with lettering or blend in another color or whatever. The knowledge I picked up was invaluable. Every time I applied custom paint to a race car it was as though I was working in my own personal "R and D" (research and development) center. Little did I know that I would be part of an "Evolution" in the years ahead. As the race cars became better looking, I had also become involved in painting custom show cars as well. As I said, the knowledge I picked up was valuable and I finally worked my way up to "Best Paint" awards at several car shows, as well as national recognition in major custom magazines. Strangely enough, it seemed like the classy looking stock car syndrome "caught on" and eventually both race cars and the custom cars came together, boasting custom paint, pinstriping, and lettering not only at their own "shows" respectively, but often displayed in the same shows. The two industries had come together and I had played my part in the transition. (More about custom paint later.) The race cars provided a special "playing field" for me, unbounded and limitless. They became my "laboratory" for experiments. The cars needed to be painted before I could letter them, so why not experiment?

Pete Corey had opened his own shop behind his home out in Crescent, N.Y. This became my new base of operations. After bouncing around the race car circuit and working with so many different people, I felt I had a lot more skills and ideas to work with now and Pete would provide the best environment to work them. Out of all the race car people I came in contact with, Pete was the one person who understood "philosophy" regarding ideas. As I said earlier, he was especially open to experimenting. He loved to work a new idea and he used "philosophy" in his thinking. Once again using me as a "sounding board." He would run ideas by me and we would discuss them. I was honored to be part of his thinking and often ran ideas by him as well.

He told me once… "Your lettering is very different than any other work I've seen, I just can't put my finger on what it is though." I told him that when I letter a car, whenever possible I place the lettering on that car as it would appear through the lens of John Grady's camera, as it was coming off of the second turn at Fonda Speedway. Clear, striking, and camera active. He got a kick out of that.

It felt good once again working with Corey. Iron sharpening iron. Iron tempered with philosophy. Once again I found myself in a world unbounded and limitless. My brush was working its way onto Sprint cars, Grand National cars, Dragsters, and Custom cars. It seemed that somebody always had a friend of a friend or someone who knew someone who wanted something done.

Getting work was never a problem. Getting the work done in a timely fashion was *always* a problem. I loved what I was doing and each job would consume me. I often lost total track of time, especially when I was pinstriping. I remember one time pinstriping a car (I started on it early that day) and as I finished, I looked out the window thinking it was about to storm because it was getting dark outside. There was no storm, it was evening. Many times I have experienced "time standing still." I read somewhere that when a person is in the "zone" that for that moment everything is suspended. Maybe that's why at age sixty eight, I still feel like I'm thirty. Anyway, this did not fare well for those who were growing old waiting on me. Each day it seemed I would make one person happy and piss off three others. Human nature dictates that people generally want what they can't have, so I always had a large group of pissed off people wanting me to do work for them. Corey had the solution for all of this but somehow I just wasn't tough enough to implement it. You can probably see the "rub" here. So to preserve our friendship, Davie moved out of Corey's and on to more undeveloped territory.

✎ GRANT'S SPEED SHOP

One day Jack Muldowney called and said that he wanted me to meet someone he thought could be very beneficial to me. His name was *Erv Grant*. He was running Grant's Speed Shop over on Guilderland Ave. Jack's exact words were "this guy is quite a character." Well, Jack wasn't exaggerating; to this day I can say I've never met anybody quite like Erv. Most businessmen are businessmen and a wild man is a wild man. Grant was a businessman, but when he would get behind the wheel you would experience the wild man. Erv Grant enjoyed both to an extreme. All kidding aside, Erv was a very bright guy and when I met him he was handling a huge tiger by a very large tail himself, not to mention raising a family at the same time.

The thing that differentiated this shop from any of the others I worked around was that this was "high level" crazy. The clientele that this shop attracted were big time players. My lettering, and especially the pinstriping, fit in this place like the frosting on a wedding cake, or so I thought. Erv was very particular about his shop and his equipment and kept everything neat and in perfect order. Whenever I lettered something for Erv, I often ended up changing the letter style or colors three different times before he liked it. I went through a kind of "boot camp" with him that actually prepared me to work for his customers. I was coming from enjoying free rein at my

creativity to having to take very strict orders, and many times using colors and styles I didn't agree with. Just about when I didn't think I could take any more, the fun would begin. We would all take off for some drag strip and have a great time. Shirley Muldowney was gaining fame, she had moved from running her Corvettes at the local drag strip to competing with a "top fuel" dragster at major events across the country. Erv himself became popular as a dragster driver, especially in Canada. I remember one time we were up there racing and Erv won top eliminator. If I remember correctly, he set the track record that day but anyway, this group of Canadians wanted to buy his car. I mean really wanted to buy his car. Erv had no intentions of selling the car. They just kept offering him more and more money, until he finally agreed to sell it. So here we were, on our way home, heading for the border and he realizes he has an empty trailer behind him. He had gone through Customs at the border each week with a race car, everyone at the border knew him.

You just can't bring a car into Canada and sell it without going through reams of paperwork, not to mention the taxes that might have been due, etc. He had to do something quick. All of a sudden he pulled off the main road and headed for this junk yard where he had gotten some parts once before. He drove around the yard until he spotted what was left of a sports car that was completely destroyed in a fire. The owner of the junk yard couldn't speak English and Erv is trying to convince the guy that he wanted the car. The guy's wife spoke a little English, so she got involved and went back and forth with Erv for a while, then finally she looked at her husband and I heard her say the words "coo-coo" and then her husband fully understood. He made the sale.

We approached the border with some apprehension but it was the only shot we had. The guys at the border came out and quickly surrounded the charred mess of a car. One of the men said… "Monsieur, you had an acc-i-dente? Your car, it was so beautiful… and now… it is gone." Erv said… "I don't want to talk about it!" (I'm sure he didn't) The guy came back with…"Wee Monsieur, I understand."

Across the border we went, homeward bound. I heard later Erv even made a couple bucks on the charred piece. Scrap iron was doing better in the States than in Canada.

While working around Grant's I was introduced to a very different life style. Up to this point, the guys I had been around were "working class" folks. The customers at Grant's were "high rollers." This was a new world for me. At first the life style seemed very appealing, but after a while I could see it wasn't for me. Everyone seemed "uptight" all the time. The vehicles I was now working on were no longer created from nothing and hand built to become something. Everything in this arena was big bucks "special order." I never saw so much money being thrown around.

One day in the middle of winter I was at Grant's, lettering and pinstriping parts to a dragster. In the other garage there were two "Muscle cars," both there to have racing motors built for them. Jack Muldowney built one engine and an old stock car buddy of mine, "Lefty" Colgan had built the motor for the other one. The owners were there and they started bragging about how they were going to blow each other off the track. The racing season was months away and they were obviously frustrated waiting to unleash all of that power. Jack had many winning motors out there on the drag strip and Lefty had his share of winning circle track motors, so this was going to be interesting to say the least. Well, as the day went on they got into some booze and the argument intensified. At one point one of them said... damn it I'll race you right now, right here! With three feet of snow outside I had no idea what this guy meant. What took place next was pure insanity. Two drunks in high-powered drag cars backed them up against the overhead doors. One of their buddies decided he would be the "flagger." They raced twelve feet to the tool boxes. A hundred bucks a run. All we could hear for the next half hour were a series of squeals and crashes, squeals and crashes, over and over until finally it stopped. When they opened the overhead doors and the smoke cleared, we were looking at ten thousand dollars worth of damage on two cars and a couple of tool boxes so destroyed that we needed crowbars to open the drawers. Erv never got upset, he'd just laugh and pull out his estimate pad and start writing.

The winter months were dangerous times around the speed shop. You would think these guys would play cards or something. No, they were way beyond that. Anything could set off a fiasco. I remember Erv going out to his car to get something and Shirley hit him in the back of the head with a snowball. He quickly returned fire. Then we all joined in, me and Erv and our guys against Jack and Shirley and their crew. Then, as customers pulled in, we would quickly recruit them into battle. The snowball fight, which was probably one of the largest I have ever seen, lasted for hours and got totally out of control. What began with snowballs turned into ice chunks and whatever else could be thrown. It took the better part of a day for the guys from the glass company to replace windows in cars and the plate glass in the front of the building.

It was obvious that a person could make a lot of money in this environment, if you could stand it. I got to know my customers quite well and the theme for most of them was that they worked at very stressful high paying jobs. They played hard on weekends and God help you if you didn't have their "fun machine" ready Friday night. During the week, the veins in their bodies were "tweaked" like piano wires, stretched to the max. But ah... the weekend would come, bringing relief and they could play. Then back to the money grinder again so they could get a new toy. What a life. Eventually their hearts would just explode with joy.

Jack Muldowney and I had talked about this many times. We both came from meager backgrounds and were aware that this environment could be a gold mine, if handled right. Shirley was clearly carving a path to the big time. She saw opportunity presenting itself all over the place.

Grant was very talented when it came to handling these types and I give him all the credit in the world. But it wasn't for me. I quickly did the math… let's see, I could do one job for the rich guy and put up with all the stress, or I could do three jobs for working class with no stress for the same money. I'll do the three, enjoy the work, the people, and no stress.

Eventually, Erv moved on as well and proved that he could be successful at just about anything. I ran into Erv recently at an event where he was guest speaker. He touched on a few things that happened back in those days, but later we got together and laughed for a couple of hours about what really happened back then.

1963 Northeast Speed Shop (left to right) Jack Muldowney, Lew Tizzone, Bill Rubin, Gene Mangino, Stan Newman, Shirley Muldowney.

Left: *Shirley Muldowney and her double engine dragster.*

Below left: *Shirley, John (son), and Jack (husband).*

Below right: *Shirley wins at Fonda Speedway.*

1965 Napierville, Canada Erv Grant (left) Ed Geier (right)

Chapter 16:

LOOKING FOR LOVE

Now that I had wheels and a few bucks coming in, I thought I might give Debbie a call. To my surprise she was involved with someone else.

"Things left alone have a tendency to deteriorate," even relationships (especially relationships)

Well, a kid, sixteen, with wheels and some talent that could generate income, is not going to have too much trouble finding "chicks" (that's what we called them back then.) After hanging out with older guys and being around garages most of my life, it was as if I had advanced training in this field. Or at least I thought so. It wasn't too long before I met "Josie." She was a little doll. Tiny, beautiful, and what a body., It seemed like everyone was after her, but I had the edge. I had wheels, bucks, and a line of bullshit forty miles long. Oh, and I knew how to have fun.

On our first date I took her out to an airport where I had lettered a plane for a buddy of mine. He took us for a little spin around the area. The next date, I took her up into the mountains to visit this old couple who lived in a cave. They could tell your fortune. Then I introduced her to famous race car drivers and a few really cool biker buddies. I figure by this time I had put some distance between me and any other "jamoke" that might try to impress her. Josie turned out to be quite receptive and talented in ways I had never experienced before. She had been around. She was like a little sports car, four speed with overdrive. Push the right buttons and the top would go down. The only problem, it was kind of like the rental variety; as long as you were putting fuel in it and driving, she was yours, but if you left it alone for any length of time, someone else would quickly get behind the wheel. This was a different kind of stress for me, I had never had to balance my work and the pleasures of life separately before. They had always been basically one unit. With Josie, if I went off to paint something, you wouldn't want to be gone too long or there were surprises when you returned.

There was a new speed shop that opened down on Albany St. and I had the job of lettering the signs and vehicles. I just finished the sign on the store front and had come down off of the ladder when I noticed this girl, "Diane" who I knew from roller skating... She had another girl with her. I never knew where Diane lived. It turned out to be right across the street from the speed shop. I said hello and we talked for a moment but she didn't introduce the girl with her. I couldn't take my eyes off of that girl, she was strikingly beautiful. She had on white shorts and a pink top with the shirttails tied in front. I can remember it like it was yesterday. The girl kept looking back at me as they walked away. The next day I saw Diane again and asked about that girl. She quickly said, "Never mind, she is definitely not your type." I thought to myself, I'll decide that.

I found out her name was Linda and she lived upstairs from Diane. A couple of days went by and I saw her (Linda) coming back from the store. She was carrying groceries. I was quick to say hello and apologized for Diane's not introducing us. She was very friendly and even more beautiful up close. She said she had been watching me lettering the building and said what a great job I had done., I told her I had vehicles to letter and pinstripe and she could watch me any time she wanted to. She said she'd like that if it would be ok. She said she had to get some things into the refrigerator and had to go but hoped we could talk some more later. I was hoping for that too.

It really bothered me what Diane had said about her not being my type. What kind of impression did Diane have of me? Was I that bad? What if she asks Diane about me, what would she tell her? All these things started running through my mind. This was a really nice girl, would I not be worthy of a "nice girl?" I got thinking, if Josie was a sports car, this girl was a Mercedes Benz. Well, over the next few weeks Linda and I became friends. I found her to be friendly, compassionate, and very intelligent. I noticed that it didn't take much to make her happy. If we just took a walk and talked about something she seemed to really enjoy it. This was new for me. The girls I had known were not like this, they had to be entertained continually. I found myself truly enjoying being with her. I envisioned her having a very good family and home life. This was not the case. It was quite a while before I met her family, and I started to detect there being something wrong. It turned out that her dad had walked out on her mom years ago, leaving her with five children to basically fend for themselves. They were doing an amazing job though, with little or nothing. I could see why Linda was so compassionate and could enjoy the little things; let's just say she hadn't been spoiled, that's for sure. I had never met anyone like her. She had three brothers and a sister. Linda was the second oldest. I really liked her family; they were quiet but friendly and very talented. Her older brother David was (and still is) a very gifted artist. He also excelled in sports. There is no doubt that had he had some help from a dad, he would have gone to the major leagues.

There were very distinct differences between the sports car and the Mercedes. The little sports car was ready to go at any time and it took me down roads I never knew before, but it was never truly mine. The Mercedes on the other hand was still in the wrapper. I could admire it, show it off, buy a few accessories for it if I wanted to, and eventually it would be absolutely mine and no one else's, with one stipulation... I wouldn't be actually *driving it* any time soon or at least until all the specific paper work was in order.

There were several guys interested in Linda for sure, but she said her interests were in me and that if mine were in her, we would have a relationship. She would invest in me and I would invest in her, specifically with no "side deals." That's the way it is and if it worked out, someday the keys to the Mercedes were mine. This would have been perfect if I was twenty five years old but for a kid sixteen? What a dilemma. Linda was very mature for her age and her contract was bullet proof. Also, I had too much respect for her to try to bullshit my way around it. Plain and simple, I had a decision to make.

I chose the Mercedes. The little sports car was not at all happy about my decision.

Illustration by Bill Carney

She thought she would show me what I was missing by taking all of my buddies for rides. It seemed like everywhere I went there she was with another one of my friend's, cruzing with her top down.

Just holding hands with the Mercedes would have to do for now. I accepted that.

Although one day I did "slip" a little bit and thought … just a little peek under the hood wouldn't hurt anything. Once again I was stopped short and informed that the latch for the hood was on the *inside* and we weren't there yet.

I felt like I had been thrown from a high-powered sports car and landed in a pressure cooker. I honestly thought I would explode. But after awhile I found out what love is really about. Actually, I found out what a lot of things were about.

Linda and I would sit on her front porch and look out on the world below. It was much like being in the tree again but this time I wasn't alone. As I sat with her everything started to come into focus, exactly like when I would sit in the tree. I would see clearly what had happened in the past and before long, see a bit into the future and now there was someone to share it with, to dream with.

As things started to come into focus, I realized how long it had been since I had thought about philosophy. I hadn't been able to use it in working with the big money people at the speed shop; they dictated everything. To discuss philosophy with Josie would have been ridiculous. It was clear Linda was providing an oasis in my desert. From this perch I could see clearly how far I had drifted off course. I also felt some pangs of addiction regarding the pleasures I had with Josie. I realized that anything pleasurable or even fun can become a kind of addiction. I realized how many times when I was working under stress, how I would often think … "just a couple of more hours of this and then I can go find Josie and we can have some fun;" that is no way to live.

Now, I had someone to talk to and when stress built up, I didn't have to turn to some form of pleasure to help me cope with something I didn't want to do in the first place. I could just walk away. It seems like if you don't stop and think every now and then, and understand where you are and what you might be doing, the world will just swallow you up before you know it. The quiet time with Linda turned out to be very revealing. I could have been swept up so easily into a lifestyle that would have ruined me.

I could actually see in the distance, my boat sailing off to Hell and because of an Angel named Linda, I wasn't on board.

I wasn't the only one falling in love with Linda. My folks were as well, especially my dad. When I told him the situation I was in with Linda vs. Josie, he (in his infinite wisdom) said… *"You mean to tell me that you chose " peace of mind" over a piece of ass? There might be hope for you yet son!"*

At this stage of the game, my folks needed a considerable amount of help and Linda was right there for them. I tried to help her family as well. They had no car, so transportation was a big deal — with five kids you can imagine. Linda helped me a lot more than I helped her. I seemed to mess things up a lot.

I remember one day I was coming back from East Durham (a little town in the Catskill Mountains) where I lettered a truck. I was driving along through the countryside and noticed all these corn fields. They were right alongside the road. I got the idea what a hit it would be to bring her family some fresh picked corn for supper. Right off the old stalk. I immediately pulled over and helped myself to a trunk full of fresh corn. I'll be the hero of the day! Maybe this'll open the door on the Mercedes? (Why do I think like that? What's wrong with me?) Anyway, when I got to Linda's I got the boys to help me unload the corn while Linda put a couple of pans on the stove and got everything ready. The kid's mouths were watering. A half hour later we slapped the butter to it and dug in. I noticed it was a little chewy, almost like corn flavored bubble gum. Nobody said a word, they just chewed away and then Linda said… can I speak to you for a moment? We went into the kitchen and she asked me, "Where did you get this corn?"

I told her, "Out in the country."

"At a stand?"

"No, I picked it fresh myself."

"David! It's cow corn!"

I apologized to her mom and the kids and told them I would personally have somebody kick the guy's ass that sold me that corn. Then we all piled into the car and drove to "Jumpin' Jacks" for burgers.

They seemed to appreciate everything and anything. It was a pleasure being around them. Having Linda for a girlfriend was really great. We had a lot of fun together. Everywhere I took her everybody just loved her. They would say… "Where did you find her?" and "Don't let her get away."

Linda especially loved old folks and they took to her right away. Happensburg gave his stamp of approval immediately. He loved the Mercedes story, and added… "It sounds to me that Josie was an '*object*' and Linda a '*subject*.' You realize that objects must be manipulated and subjects are studied. You have made a wise choice. I have a feeling you'll find your study most interesting."

It can (and should) take a lifetime to study just one human being.

As I'm writing this book, Linda and I have been together fifty years and I'm still studying her and still learning.

A year had gone by and Linda and I were closer than ever. By this time we knew much about each other. We kept no secrets. I knew all about her family and she knew about mine. She was very understanding. I knew she was the "one." She worried about me and I worried about her. I was growing emotionally and spiritually because of her. When I saw her working so hard cleaning someone's home, or doing whatever she could for a few dollars, it did something to me. My heart went out to her. This was in sharp contrast to my hearing people whining and complaining that they didn't like the way the mag wheels looked on their car, or the most important decision in the whole world they would have to make was what color pinstriping they wanted. I could not believe that in this insane world there was one unspoiled girl left and she was mine to have and hold (hands with). I finally stopped complaining about the "all I could do was hold hands" thing. It was after our first kiss. It totally swept me away. My heart didn't stop pounding for half an hour. I decided, I'll wait, no problem. Here was another example where hurry would have put a damper on things. Clearly, slow was the way to go. I was about to learn the monumental difference between a *Fanciful, Fake, and Phony* lifestyle and a *Foundational, Faithful, and Fruitful* lifestyle, a concept we would design our lives around.

"The immediate is often enemy of the ultimate." (Indira Gandhi)

I had a chance to take a good look at where I had been and where I was going. I also received my "credentials" as a full fledged "Non-Conformist." Think about it: to call yourself a non-conformist because you didn't agree with the programs and rules in school was one thing, but to be able to walk away from the pleasures a beautiful girl can offer, in anticipation of moving to a higher plain — how many guys could do that? I was on the right road and I knew it. If it sounds like I'm bragging... I am absolutely bragging.

Chapter 17:

SPIRIT

If you think deeply enough, *everything* has a "spirit nature." My artwork had (and still has) a spiritual component. The component I'm talking about is more clearly defined as having *animation,* or possibly *motivation.* A person may be beautiful or handsome but a close investigation of their spirit may reveal they are evil. The opposite would hold true as well. A person who may be relatively unattractive may have a very good and wholesome spirit.

Think about it, even a simple conversation has its own *Spirit.* As you're talking with someone ask yourself "is what we are discussing going in a right direction, is this worthwhile, joyful, hurtful, or deceptive? Good or evil in spirit?

With the exception of "Debbie," most girls I had known up till now were burdensome and often stressful. They were spoiled and needed to be continuously pampered. The situation with Josie was more stress than it was worth, although I didn't realize it at the time. All of the time I had spent with Josie, I hadn't come up with a single good idea. I was too busy keeping one eye on my work and the other on her. I was courting a beautiful, attractive person with a very *"Difficult Spirit."*

The situation was completely opposite with Linda. She was a stress reliever. I didn't have to worry about her. The reason for this was because Linda had a very different kind of *"spirit."* Often, when people don't get along for any apparent reason, you might say their spirits "clash." Linda's spirit and mine seemed to get along just great. After a year we had grown very close. We were now seventeen and decided that as soon as we were eighteen we would get married and begin a life of our own.

Some more of my Dad's infinite (bar room) wisdom...

There are many women out there who can make a fool out of a man, but David, you have found a woman that is making a man out of a fool! God bless her.

The Mercedes (Linda) and the author (Dave Sr) 1960's

The Mercedes and Me 2010

"Love, in and of itself, holds the key to understanding"

More about this later.

"When we have to go without, we often learn what can be accomplished from within" (Dr. Denis Waitley)

Another Spirit that seemed to be around back then was the Entrepreneur Spirit. It was as though everyone was into some kind of business venture. Many of the signs I painted and trucks I lettered back then were for businesses that began operating in the late fifties or early sixties. I was nineteen or younger when I lettered or pinstriped for many of these companies:

Dick's Glass Shop, Tony's Trim Shop, Frank's Body Works, Rotterdam Body Service, All Season's Equipment, Mohawk Ambulance, Dick's Auto Sales, Bellevue Auto Parts, Village Auto, Yankee Motor Co., Crescent Auto Body, Morris Body Service, Ultra Body Works, American Body Works, Erie Body Works, Neenan's Garage, Uber's Garage, Young's Garage, Kugler's Auto Repair, W. Steria Oil Co. Grant's Speed Shop (later to be North East Speed Enterprises), J & R Speed Shop, Villano Bros., Emil J. Nagengast Florist, F.W. Cernik Painting, Bobar's Towing, Grandview Block Co., American Glass Co, Roland J. Down Heating and Cooling, Empire Paving, American Paving, Jim Meisner's Auto Parts, Jimy's Tree Service, Lawnwood Farms Dairy, Nils Engvold Excavating, Ralph Byer Trucking, Produce Express Trucking, Wade Tours, Schenectady Marine Supply, Town Construction Paving, Bellevue Builders Supply, G&A Construction, Char-Lew Builders, Reutter Bros. Construction, Lucky Penny Trucking, Westcott Coal & Oil Co., Mohawk Chevrolet, Marsh Hallman Chevrolet, Webster Motors Ford, Orange Motors, Al Mangin Auto Sales, Autobody Supply Co., Stan's Autobody, Denny's Fuel, Cuomo Meat packing, Towne Diner, Towne Decorators, Spitzies' Harley Davidson Sales, Brownies Indian Sales, Howard's Cycle Shop, Henry's Cycle Shop, White Eagle Bakery and Mt. Pleasant Bakery.

🌦 *WHAT I HAD LEARNED*

At this point, I could see the magnitude of the "Creative World" and what it held. I could clearly see by using "Creativity" and "Imagination" we can create our own world within this world.

It was obvious how situations repeat themselves, though they may have a different "face" or circumstance. How knowledge from the past (including older people who have that knowledge) can be so valuable in changing circumstances to shape our future. It's not just talent or ability; that's only part of it. There are things like self-discipline and perseverance that hold it all together.

But above all, it's the "mind set" of… *"What can I Give"* not *"What can I Get"* that is so important to understand. These are at opposite poles. Obviously, I received much from my world back then, but I also *gave* a fair amount of talent and ability.

Do you think philosophy might play an important role in our lives? Understanding this world and the people that live in it can give us leverage and control over **our** lives. If you don't understand this, there is a distinct possibility that others will have control over your life.

"If you can create something that would be of value to other people, then you would have income. They get what they need, you get what you need."

Sounds simple enough, but this involves a *"Spirit of Contribution."* Many people have given **nothing** to society and then complain because they have nothing. *"What can I give"* is a foreign language to them. They suffer from *"Reverse Polarity."* It's the equivalent of hooking up the battery in your car backwards — hooking up the negative side where the positive should be. The car will run for a time but nothing is being returned to the system and before long, everything shuts down. This is one of the major problems with the economy today. So many people are concerned about what they can get and so few are concerned about what they can give, therefore putting a tremendous drain on society.

I learned there must be a connection between EDUCATION and APPLICATION — how important it is that we put to **practical use** what we learn.

I had used creative thinking to "compete" for "Josie." But it was interesting that I did **not** have to compete for Linda. She was a "Gift," and **what I had been taught helped me recognize and appreciate that gift.**

I hope this all makes sense to you. What I'm trying to do is open your mind and make you aware of certain things that are foundational in order to move to another level. I hope you find this book entertaining, but it would mean more to me if you gain knowledge and raise your level of consciousness regarding what these pages reveal.

Although we pop along as though everything was so easy for me, please understand most things were very difficult, but I chose not to dwell on that aspect. If you don't believe me, pick up a brush, dip it in some paint, and attempt to form a dozen alphabets right out of your head. Then take a striping brush and run a freehand sixteen foot line down the side of somebody's new car. Then you might understand.

ᔌ ULTIMATE FREEDOM

When I left school, I wanted "freedom." It didn't take long for me to realize not only that freedom wasn't free, but that too much of it could be dangerous. Look at it this way…say you wanted to experience a day of "Ultimate Freedom." This would be a day with no restraints. You could do anything you damn well pleased. No discipline whatsoever. No one would tell you which side of the road to drive on, no sign or color of a light would make you stop or go. It would be a very short time before you would have absolutely no freedom at all. You would either be killed or incarcerated. On the other hand, if you were willing to adhere to certain disciplines, you could enjoy a life with a tremendous amount of freedom.

"The more self-discipline you have, the more freedom you'll enjoy."

---

also…

"Discipline summons Order"

I gave you an extreme example but I'm sure you get the point. It took much time, effort, and discipline for me to develop my skills as an artist. That effort gave me not only income but great freedom. I hope that any young person reading this would comprehend what I just said.

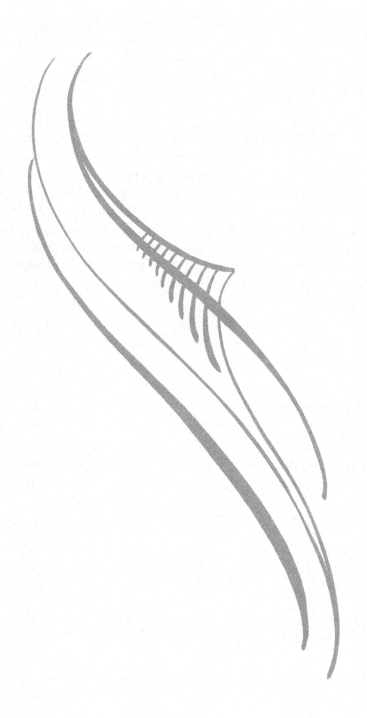

Chapter 18:

THE PROMISE

Linda and I had discussed many things, not the least of which was our family's backgrounds. Both of my grandfathers came from Wales and were quite successful over there. My mother's father was an engineer and built coal mines. My dad's father was very talented in many fields. Their main purpose for coming to the States was so that future generations could have a better life. This involved putting many of their own personal desires aside. They found work in the quarries near the New York-Vermont border, now known as "Slate Valley." They settled there with their families. Ironically, both my grandfathers were killed while working in those quarries.

Linda's grandfather (on her mother's side) brought his family here from Germany before the turn of the century. He worked at the General Electric Co. and, on several occasions, worked with Edison. Obviously our families had come from "good stock," but what happened to our parents? They were not continuing in the manner intended for them.

I could only imagine what it must have been like to leave your home and sacrifice everything to come to a strange country so that future generations would have a better life. Because of my grandfather, my dad did not have to work in a coal mine and neither did I. The life I was living was far from a coal mine or quarry work. I owed my grandfather a great deal.

One day I took a ride up to the cemetery where just about all of my relatives are buried. I stood in front of my Grandfather's grave. I was on a mission. First of all, I gave thanks and acknowledged all he had done for his family and all he had sacrificed. I also acknowledged that it was because of his efforts that I was living in this great country and had the opportunities I had. Then I made a promise that...

I would develop and use to the fullest, every ounce of talent and ability that I had been given. Also that I would teach my children and others (who were willing to listen) about the importance and value of using their talents as well, so that his efforts would not have been in vain.

That was many years ago. I am still fulfilling that quest.

It was at this stage in my life that I had come to the realization that just about everything was "double-edged." It seemed that everything I was involved with had two sides to it. It was as if there were two mentalities. On one side, the *constructive mentality* and on the other side, the *destructive mentality*. I was free to make my own choices but what was so interesting to me was the **importance** of the choices we make.

Where we stand in life right now is the result of the choices we have made thus far. "Choices cause circumstances."

To make intelligent choices we need truthful information. Remember, with regard to information, *Truth* is the only thing that is "Real."

Truth is the "benchmark," the needle in the compass. "the point" of reference. Truth is an absolute.

It seems today the world has a nasty habit of "dissolving absolutes," as well as "justifying" anything and everything we do.

"The driving force behind wisdom is understanding the value of truth"

It has been my observation that those who put a high value on truth fare better than those who don't. Those who don't seem to be disconnected and are not grounded to anything substantial. They often wander aimlessly and if need be, what if anything can they return to? There is no needle in their compass. They have no reference or benchmark.

It is easy for me to write about this now, after living much of my life. The irony is that as a kid, I would bullshit my way along with a certain amount of effectiveness. But, "when the rubber hit the road" or "when the brush hit the object," the Truth would be revealed and sometimes I knew what I was doing, sometimes I didn't. I guess it kept me in check with my limitations and respectful of truth.

It is very difficult to grow talent, ability, or skill without embracing truth. Again "It's the only thing that is real." Many folks end up going down the wrong road because they ignore this very concept.

Chapter 19:

OTHER FORMS of INTELLIGENCE

I started to realize that there were other forms of intelligence; I'm not talking about science fiction. There was *"Creative Intelligence"* (I grew up around that), but now I was experiencing *"Artistic Intelligence," "Intuitive Intelligence," "Imaginative Intelligence," "Emotional / Spiritual Intelligence,"* and *"Marketing Intelligence."* I had never looked at intelligence in these forms before.

This broad view of our human intelligence gave me a new perspective on Creative Thinking. You may substitute the word "awareness" for intelligence if you like. But basically, what I was viewing was an understanding of talent and abilities separated or individualized, so they could be more easily recognized and understood. The interesting thing was that some of these forms of intelligence were born of other intelligence.

For instance, Artistic Intelligence could be formed from Imaginative Intelligence (or Imaginative Awareness.) Intuitive Intelligence could be developed from pure experience, or any other intelligence, or just a keen sense of awareness. There are embryos of different talents and abilities in all of us.

Any singer or songwriter of any caliber would understand the value of a well-developed emotional intelligence in his or her work. Actually, if you remove intelligent emotion from music, or art, you have little or nothing. Think of it this way; emotion without intelligence is "mumbo-jumbo." Although, with the low standards we have today, I suppose someone with some Marketing Intelligence could probably sell that.

On a more serious note, because of the time spent on computers and the lack of personal contact, many young folks are lacking in emotional intelligence, the main ingredient in developing social skills. Patience and compassion are also linked to emotional intelligence.

Whenever I would "overcome" something, there were always rewards. The rewards often came in a form of *deeper understanding*, as in the situation with Josie and Linda. Incidentally, I made light of overcoming my attraction to Josie. It was very difficult for a young guy with a sweet tooth, who had free run of a candy store, to suddenly have to go without sweets. The emotional pain I endured is hard to describe, but it was worth it and the rewards were there. I never regretted making that decision.

In this life we must experience "growth." "Overcoming," in my opinion, is a powerful form of growth. Not all growth has rewards, but overcoming definitely has its rewards. Overcoming an addiction or walking away from a bad habit, or overcoming a fear can be a life changing experience. I don't know a single person who, having overcome something, regrets the experience, no matter how difficult it might have been. It would be like a person regretting time they spent at the gym or time spent with a mentor learning a new skill. The rewards far outweigh the pain and difficulties.

Life is about learning and growing. Everything is constantly in motion, though sometimes we need to just step away, "Be still" and listen to our inner self. Two obstacles to avoid are "complacency" and taking things "for granted." Don't become *"Cattle-ized."* Like cattle herded around and led to places they really don't want to go. Separate yourself from the masses. Cultivate those tiny embryos of talent and ability. You'll be surprised how fast they'll grow. And remember to think… *"What can I Give?"*

I was happy with what I was doing and had plenty of work. I had something to give and that gave me a position in the game. The question was, could I support Linda, have a home and a family, and still enjoy what I love so much. If I could pull it off, **we** would have a life.

In the summer of '64 I turned eighteen. Linda had a few months to go before her eighteenth birthday. My dad and mom were very ill and both were hospitalized. They would make it through but never again to be at full capacity, so my sister and I settled them in a small but very comfortable apartment where things would be easier for them. I was to assume responsibilities for the house. While my parents were in and out of hospitals, many things were neglected. There were repairs, bills unpaid, and taxes, etc., so Linda and I would be starting out with a heavy burden. Little did I know how much having to "struggle" can pull two people together?

I felt the need to "stretch" myself in many areas in order to accomplish what was ahead. Fortunately, I had great friends and wonderful council that I could tap into. One of those great friends I had been doing a considerable amount of work for at that time, and had become very close to, was the owner of Henry's Cycle Shop, *Bill Himmellwright*. I had been doing signs and truck lettering for him since he bought the bicycle business, which was located a few doors from where Linda lived. Bill was of the same mold (or should I say **spirit**) as Carl Borst. He was (and still is) a man of character and integrity.

I watched closely how Bill Himmellwright handled his business and customers. He was truly remarkable at his craft. His business flourished and it was no surprise. I can remember watching Bill using his skills in salesmanship many times. He truly believed in his product, which at the time were Schwinn Bicycles. What stands out most in my memory was the time he was showing a bicycle to this couple. They had been looking for a bicycle for their kid for his birthday. They made it clear they had been to other stores and Bill's price was higher than the others. He explained that they were looking at "more bike" than the others. As he was casually talking about the structure and manufacturing of this bicycle (and it was just a kid's little bike,) he grasped the handlebars, stepped one foot on top of the tiny little chain guard and suspended his weight there. His entire weight was supported by the little chain guard of that bike. I saw the lady cringe when he launched himself up. From that position he continued to explain all the unique characteristics of that bicycle, and ended with… "You see this is not just any bike, this is a Schwinn!" The lady pulled out her checkbook and bought the bike. Was that impressive? Well, that was over forty years ago and I never forgot it.

Bill Himmellwright was an amazing person. One day, Linda told me she heard that Bill had gone into the hospital for back surgery. We were very concerned and I remember her saying a little prayer for him. (Is there such a thing as a "little" prayer?) Anyway, we were imagining a long recovery and hoped his convalescence wouldn't affect his business, etc. I stopped at the store to find out how things were going. His dad was there filling in for him and he was very busy with customers, but managed to take a moment to tell me that Bill was doing great, not to worry. A few days went by and I'm driving down Balltown Road, heading to a job and there's Bill, walking briskly along the highway! I pulled over and rolled the window down and he looked in. After we said our hello's I asked, "how are you doing?" He returned with ... "Great Dave, just working some of the kinks out, I'll be in the shop next week — stop in, I've got work for you." Bill Himmellwright never complained and never explained, he just kept moving on. I see him every now and then and he hasn't changed a bit; that tells you something about a person's true character.

Chapter 20:

LIGHTHOUSES

I started to become aware of "patterns" that were forming in my life. It was as if I was out there navigating the ocean of life. Some days the sea was calm, some days it was very stormy and even dangerous, but along the way there were lighthouses, the likes of which were in the form of Happensburg, Borst, Himmellwright, and others I will mention as we go on. They not only kept me from crashing into a rocky coast, but helped me chart a course that would allow me to sail on to ports explored only by a select few, very fortunate individuals.

Happensburg helped steer the ship; Himmellwright was more casual and helped when needed; Borst just had to "**be** who he was," providing an excellent example. Amazingly, Linda had people in her life that were lighthouses as well. We realized early on that we were both "blessed" and had much in common. We were very sensitive to our world, the gifts we had been given, and the value of those close to us. The respect that we had for those older folks around us was rock solid. It was like having your own gold mine to tap into. The information and wisdom these folks were willing to share was invaluable in the shaping of our lives. We often heard the term "Generation Gap," meaning the space between young and mature folks. The term "Generation Connection" worked better for us.

"In the Creative World, each day becomes an integral part of the Ultimate Masterpiece we call life"

Through everything we had been sharing, Linda and I could not have been closer. Well, maybe a *little bit* closer, so we decided to get married as soon as possible. I had a friend that I called "The Arranger," another guy that didn't know everything but knew "everybody." He told me that if Linda's mom would sign some papers, we could take a ride out of state and get married.

He could set it all up. He did, and we did, and the rest, as they say, is history. We would have a church wedding later when we could afford it. From that day forward, it was the Mercedes and me, forever and ever.

We continued to help out each other's families and grow a business as well as build a life of our own. We had been blessed with good people and great models in our lives. Understand that it wasn't as if we didn't have problems, too many to mention, and if we overcame our problems, why give them credence, why revisit the negative? This book and the value herein are about "growth" and solving problems, not dwelling on them.

"Nothing of value will grow in negative soil" ·

The pinstriping was seriously becoming my little "money maker." It was also taking me to some very interesting places. Race cars and truck lettering were still an important part of my life and income. I realized that I needed a shop of my own, a place where I could work and make a steady income. Bouncing around was great for a single guy but that had changed, so now "stability" was becoming a priority.

Rollie Johnson knew some people that owned a building on Curry Road. At this particular time, the building was vacant. It would be a perfect place to set up shop, although up until now, I had been working my expenses "out of pocket" and now with the accumulation of other responsibilities and expenses, this was going to be tough. We (Linda and I) wanted to buy my parent's house, but it needed a lot of work, so we decided to put it on hold and concentrate on the business, because the business could pay for the things we needed, if it prospered. It would be a stretch, but we went ahead and rented the building. The difficult part was always working without help. I should say skilled help, because I always had buddies around to do basic things but they were often in the way when skilled things had to be done. I always found myself having to explain every part of everything I was doing. This slowed me down tremendously, so most of the time I worked alone. Linda worked with me when she could, but she was helping with my parents and her mom, which left little time for anything else.

A year went by very quickly and the shop was super busy. I also learned back then that "busy" does not always mean success. I was busy but not really making money. The interruptions during the day were something

I hadn't planned on, and it was difficult trying to get things completed. I found myself wishing I could just take the work someplace where I could do it without being disturbed. I could only get paid for what was completed. There were always people coming in and out (actually there was no "out," they just came in and hung there.) If I had a brush out, they were being entertained and they weren't leaving. I would work like that as long as I could stand it, and then I'd blow up and throw everybody out, lock the door and seriously work. I tried hiring someone for the office to talk to the customers and keep people from bothering me, but the people I hired usually didn't know anything about layout or colors, etc. so I ended up talking to the people myself, anyway. I must have had a dozen different people working the office for me that first year. One guy worked one week and booked two and a half months work. What was I to do with the next customer coming through the door? It seemed impossible. At least before, when I was bouncing around, I could control the flow of work. I just couldn't find the right people to help. I had grown up with a diverse background and knew how to deal with different types of people. If I had a person working with me that knew office work, they usually couldn't understand the different types of customer's needs and vice-versa. Talent needs management, but how do you manage subject matter you don't know anything about? What kind of striping would look good on this car? Where would I put it? What colors? How long would it take? It would take years for me to train a person in these areas. Remember, we're talking the 1960's and there was little or no reference regarding these skills, and much of the concepts were my own that I developed as I went along. It seemed like the tiger I had by the tail kept turning around and biting me.

❧ "HELP WAS ON THE WAY"

One morning, Linda informed me that help was on the way. She was pregnant and in eight months or so I would have my own personal little helper to work with me, after a little training that is. Wow, I was going to become a dad! Now more than ever I had to come up with a solution for the immediate problem of getting the work DONE. These were times when I thought the whole world was on my shoulders. I had gone from being a free agent to a businessman, a husband, and now about to become a father, all of which I knew little about.

Isn't it strange how we can be so smart in some areas and so lacking in others? I guess that's just part of being human. At one point I had everything under control and now it seemed that I didn't have control over anything. I needed time to think, but there was no time. Bills were piling up and there were deadlines on everything I was involved with. The burden on us was tremendous. There were many lessons to be learned in those years. I was thankful that Linda was accustomed to tough times and difficult circumstances. She could adapt to any situation and always looking toward the future. Always "planting" like a good ol' farmer.

The world seemed to be changing all around us. We were experiencing first hand "being **IN** this world, but not **OF** this world." We were like a couple of "old fashioned kids." The busy-crazy world didn't make sense to us. It was filled with what I called "Insta-Grats," (people wallowing in instant gratification.) Everybody wanted everything now, right now. When David Jr. was born, we experienced many changes ourselves. Things that were so important before didn't seem important at all. I came to the conclusion that I was not a doctor and there was no such thing as an emergency pinstriping job. Well, except for one time when a buddy of mine who owned a body shop called and had just completed a $3,500 job that needed to have the original stripe put on the car. The customer had the check in his hand but refused to pick up the car until the final stripe was on it. My friend said it was an emergency and I suppose it was. But, for the most part our (or my) priorities had certainly changed. Becoming a parent is life changing, in a good way.

✎ *DEBT*

Not since my little lemonade stand had I experienced real serious DEBT. Debt can be a destroyer, a destroyer of "**free time**" (the true definition of wealth.) Debt can also destroy happiness. When people are in debt, they think differently than when they are free of financial burden. There is a stress that goes along with debt that is difficult to explain. With the advertising and marketing today, we can all understand how so many people get into debt. Getting out is the difficult part. Our situation was a little different than most. The things that had us in debt were not luxuries. Most of our burden was in the form of business expenses, taxes, and repairs on property we didn't even own yet. Nonetheless, we were burdened and it was something we had to deal with. My dad would often repeat an old saying… "Necessity is the mother of invention." I knew that to be true. So, my necessity was to increase my income and clear some of this debt. I was already working day and night lettering trucks, signs, pinstriping cars, etc. The problem was always getting the jobs to completion. It was taking six to eight hours to do three or four hours of actual work. I often had to go into the shop late in the evening and work through the night to get things done. It was the only time I could work uninterrupted. This threw my life into turmoil.

It had been a while since I had done any custom painting (complete paint jobs on cars) as I just didn't have the time. There were a couple of people that had asked me several times to paint their cars, but I was always too busy pinstriping or lettering. As I said earlier, debt can really mess with the way we think. I knew these guys were willing to pay decent money for complete paint work and maybe I could have some of the guys that were hanging around the shop help with prep, masking, and sanding, etc. Maybe I could jump ahead. I had the chemistry experience from experimenting painting race cars, and it just seemed like the logical thing to do under the circumstances. The next couple of years would prove very interesting.

The true artist gets "into" his or her work and this was no different. Taking on custom paint work presented new challenges and problems. The cars to be painted were no longer race cars but high end, very expensive show cars. Our ultimate goal would be to attend the car shows and compete for "Best Paint." I thought it would be interesting to use "creativity" to "compete" in this arena. I had a reputation for lettering and pinstriping, but few people knew me as a custom car painter. If I could grab "Best Paint," it would establish me as a "player" in the game. From that position I could get the customers I wanted for paint work. Once again, I had a tiger by the tail.

Custom Paint turned out to be a huge "playing field" with plenty of room for ideas and creativity. The things that could be done with paint were amazing. I had entered a whole new world. There were other things that were amazing as well… the cost of materials for one. Up until now, it hadn't cost me much to complete a lettering or pinstripe job, and if I painted a race car the owner picked up the cost of materials. Working with Metal flake and Candy Colors involved spraying the car with clear several times, sanding the finish between coats, and the final buffing to the "show shine" with expensive compounds, etc. Then, with time and labor added in, this could be a very scary place to be. Looking back, I remember learning two things; one, that it was true that "all that glitters is not gold" and two, "bigger is not always better." I worked harder at custom painting than anything I had done before. It was "labor intensive" and very stressful. You could work your way through several colors and designs and lose the job in the final painting if something went wrong chemically; this would keep you "on edge" through the entire process. Some chemicals would react differently with others. I had learned much from the stock car painting, but not nearly enough for big league custom painting. In the beginning it was mostly trial and error. This was just fine, because even though it was difficult finding my way, the results would always be "original work."

After about a year or so we had competed in many shows and, while we managed to win runner-up for Best Paint several times, we still hadn't received top honors. We knew we needed the right car to pull it off.

Chapter 21:

A PARTNERSHIP THAT PULLED IT OFF

During my years spent custom painting, I had done much pinstriping and lettering for a friend and fellow painter by the name of *Fred Traegler*. Fred was a design engineer for the State of New York and had dabbled at custom painting and body work. He had done some great work and we often found ourselves "teaming up" doing work for the same customers. Fred and I got along great and we both attended car shows, often discussing working together and taking a shot at "Best Paint." As luck would have it, Fred had ordered a new Corvette and expected delivery a month or so before the car show circuit was to begin. This was late 1967 and the new '68 body style would present a new look and lend itself for all kinds of creative paint work. Fred suggested that we paint the new piece and enter it in the shows competing for "Best Paint." For someone to have the courage and faith in our combined ability to take on such a challenge was amazing!

One thing I knew about Fred Traegler was that he always said what he meant and meant what he said. So when Fred said he would be willing to bring his brand new Corvette into the shop and take sandpaper to an already new surface, custom paint it, and enter it into the running, I knew he wasn't kidding. I also knew that with our combined talent, no one could possibly beat us at Best Paint. Especially with the new style changes that GM was offering on the Corvette that year.

Fred's Corvette came in on schedule and he drove it directly from Marsh-Hallman Chevrolet in Albany, seventeen miles to our shop in Rotterdam. We had just about thirty days to get ready for the first show in Albany. Ed Bobell the owner of Autobody Supply of Schenectady heard about our endeavor and "sponsored" us with the paint and materials. We closed off a specific stall in the shop for our project, covered all the windows and attempted to conduct a covert operation painting this car.

Did you ever notice that the less you want people to know, the more they find out? Well, the word about our project spread like wild fire. People were coming out of the woodwork. We would often work through the night in order to get things done. Fred was both creative as well as methodical and we would plan out things very carefully before implementing; this was different territory for me having the habit of shooting from the hip most of the time in my work. This was a great learning experience for me especially in avoiding mistakes. Fred had a college background and my working with street education turned out to be a masterful blend of respect and capability. It was truly magic how everything came together.

As I said Fred was very creative. We had the challenge of "balancing" this multi-colored paint job on this new body style. The one particular obstacle was the rear deck area. The gas filler was centered on the deck and we were trying to cleverly surround the filler with colors but kept changing the layout, not being satisfied with any attempt so far. One day Fred came up with the perfect answer (or solution) to our problem. He had brought from home an antique lace, round table "doily" originally from Germany that his grandmother had crocheted. It fit like a glove over the filler cap and the pineapple design of thin lace would serve as a "masking."

I'll explain how we did this. We first put down a silver metal flake "splash" then carefully laid the crocheted lace onto the metal flake and taped each point in place using string to pull the doily into shape and allow us to tape far enough away so the tape that held it in position would not interrupt the airbrush work that had to be done in between each crocheted sequence in the design. This was tricky because if any of the individual strings that were held by the tape ever let go, it would distort the design ruining the entire job. It had to stay absolutely in place with no margin for error. This took many hours to set up and any distortion would set us back considerably. Once this was accomplished, we would enter in with the airbrush as many colors as were physically possible into the design. When we lifted the doily from the deck the thread would divide any and all colors with very thin silver metal flake lines. The silver metal flake splash would also provide the base for the candy colors turning each into a blend of metal flake colors never seen before.

The next scene was like that of an operating room with surgeons working diligently. I had the airbrush filled with the first color. Fred stood close by with the change-up for the next sequence of colors. A couple other friends stood by cleaning the airbrush containers and readying them for more colors; the operation was underway and lasted several hours. There was no stopping because all colors had to blend into each other. We all watched the strings and their respective tape carefully, hoping they would hold through the tedious process. At one point one of the strings started to let go, I remember seeing a hand reach over and hold down on the string. I can't remember who it was that held that string, but I do remember "that hand" never moved until we were completely finished. (How often the real heroes don't get the credit they deserve.) The operation turned out to be a complete success, and we went on to win "Best Paint" not only that year but several years in a row and many shows as well. There were spots in national magazines and paint journals, numerous articles and interviews as well that would follow. Our combined efforts paid off and we went on to paint many more cars and were in many more custom magazines. As much recognition as I had gained from custom painting, and I have to admit it was much fun, I couldn't say it was all that profitable. There was nothing more profitable that pinstriping. When you weighed time and materials against profit margins, pinstriping was unbeatable. Under the right circumstances, free hand lettering also produced tremendous profit.

Wild Imagination...

Dave Davies has been painting since he was a kid. He started lettering and striping when he was only thirteen.

Davies and Fred Traegler, both from Schenectady, New York, teamed-up to customize Fred's "vette". The result was the first place award for best paint job in the Albany Auto World Show, Albany, N.Y., last December.

Davies, who does all the layout and finish paint work, used a round lace tablecloth that was imported from Germany. Great care was exercised to stretch the cloth and hold it in place, undisturbed. *Duracryl* DMA base colors were applied with an air brush. Thirty-

four colors were used on the entire job.

At the Albany Show, a man came up to Dave and asked how he got that "decal" on without any air bubbles. The man almost fainted when he learned that it was all paint.

Davies uses a full line of *Ditzler* products. In addition to *Duracryl* colors, his solvent choice is DTA-105 Extra High Gloss Acrylic Thinner. For undercoats, he prefers *Duracryl* DZL primer-surfacers.

"I do a great deal of custom work and this type of painting demands a durable but 'glass like' finish," explained Davies. "Using *Duracryl* DCA-468 Clear and mixing toners, I am able to establish just that."

"In California they have excellent climate conditions for paint, but in New York you must have a paint that can withstand temperature changes," Davies remarked. "I find that *Duracryl* acrylic lacquer is the only paint that can take this type of punishment. In the past I have had much trouble with other brands as far as 'checking', 'fading', etc. On race cars and dragsters there is a great deal of vibration and flexing.

"I don't like to 'baby' the paint," Davies. "In other words, we like to lay it on. *Duracryl* acrylic lacquer enables us to do just this."

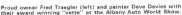

Proud owner Fred Traegler (left) and painter Dave Davies with their award winning "vette" at the Albany Auto World Show.

Thirty-four *Duracryl* colors were used on this exciting paint job.

Chapter 22:
CREATING THE RIGHT CIRCUMSTANCES

We must remember that our past (good or bad) will always serve as a reference. I remembered from my past, that *"the money I could make would be directly proportional to the value of the object that I was pinstriping."* This is a basic principle and other things have to be considered as well, such as time and materials etc. But having said that, pinstriping separated me from the "starving artist crowd," that's for sure

(I was about to create a "niche" but I didn't know it yet.)

Anyway, motorcycles were the most profitable thing I could pinstripe. So when you find a good thing that produces profit, the logical thing to do is more of that. I had been pinstriping occasionally for some of the motorcycle shops in the area and had done well with them. I only wished I could do more. The only answer that made sense was that if there weren't enough motorcycles to pinstripe around here then I would have to go to where there were more of them. It was time to return to Laconia and do it right this time. This would be the new venture and I had to prepare for it. There were thousands of "bikes" up there in the Lakes Region of New Hampshire during the Laconia event. If I could "position" myself accordingly, there could be huge profits. Laconia was traditionally a weekend event hosting the races in Loudon, N.H. This event had been going since the 1930's and drew huge crowds. Back then there were few "vendors" but if you were selling something you could just set up along the road someplace and start making money — there were no ordinances or laws against gypsy vendors setting up or even gangs hanging out in the wooded areas between the track in Loudon and Weir's Beach (an amusement park on Lake Winnipesauke.) Laconia could be a dangerous place during bike rallies, especially for vendors that were set up alongside the road. The police usually had their hands full with rowdy bikers. I thought that if I set up in town somewhere it might be safer and to my all around benefit. The corner of a gas station lot or an empty lot would work well if the rent was cheap enough. No "biker bars" or tavern locations; I had too many bad experiences of working around drunks.

As I rolled slowly down the road from Laconia toward Weir's Beach, I noticed a car wash coming up on the right. A man I thought might be the owner was out in front sweeping up. I quickly pulled in and drove up to where he was standing. After introducing myself I explained that I was a pinstriper looking for a location to set up, and would he be interested in having me on the corner of his property during the rally? I further explained how it might generate business for both of us. He turned out to be a great guy and welcomed the thought of having a vendor on the property. Now, the big question… how much? He said he had no idea; he never had a vendor there before. I thought for a moment and said; look this is a new thing for both of us. I never set up at a car wash before, so why don't we do this… let me set up, and work the weekend. Sunday afternoon you and I will get together, we'll see how each of us faired. I'll tell you how things went for me and you tell me how much I owe you. If it's too much I probably won't be back, but if it's fair to both of us we may have the beginning of a good thing. He agreed to my proposal and we set up shop which was basically a makeshift tent extending off the roof of my camper, with an area roped-off where we could pull bikes in and work.

Bob Pelletier and Dave in Laconia early 70's

Chapter 23:

WHEN WHAT YOU WANT — WANTS YOU

It was almost as though Laconia wanted me there as bad as I wanted to be there. This concept has presented itself many times in my life. It was not surprising to have experienced it another time. Many times, I have wanted something and it appeared as if it wanted me as well. From the lettering of race cars for famous drivers to getting to hang out at speed shops and travel with some very interesting people. This definitely has something to do with the creative environment.

Clearly my place in Laconia was pre-destined. It wanted me as badly as I wanted to be there. The car wash not only provided me with a captive audience, but if it rained, I had four stalls to either work in or to use to park bikes for drying. Strangers came over and were helping me set up, customers were lining up for striping, and it was as if they were waiting for me before I arrived. They seemed to know what I was there for before I even told them or sold a job. This was truly amazing. Did you ever just know that you're in the right place at the right time?

Well it turned out to be a great weekend. I made many new friends and enjoyed much of the excitement that Laconia has to offer. Sunday afternoon came quickly and the owner of the car wash came by as we had planned. I told him that I did very well and that if he could be fair on what I owe him, I'd be back again for sure next year. What he had to say surprised me. He said that every year he has to deal with damages on the stalls of the car wash and that sometimes they pull a hose off of the wall or break into his change machines. The damage usually runs several hundred dollars. This year he said he had no damage, probably because I was parked there and striping bikes well into the night. So he said "I'm ahead several hundred, so how's 'no charge' sound? Hope to see you next year."

This began a friendship that lasted ten years until the guy retired and sold the car wash. During those years we had so many wonderful and exciting experiences. I'll share just a couple of the stories that stand out in my memory.

✒ PINSTRIPING SAVES THE OUTLAW

I remember one year in particular, we were right out straight striping bikes and there was a large crowd made up of folks that were either waiting for striping or just watching. Bikes with loud pipes were going by all day long, but all of a sudden we heard the sound of a bike coming not only with loud pipes but really rolling at an unbelievable speed. We all looked up to check it out. What we saw looked like a scene from a Hollywood movie. Here comes this young guy, running flat out, a frantic look on his face, his beanie helmet pushed to the back of his head barely held by the strap around his neck. Off in the distance we heard police sirens. There were several girls there and their hearts dropped as the rider disappeared down the road. They knew he was in big trouble. If those cops got that kid, they'd probably lock him up and his bike would be impounded. The police in New Hampshire in those days were tough.

In a minute or so the police car chasing him came by. Then things were quiet for a short time. Then all of a sudden we heard the biker coming again. This time he was heading back in the opposite direction. The girls ran out to the road to get a closer look at the handsome outlaw. An idea flashed into my mind. I yelled out to the girls, "If he's got a good lead and the police car isn't in sight, flag him in! We'll hide him here, it's his only chance!" Hearing that they ran out into the road and as the rider approached they waived him in. We quickly pushed the bike that I was working on out of the tent and opened up a "hole" for the frantic rider.

I guess when he saw a bunch of beautiful girls standing in the road waving him into a hiding place, it must have been a welcome sight. He obliged immediately. They guided him in under the tent and I immediately put a brush to his bike. The crowd closed up around him and he disappeared from view. The young man, soaked with sweat collapsed on the ground. The girls quickly comforted him and one took her kerchief and began wiping his brow. A moment later we heard the sirens and the police cars. As they approached, everybody pointed down the road away from the car wash. They sped off. We thought, maybe our outlaw was home free, but a short time later a police car came slowly down the road and stopped right at the car wash entrance. Then another pulled up behind that one. The one officer motioned to the other officer to go on ahead, that he would check this location out. As he was leaving, the second officer yelled to the first one "I

166   DAVE DAVIES, SR.

didn't get a plate, but he had a grey beanie helmet with stickers all over it, I know that." The first officer acknowledged and the other car left. With little strength, the exhausted outlaw didn't move. The grey beanie helmet lay on the ground beside him. But the girls would not let their hero be taken! One of them grabbed the helmet and quickly stuffed it under her sweatshirt, instantly appearing pregnant. She then boldly propped up the young stranger and wrapped her arms around him. The officer approached the tent. I recognized him, he was local police and I had pinstriped an antique motorcycle for him.

"Hello Davie. How's it going?" He asked.

"Hey, great how are ya?"

The motorcycle was so hot that the engine was "crackling." I continued to pinstripe the bike and pretend everything was "cool." The officer looked around and then fixed his eyes on the "pregnant" gal and the young man soaked with sweat. Then the officer leaned over putting his head along side of mine, while still starring at the young couple, and asked… "Do you always pinstripe bikes when they're so HOT, Davie?"

What could I say? I came back with… "Only when it's absolutely necessary."

Everybody laughed, including the officer. Then he said … "Well it's just that you could really get "burned" working on this one. I think you should let it cool down a bit, don't you? I'll bet a few of the boys would really like to see this bike when you're done, but… if it isn't finished by 3:00 when there's a shift change, I guess they won't get to see it. Well, so long for now Davie, keep up the good work."

The officer walked to his car and drove off. We all breathed a sigh of relief. The young outlaw thanked us for saving him. He explained that the whole thing had begun when he had done a "Burn Out" in the middle of town filling the intersection with smoke and took off with the police in hot pursuit.

He gave me his business card. He and his dad owned an auto sales in Maine. He said if I ever came to Maine he'd return the favor. His dad had antique cars and was always looking for a good pinstriper.

Several years later while heading through Maine on our way to a rally in Bangor, we passed by a sign reading Lisbon Falls. It sounded familiar; I pulled out my stash of business cards. There it was. Immediately I called the number on the card and after identifying myself, the fellow on the other end told me not to move! He would be there in three minutes and I could follow him to his shop.

He made reservations for dinner and then gave me a tour of the dealership and his dad's stable of antique cars. (I ended up pinstriping several of them.) We're still great friends and we manage to have a "Lobsta" dinner whenever I visit that area in Maine.

❧ THE PROFESSOR AND THE LOW RIDER

One thing's for sure, we met all kinds of people at the Laconia Rally. There were folks from just about every walk of life. This particular day I was pinstriping a very expensive BMW for a professor. He was a customer from the previous year and he was back with another new "ride." There were several other people waiting in line for striping, one of which was a guy I had done work for before as well. He was a hard core biker and he had his "home built" chopper there and wanted a little more pinstriping on it. The year before I had worked on it and this year he wanted a little more with the words "Low down Rider" written on both sides of the tank. This was long before Harley had come out with the production model Low Rider. What took place next was like a scene out of a comedy movie, although it wasn't intended to be.

The professor stood over me dictating every line and every stroke of my brush. Each year I would go through this agonizing neurotic ritual with this guy, but he always appreciated what I did and paid me well, so I would just suffer through it. The chopper guy was watching me and began suggesting what he thought I should do on the professor's BMW. It went something like this...

CG) (Chopper Guy) "Hey bub, you going to have Dave 'squiggle' on that thing? You need a few more designs on that baby to 'set it off.'

Prof) (Professor) "No, there'll be no squiggles on this motorcycle."

CG) "Aw man, it's just too plain lookin'. No pizzazz man. Let him 'do it up!'

The professor, becoming irritated, ignored the comment and continued to dictate where he thought the next line should go (this was "trial and error" and driving me crazy.) Well the chopper guy just kept going on and on telling him he should have something here or there. Then he told the professor to look at his bike and see what pinstriping is supposed to look like. The professor was becoming more and more irritated by the minute.

Finally the chopper guy asked him ... "Now tell me man what do you think of my 'ride?' Seriously, what do you think of it?"

The professor turned, looked at the man's motorcycle and said, "You want my honest opinion? What do I think of that motorcycle? Why, I think it is absolutely grotesque."

Everyone was silent, no one said a word. The chopper guy continued wiping it down with a cloth and answered...

"Well thank you sir, I built it myself except my brother Bobby done most of the weldin' on it."

The guy actually thought the professor had given him a compliment! Everyone laughed quietly to themselves. Then this dialog opened up between the two of them that was hilarious.

CG) "It's different, my own design, I ain't seen nothing like it nowhere."

Prof) "It's utterly amazing how much you have accentuated the obvious."

CG) "Yea, and still kept it cool lookin' too!"

Prof) "Indeed and you have obliterated everything that a well engineered motorcycle should represent."

CG) "You noticed that huh? You got a good eye bud! I wanted to build something that was not just different but 'bad ass.'"

Prof) "Oh, you certainly have accomplished that! I think it's about as bad as it could possibly be."

The people were bent over laughing; you would have thought this was a comedy act. I could hardly stripe the bike I was laughing so hard myself. It continued...

CG) "So, if you know what's cool and all, why ain't ya letting Dave 'do yours up?'"

Prof) "It's not so much me as it is my wife, she's very conservative and if I go home with my ride 'all done up' she'll 'freak' on me. You understand."

CG) "Let me tell ya right now, if my ol' lady even begun to tell me what I could or can't do with my ride, I'd thump her!"

Prof) "I see, well I assure you that if I ever tried to 'thump' my 'ol' lady,' the results would be... well let's say... more than I could handle!"

CG) "Oh... I'm feelin' sorry for ya man. I know right where you're coming from. I had a buddy and his ol' lady would beat him wicked. That really lowers a man's feelings of himself. It's a tough thing to have to deal with. Forget what I said sir, your bike would look nice done up, but it ain't worth her givin' you an ass woopin'"

The professor didn't say another word. He paid me, got on his bike and drove off. My chopper friend apologized for having hit a "sore spot" with the professor's situation with his ol' lady.

Laconia always presented a variety of people and challenges. Between the weather and the crazies, you would earn your money up there, but the trip was always exciting and profitable. It was to set the stage for the road shows we do today. Daytona, Myrtle Beach, Sturgis, and numerous rallies followed the Laconia Event.

Once a 1951 Buick Hearse, transformed to The Davies Creative Camper, which made many appearances at various rallies

Once again I would use simple philosophy; if this idea works, then duplicate it. Do it again, and again. Each time "sharpening the saw," making it work even better. I started going anywhere there were motorcycle gatherings. There were motorcycle "hill climbs," "swap meets," drag races, motocross races, etc. Some were better than others and it took time to decipher which rallies would be better for a pinstriper. Surprisingly, racing events turned out to be the worst places to set up. The dust and dirt were a problem along with the fact that people came to watch the races and that was their main focus. Other rallies were "parties" and everyone got drunk. Esthetically enhancing their motorcycle was the furthest thing from their clouded minds. So a select few events would work and it was important to find out which ones they were. I then set up criteria that an event would have to meet. Now I had a gauge to work from, a "benchmark." I won't go into details because it only pertains to my work and a particular approach to my craft. The important thing is that I convey the basic principle used.

Once again, if I were to write about all of the stories of my experiences as a traveling pinstriper at just motorcycle rallies, it would take hundreds of pages. This book is about a life. A life that isn't "stuck" in any particular place in time.

It seemed that unconsciously, I was fulfilling many desires in my life simultaneously. I loved to travel and see the country, I loved being around interesting people, I loved my craft, I loved coming up with ideas and implementing them, I loved making money doing what I enjoy so much, I loved bringing my family along when possible, I loved the knowledge we could all gain from the experiences.

It's been said, *"traveling broadens the mind."* This statement is absolutely true. There was something else that was also true that once again crossed my mind: A truly creative person with the proper foundational principles could...

"Create a world around them" and avoid (for the most part) being "victim of their surroundings."

How many times must I experience this before I would begin believing it? I had gone from having serious difficulty paying bills and keeping commitments, to having much more control over both, thus creating a different playing field, yet not changing my craft or skills.

Now you might say people often change jobs or reeducate themselves. I understand, but are they able to keep everything that means the most to them in tact through the entire process? It is so important that we hold on to what is so dear to us. So many of my friends had started out pursuing their dreams, some were musicians, some were artists, or dancers, race car drivers, but they veered off course and never pursued their dream. Don't get me wrong, often there were valid reasons for the changes they made. Things like debt, or sickness, or unforeseen circumstances, are legitimate reasons for setting a dream aside, but to give up the entire dream forever?

I've dreamed of writing screenplays. Over the years I have had to put that dream aside. That did not stop me from gathering books on the subject and attending a class whenever possible, though. Poetry and writing have always been an important part of my life but very few of my friends knew this side of me. The circles I was traveling in did not provide a healthy environment for discussing these things. If I recited a poem about Pete Corey (and there were many) or read a story I wrote about the Hell's Angels I probably would not have gotten the response I was looking for. So you might say I was a "closet writer." The important thing is I never stopped writing. Just because you don't have the luxury to be surrounded by a level of consciousness that will support your endeavor doesn't mean you should not continue. My career as an artist spans over half a century, I have also been writing for over half a century. Now is the season for writing. Now after going through the refinement process we call life. In the beginning of the book I stated that in the Creative World the older you are, the *more* valuable you are. Am I not more valuable than twenty or thirty years ago? As an Artist? As a writer? As a person? As a friend?

There is a situation that prevents people from pursuing their dreams...

Chapter 24:

THE PLATEAU

The plateau is that place where we get "stuck" or at the very least "bogged down." It's the place quickly brought up in conversation when you run into an old friend that you haven't seen for years. It usually goes something like this...

"Hey, remember back in school when we were on the football team?" Or remember when the kids were little and we lived on such and such street? Then they go on about how great times were back then and although they don't always say it, they give the impression that things have kind of gone downhill from there. They "plateaued."

Don't "plateau!" I could easily say that the days when Tom and I terrorized the neighborhood, or Debbie and I went fishing, or the years I spent with Pete Corey, or when I first met Linda, were the greatest times of my life. But I am still living the greatest time in my life.

I never dreamed that I would or even could, write a book. I have enjoyed many projects but writing this book and sharing my life with those who may be benefiting from these words gives me not only great pleasure but a **new pleasure**. There are many of you that should still be chasing your dreams. Many well meaning friends told me that writing a book would be a waste of valuable time, distracting me from my art work. Others made it clear that with a ninth grade education that my attempt would be less than successful. What they didn't know was that I would rather try and fail, than not try at all. I have failed many times at many things and have few regrets, but to not try and go through life thinking "maybe I could have" will tear you up. I can look back at things that didn't work out for me and laugh, but something that I thought I could do but didn't try, would be no laughing matter.

Over the years I have taught many people free hand pinstriping. I even produced a "how to" kit with brushes, paint, step-by-step booklet, video, etc, so that people could learn this skill. Many folks had asked how they could learn striping. I thought it would be a big hit. Well "when the rubber hit the road" and they were presented with the "real deal," the excuses came popping up. "I could never do that, not in a million years, I don't care how much information I had." "My hand isn't steady enough," etc. etc. They seemed so sincere when they asked about learning but they really didn't want to learn the craft. What many wanted were the results of the craft. They saw what I had done with the craft and where I could go with the craft, and they wanted "that." They hadn't experienced the "Reality" of the situation — the rubber hitting the road. This stems from the ravages of "instant gratification." In today's world it seems everyone wants everything instantly. "The quicker — the better." Years ago a person would take the time to learn a skill, a guy would date the same girl for years, and they enjoyed the "process," always looking forward to anticipated results. A joy that "Insta-Grats" will never experience. Some "Old School" advice would be to think... " Later-Greater."

I have heard so many times... "I would give anything to be able to do that!" (freehand pinstriping.) This usually takes place while we are transforming the dynamics of a car or motorcycle at a rally with a huge crowd hanging over us watching in amazement. Many of the people had never seen a human hand form lettering or pinstriping with a brush and paint. When I was growing up it was very common to see a man lettering a sign or a window. People walking by might gaze for a moment, but it was just a man busy at his craft. These days if I have a brush out painting anything, it will always draw a curious crowd. One time I was lettering a sign for a friend who had a business in Lake George. Two kids vacationing for the summer came walking by. They stopped and almost appeared to be mesmerized as they watched me forming the letters on the sign. "Where are the letters coming from?" The little one asked. "From that brush." The older one answered. "The letters are coming out of that brush."

He thought the letters were inside the brush and I was transferring them onto the background. I explained that I was "forming" the letters with the brush. (I was lettering "freehand" and had no letters marked out on the board, so I think that caused the confusion). When I told them that I was working from an alphabet in my head they were amazed. They understood computer generated letters but to think a person could hold alphabets in their head and then form them with a brush was beyond their comprehension. This brought to my attention how quickly things can "go away." This really bothers me. We are losing so many wonderful things that made life rich and wonderful. I also noticed something else (and this is only my own observation), there may be a connection between working with your hands and mind and enjoying good health into your elder years. I intend on doing some research on this.

Chapter 25:

FAMILY

The concept of "Family" has special power. It has strength, support, and can provide a nucleus of energy and creativity among other things. TV shows that represented a family were more successful than others. Family businesses seemed to have a much better chance at succeeding. Family represents unity, all members having a common understanding, working toward common goals.

In today's world the concept of family has taken a terrible beating. There is this "independent" mentality manifesting itself in people today that is detrimental to everything family represents.

Common sense dictates that most often "Whenever we DIVIDE" we must SUBTRACT. There is no addition to division."

Because Linda and I were of the "Constructive Mentality" we erred toward *unity* and had a high regard for everything that represented "Family." So why not *create* one. That August "the Mercedes" produced an exact duplicate of the original. **David Jr.** was born. As he grew I could see even more evidence that he was just like the original. He would keep everything neat and orderly, he was careful about saving and spending money, he was very resourceful, *he was just like his mother!* David also had many of my traits as well; he was his own person and very creative, and from past experience we knew this must be handled properly. Our dream was if he could develop the family talents and use them resourcefully, that would be a dynamic combination. . We were aware that the world was a difficult place and that if children were not properly prepared; life could be not only difficult but hazardous. If this little guy was to be able to survive in this jungle he would need to be armed with a sharp mind and some very specific skills. He would need to develop a spirit of contribution, and understand the needs of those he would be serving.

My dad believed that having skills were vitally important to life. By developing valuable skills you could create income. If you were to create valuable skills that you *enjoy* there is a good chance you could create a level of happiness and health as well. I found this to be absolutely true.

Even though Linda and I were relatively young we had experienced more than most people our age, and there was something that concerned both of us. Something that we had seen throughout our lives that was very disturbing Something that, if possible, we wanted to avoid.

Chapter 26:

THE SPOILED CHILD

The Spoiled Child is no Joke
The Spoiled Child has little Hope
The Spoiled Child Can't Cope

This is very serious stuff. Many of our friends would joke about their children being spoiled. Linda and I had experienced firsthand, often on a daily basis, dealing with spoiled people. The insensitivity, lack of compassion, self-centeredness, and general demeanor was brutal to have to deal with. We both have had to "wait" for many things. This always gave us something to look forward to, to hope for. Many things we thought we needed so badly, after some time would pass we realized we didn't need them at all. Often something better would come along to take its place. When we did have to wait patiently or had to save for something and finally received it, the joy was often indescribable. There were times when we had to go without things. We simply could not afford something or it might have been beyond our reach. It simply worked best to cope with the situation until things changed. It wasn't in our best interest to argue with each other, complain, or have a tantrum; we would simply cope with the situation. As we look back I would have to say that the *reward* for coping would be the building of an *"inner strength"* through the process and inner strength can be very comforting during difficult times.

"When the dessert is served before the meal, all that would be nutritional and good loses its appeal."

Listen, we can't be with our children every moment of every day. As they get older they will be introduced to everything from sex to alcohol and drugs. If they haven't been able to experience life outside of their comfort zone how would they have the inner strength to walk away from these things that could destroy their lives? The feeding of "instant gratification" side steps the building of inner strengths. You would be sending the child into the world unarmed against things that could seriously harm them.

If you still think that a spoiled child is a joke, let me take it to another level. Today because of the powerful influence Television, the Internet, and the environment projected by our school systems upon young people, many become... *Self Centered, Pleasure driven, Image based, Comfort Creatures, with a Hollywood Mentality, Prone to Addiction, often receiving much of their (so called) knowledge from Advertisers rather than genuine Educators or Mentors.*

In these times with so many choices, advertising everywhere, and credit available, it's difficult to avoid spoiling a child, but we must be careful. When do you know you have gone too far? When there is clear lack of appreciation. When children start taking things (and people) for granted, and they become insensitive to others' needs. They become unreasonable and seem to lose the ability to reason right from wrong.

It is my opinion that in certain spoiled children there is manifested a form of mental illness not yet explored.

I remember being at a wedding reception and sitting next to this elderly lady. She was obviously very wealthy and had been bragging how much she had contributed to the newlyweds (she was a relative of the bride). She said something that really upset me.

She said "One thing is for sure; when I'm gone my children will be well taken care of." (Meaning she had plenty of money, insurance, etc.) I thought... don't say a word, keep your mouth shut, you may offend her.

I couldn't hold back. I looked directly at her and said... "Do you really believe that? That a large sum of money dumped on children will 'take care of them.' That's like leaving the devil himself there to watch your children! Let me explain something to you."

"Money is a magnifier. It often makes things larger. There have been families where there was a little drug problem, or alcohol problem, or a gambling problem, and large amounts of money from inheritance blew those little problems up and sent them through the roof. On the other hand where someone was trying to build a business, or secure a home, some cash could help out immensely. The point being that depending on the circumstances a magnifier may help or possibly hurt the situation."Money is like gasoline. In the tank it can fuel the engine and take you where you need to go. It must be stored properly and kept away from sparks and open flame, or you may have to deal with the adverse effects of it. To be more "pungent" let me say this

"When someone receives a large sum of money and has not the preparation, knowledge, or level of consciousness to handle it, it's the equivalent of receiving a ticket to dance with the Devil"

I then mentioned to the lady… "Now, I heard you use the term *"taken care of,"* and I would strongly suggest you rethink that. It's wonderful that you are kind enough to want to leave the people you love something to help them in their lives, but without the proper knowledge and understanding, money can fuel the wrong things. Besides, would you rather be worth more to them dead than alive?" She was offended that I questioned her judgment and ignored me the rest of the evening. Some people get it, some don't. I said what I had to say. Older folks were always worth more to Linda and me if they were **alive**. With their knowledge and wisdom we could create our own wealth.

You may be wondering, how do you "un-spoil" a child?

Very carefully and very cautiously. You are dismantling a bomb! "Say the wrong NO and the whole thing could BLOW."

Obviously this is a subject I am very passionate about. I'll be taking this to another level and going into depth on this subject in another book. For now… enough said.

Obviously Linda and I were going to try to be very cautious in bringing up our children. When David Jr. was young we didn't have much to spoil a child with. Back then we experienced a few of those "Charlie Brown Christmas's" and Creativity became a treasured friend. Winter always presented its own problems but I remember one particular year that things were especially tight. With Christmas approaching we knew we had to come up with something clever to get some extra cash.

As luck would have it a friend stopped over with an old familiar request. He had purchased a new bowling bag for his wife. Both he and his wife bowled on a team together. I hadn't lettered a bowling bag in years. I would usually letter the name in script and shadow it in another color. Back then ten bucks would cover it. You couldn't go wrong for that, especially since it gave insurance that no one would steal a bag with a name on it. Some of these bowling bags were very expensive. This would also give young David a chance to watch closely how I formed the letters with a brush. I showed him how to find center of the lettering space and count the number of letters then divide to find which letter would fall in the center. I let him make the top and bottom guide lines with the ruler. He watched every move I made and truly enjoyed the process.

The only problem was that the whole process seemed to end too quickly. David and I were having such a good time that I told Linda that I wished I had a few more to do. She thought for a moment and came up with a great idea. She had a friend that had told her she was looking for something to get extra money for Christmas as well, but hadn't come up with anything as yet. Linda suggested that we letter her brother's bowling bag for an example and then let her friend go to various bowling alleys and bowler's clubs in the area. She could show the people running the "pro shops" what we were doing, even offer to do a few examples for them to display, and offer a pickup and delivery service.

If I was able to do these for ten bucks, that left room for her and the guy at the pro shop to tack on a few bucks. Well she jumped right on it and hit every bowler's club, bowling alley, and sports shop in the area. Within a few days we had a house full of bowling bags. Hey, ten tens is a hundred (do the math), the bucks added up fast. We had a great Christmas that year and David helped with every single one, putting an indelible image in his memory regarding Creativity, Ideas, Layout, and Lettering.

✎ A UNIQUE POSITION

As I watched little David carefully laying out the lines and anticipating his chance someday to pick up the brush, I found myself in a very unique position. I was in exactly the same place my dad and I were years before. But this time things were different. I wasn't about to get drunk and ruin a wonderful thing. I wasn't going to let him discover everything by himself and I wasn't going to break his heart.

What I was going to do was, to the best of my ability, harness this desire that was so evident and guide him as far as I could in developing a creative mind. With all the mistakes I had made and the knowledge gathered, there would be no problem laying down a foundation for him to work from. This would prove to be easier said than done.

The first mistake was that I thought I had plenty of time to do this. Not so. With all that was going on in those days there seemed to be less and less time to do anything. The winter months did give me a window of "down time" when things were a bit quiet (work wise) but spring would come and the world would open up and away I'd go. The years pass so quickly. Linda would drop subtle hints like "He's been eyeing my nail polish brushes and I don't think they're designed for lettering but who knows, he may come up with something creative." So, I started bringing David everywhere I'd go. My thoughts were that he could do little things to help out. (Try bringing a kid to work with you every day — see how much you get done) The little guy could only do so much and I would have to create things to keep him busy that took time away from everything I was doing.

One time we were painting a truck for a friend of mine and I was sanding the surface to prepare it for paint. David was hounding me to give him sandpaper so he could work with me. But the surface of the truck had to be sanded a certain way as not to break through to the bare metal so we wouldn't have to re-primer it. So to keep him busy I gave David some sandpaper and instructed him to sand "smooth" all the little bumps on the diamond plate bumper. He worked diligently for a while trying to get those bumps flat but soon knew he'd been hoodwinked. He began to realize working with dad wasn't all it was cracked up to be. I kept promising him (and myself) that I would take time and work with his lettering as soon as I could.

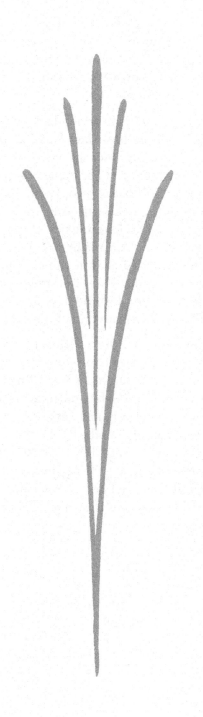

DAVE DAVIES, SR.

Chapter 27:

THE INVESTMENT

The definition of *Investment* is... CONTRIBUTION TO ACTIVITY: ("Contribution of something such as time, energy, or effort to an activity, project, or undertaking in expectation of a benefit.")

(When Happensburg suggested learning a new word every day, he never mentioned that I should ever stop.)

I knew I must make an investment in David. An investment of time, energy, and effort, and that it would pay off a hundred fold. Here we were once again involved in "FOUNDATIONAL - FAITHFUL - FRUITFUL." The message was clear, I knew what I had to do. I remembered my dad taking time to outline the lettering on my little lemonade stand. I remembered carefully painting between the lines my dad made. It was difficult but fun and as I developed the skill of transferring paint with the brush, forming letters, I can remember how good it felt. It gave me confidence to do freehand work.

We must remember that it's *resistance* that builds strength. *Overcoming* difficulties gives us *confidence*, and creates the *desire to take on more challenges. In the spoiled child, most resistance, obstacles, and difficulties are often removed for them.*

I remembered as a kid building my little homemade car; if my folks had bought me a ready-built Go-Cart, many wonderful things would have been omitted from my life. The knowledge, the fun, the confidence, the memories that came out of that experience. Not to mention learning that *"Adventure should be handled with intelligence."*

I was going to have to grit my teeth and be patient with David and allow him to make mistakes and learn from them. The student was now becoming the teacher. The responsibility was tremendous, but also the best investment I could possibly make.

I bought David a set of brushes and some paints and set him up with a little "kit." He had to learn how to take care of the brushes, how to mix paints, and the basic chemistry.

Having his own equipment and learning to take care of it is foundational and fundamental, not only pertaining to this craft but many things in life. If he learns to take care of his brushes then he'll probably take care of his other *"Gifts,"*

his tools, his bicycle, whatever. The important thing is that he puts a *"Value"* on these simple little things that have *"Use."* Especially the things that will help in the development of his skills.

Chapter 28:

THE LITTLE ENTREPRENEUR

As it usually does, time passed quickly and before long David became pretty slick with a brush. He could letter and shadow letters free hand and was only too eager to use his skill. He was lettering everything in sight. All his friends bicycles and he even lettered a stock car for the dad of one of his friends.

When his sister Sandy came along, he started teaching her what he had learned. This was especially good because when we show someone what we have learned we are reviewing it ourselves for another time. David was indeed sharpening his skills. I never thought that the skill he was developing would ever get him in trouble, but it did.

I had done some election signs for a friend of mine and we had all kinds of stuff left over from the election. There were these little round buttons with the candidate's name on them in a box. David asked if he could have them. I thought why not? He probably wants them as a commemorative thing to collect and keep. Not so, he spray painted over the existing lettering and made them all white blanks. Then at school he would take orders from kids for lettering, like "Suzy loves Tom," or a "Yankees" logo, or your favorite stock car number. Basically whatever they wanted. He was charging maybe twenty-five or up to fifty cents for each button. Well, his little venture took off and had started a fad. Just about every kid had a button with something on it. It wasn't long before the school called and we had an appointment with the principal. It seems selling items to students on school property was a no-no. I was so ecstatic when I found out that he had worked an idea all by himself and was actually turning a dollar with it that I couldn't wait to speak on his behalf. However, the school staff did not see it that way. I assured them that it would not continue but I would have to admit that it was a clever idea and that he had come up with it by himself and that, considering his age, his skill level was admirable. They were more concerned about what punishment I was going to administer. They were going to consider after-school detention on their end.

I became enraged! I said, "Look, I understand there are rules but he was unaware of them and wasn't deliberately breaking them. But if you think for one moment that I am going to punish my son for coming up with a creative idea, carrying through to a successful conclusion, not to mention making a large number of people happy, you're out of your minds! If you people cannot see the good in this then you're all educated idiots! Punish a kid for this kind of thinking? What other twelve year old in this school has ever come up with an idea of this magnitude? Something that would positively affect that many of his peers? I think I'll call the local TV station and see if they think there's a story here worth telling." With that I was interrupted with…"Mr. Davies, there's no reason to do that! Now that you have brought to light the positive side of this, it might be better to just drop the matter entirely. We were just worried that others would start selling items on school property and that this might begin something that could get out of control."

I apologized for getting upset and the thing ended quietly, but I was so proud of David and I think it was good that he saw how much his effort meant to me. It also gave me a clear picture that "Creativity" was an unfamiliar face to this administration and that if it wasn't protocol they did not consider it to be of value. In their mind it would be just great if all the students would conform and stack up neatly like little spoons. God forbid that a knife and fork may come along. I thought "nothing's changed; it's still *the non-conformist that moves the world forward.*"

The entrepreneur side of David seemed to show itself often and it soon became more than just an embryo. This young man had talent in this area and I was determined to cultivate it. It was so obvious that David had attached his artistic ability to business skills. This became exciting watching David grow and his talents develop.

"May all of our mistakes become fertilizer for our continued growth"

Chapter 29:

HEART TO HEART WITH ART

What Does Art have to do with the Heart? Everything! Or at least it should be everything. With our children, art often gave us the first glimpse of their hearts. Sandy, our second child always loved animals. She would draw animals and make unique clothing for our pet dogs. To this day she paints portraits of dogs on slate using an airbrush in perfect detail.

A friend of mine had a champion hunting dog that had passed away. His wife asked me if I would have Sandy do a portrait of the dog for a Christmas present. Sandy did such a spectacular job capturing the image that upon opening the present the man cried like a baby. Although it is just a hobby with her she has captured the **hearts** of many dog owners.

Michael, our third child, has probably evolved to the top artist in the family. He has been responsible for much of the success we have had in the motorcycle building business. Although he has been our best kept secret, he is not interested in fame or super recognition probably because of his love for the ministry. Quietly, Michael has performed miracles on trucks, cars, motorcycles, etc. with his airbrush. Then David Jr. and I would come in with a little pinstriping and get all the credit. Michael has done many displays for church youth centers throughout the country.

When Mike was just a little guy he was never a problem, no matter where we would bring him. I remember once when he was about five years old Linda was in the doctor's office waiting for her appointment. There was a woman sitting across from them and she was miserably complaining. On and on she went about everything. Linda would always give Michael a pencil and a piece of paper to draw things and that always kept him quietly occupied. Well, he drew a picture of a little deer. When he finished, he very shyly walked over to the woman and set it on her lap and returned to continue drawing. The woman looked at the drawing and melted like butter. She didn't say another word. Yes, the heart and art are very much connected in our family.

Getting back to David…it was very important that we were very careful not to completely control David's life or fight all of his battles for him. This is the point where I realized that the difficulties that Linda and I had gone through as children may have been a blessing. I truly feel that it is an indication that *you are blessed when the difficulties come first,* allowing *the rewards to follow.* I know so many kids who have had a "fairytale" childhood, only to buckle under the difficulties life presents as they grow. The tendency is, if you have had a rough start and had to struggle, you would want your child to have it easier. This concept is "half right." Of course you would want better for your children the problem being that most folks give the kids *the products* of their successes and often forget to give them the *ingredients* of their success. The classic example of this is when immigrants came to this country and struggled, then became successful. After a couple of generations living here spoiled their children they did not understand why that generation could not succeed. There are many examples where great grandchildren manage to pick up the pieces, often being quite interested in the *tools (fundamentals) that their great grandparents had used,* and actually implementing them *once again* to achieve successful results.

The concept of "Ownership" - "Stewardship," works wonders in this situation. There is something special about Ownership, and basically its *responsibility.* Maybe I should say *"response-ability."* The *ability* to *respond.* We all have a higher regard for things we own or are in charge of. Simply drive through a neighborhood where there are mostly rental properties — things are not always pretty. Other areas where folks own their homes, you'll generally see that things look quite spiffy. Let me give you an example of this in action.

If you order your child to wash the car he or she may not feel joyous about doing it. But if they were "in charge" of washing and waxing the cars and they knew that income was generated from their responsibility, they will often look at it differently. They are the boss, it's their car washing & waxing business, and income comes from taking care of it. They would have ownership over all equipment and it would be *their choice* of brands of soaps, waxes, etc. This *creates a sense of pride* and also gives some *control* over their own environment. It's an entirely different feeling. Of course they have someone above them to answer to (namely, you) but as long as things are spiffy and clean they don't need to hear from you. They can do this on Saturday or during the week, they can have some other person do it — as long as the job gets done, they get paid. Its business and they are the CEO of their own car washing/ waxing company. Can you see the value in this? Just handing your child something to win their love is so insignificant when compared to structuring something like this. This kind of love will last a lifetime.

Because of the nature of our *Gifts* and *Talents* we did things a little differently, but basically I delegated some responsibility to David. We would be doing repaint work on signs, basically refurbishing existing signs that were faded out and needed repainting. Also, we would have certain truck lettering that was basic and repetitive. We had "patterns" to work from and this could also be done by David. He was now a "junior partner" in the business. He would have a "say" in what went on regarding lettering. This gave me freedom to do the pinstriping, so we were both benefiting. I wasn't just helping him; we were both contributing to the business. David was developing skills and becoming more and more *"Valuable."* This sort of thing boosts self esteem tremendously. Also the more responsibility regarding income a child has, the more they have to lose. (Remember early in the chapters when I was young? Remember everything I had to lose?) This is a good thing, giving a person something to weigh their decisions on.

❧ SPEAKING OF DECISIONS

The "decision making process" is one of the most important tasks of the mind. It is paramount that early on we allow our children to learn the effects and power in the decision making process. Keep in mind that *"Self-Discipline"* is a key ingredient in the decision making process. The spoiled child is often void of self-discipline, and when we grow old **they** may very well be making the decisions that affect *our* lives.

The decisions we make can create happiness or in many situations are responsible for regret. The decisions we make can create a future, or they can end a life. We are living in a fast-paced world. There is a demand for quick decision making. We are living in a dangerous world, probably because of this. Quick decisions are often necessary but many times not thinking things through and deciding, without considering circumstances or situations can be dangerous. It's amazing how far we have drifted from when our forefathers were building this great country; they would often pray and fast before making major decisions. They knew they needed guidance and a clear mind because the decisions they were making would seriously affect many people. Today, high level decisions are made in a heartbeat, often devastating large groups of people. Careful thought could prevent this. Keep in mind that "DECISIONS CREATE CIRCUMSTANCES."

Some time ago I read something that the famous motivational speaker "Zig Ziglar" had written that I thought was profound. His words stuck in my head and I think that regarding decision making especially in children, they are very valuable.

Before making a major decision it is important that we ask ourselves two very important questions…

1) Is this decision I am about to make morally right, and fair to **everyone** *involved?*

2) Is this decision I am about to make going to take me further toward or further away from my major objectives?

Now think about those questions for a moment. How about a young person about to experience sex for the first time. Or experiment with drugs.

Is what they are about to do morally right and fair to everyone who has loved them and raised them, helped them and invested much of their lives in them? Could this decision change their direction toward major objectives? Or worse, cause those objectives to disappear entirely? One decision can change a life forever. Decisions are powerful. Remember earlier in my writing I explained that where we are today is, for the most part, the result of decisions we have made in our past. The decision making process is the steering mechanism of your ship. It controls direction. Don't misunderstand me; we have the right to *change our minds* if we **decide** to. Although, in the competitive environment a certain "rigidness" seems to prevail, especially when the ego is involved. Competitive types are often afraid that the **Heart** may control the **Head**. Today many people make their decisions according to *social values,* influenced by whomever or whatever may be popular. The problem is that these kinds of values **change** constantly. *PRINCIPLES never change.*

Can you see how important principles can be in raising our children? I'm not saying we did everything right, we certainly did not, but as I look back there were things that worked and some that didn't and I'm doing my best to share with you what worked for me and may be of value to you.

Chapter 30:

COMMON SENSE

Where does our common sense come from? I believe that although many people seem to be readily equipped with a fair amount, there are others totally without any! Experience has much to do with this. Tiny threads of knowledge formed together produce a base form of intelligence that is fundamental to everyday existence.

When we are **not** *allowed to experience things and especially solve small problems in our lives, the threads may become severed and the foundation is not formed as well as it could be.*

As Linda and I grew older we noticed that common sense among children seemed to be less prevalent than it was when we were kids. It was easy to blame television or maybe the fact that there are many more distractions for kids these days, causing their attention span to be diminished greatly.

I remember when I was about eight years old, one day a friend (we'll call Abie) and I were working on our bicycles. I had my dad's tools out and we were taking our bikes apart and changing the wheels, sprockets, and handlebars, etc. We would change a wheel size or a sprocket. Then when we rode the bike, it would pedal much harder or maybe it went faster because we had changed the ratio from the pedals to the rear wheel. Changing the handlebar location also changed the leverage we had from our legs against the pedals. Abie was fascinated by all of this. He couldn't believe how one small change could affect another. My dad explained *"Cause and Effect"* and how any change affects something somewhere. We were having fun and learning something. We were also covered with grease from head to toe. Later Abie's dad came to pick him up. He was driving a very expensive car, I think his dad was a doctor or a lawyer, I'm not sure. Anyway he walked over and looked at Abie and became very upset that he had grease on his hands and clothes. I remember Abie saying "Look Dad, we're fixing bikes and I'm pretty handy." His dad picked him up like a dirty rag and escorted him to the car. He had him stand there while he got some towels from the trunk, then used them to cover the seat, before carefully placing Abie in. I didn't see Abie after that for quite some time. When I did see him I asked why he hadn't called me or stopped over. He said his dad said he's not handy and he is not going to be a "grease monkey."

In many European countries a young person spends many years in an apprenticeship before entering the automobile industry and the term "grease monkey" is not in their vocabulary.

Now I'm sure that Abie is probably a doctor or lawyer himself somewhere (maybe he'd been better placed in engineering, but we'll never know, will we?) The point being, did it hurt him to learn some basic principles? As I look back I'd think his dad should have gotten a kick out of it, given that he had the path already carved for Abie anyway.

I have met many top-level professionals whose lives reveal the lack of some very basic principles. Not too long ago I was driving along and in front of me was a new SUV pulling a small trailer. The guy was weaving all over the road. I became especially concerned when I saw that he had his family in the car. At first I thought he might be drunk but as I got closer I could see that the appliances he was carrying were loaded to the rear of the trailer. This causes weight to come off of the rear wheels of the tow vehicle and without proper weight (on the tongue) toward the front of the trailer, the tow vehicle will weave from side to side. He stopped at a red light ahead and I had the opportunity to pull along side of him. I got his attention and explained the position of the load was causing the problem and if he would pull over I may be able to help. He obliged and we took a moment to move the load forward.

As he drove off, I watched him go down the road straight and true. What amazed me was that he and his wife were obviously bright, educated people and yet they didn't know this simple dynamic that most of us learned as kids. Maybe such knowledge was omitted while avoiding the "grease monkey syndrome."

Linda and I bought and fixed up houses over the years, converting old knowledge with new, applying common sense as a catalyst. One winter when the kids were little our furnace quit in the middle of the night during a below zero cold spell. The last thing I wanted to do was to call the heating guy so I thought I'd give it a shot myself. I knew about automobile engines and an oil-fired furnace is basically a combustion system as well. It needs fuel and spark. I was hoping it was a fuel problem because I knew we had fuel in the tank and I could simply trace that easier than an electrical problem. I found that the filter was plugged. I simply cleaned it with paint thinner, stuck it back in and had heat restored. Connecting auto knowledge with a furnace problem was just applying base common sense. Sheetrock taping and basic bodywork are similar. I've used some of the same tools for both. Knowledge of one can be converted to the other, etc. I'm only giving these examples to show that when you don't have the resources you are often forced to THINK your way out of problems using whatever common knowledge you may have. Even if you aren't the type of person that can perform these tasks, common knowledge of certain things can prevent you from being ripped off when someone else has to be hired to do them. Can you see the *value* in all of this?

The little things we learn growing up, the mistakes we make, and the successes we achieve represent the threads in the fabric that supports us for life. Common sense is foundational in the development of intelligence. When cultivated properly it will grow accordingly. It always amazed me that the creative world seemed to reward all of this, but in the competitive world many important fundamentals seemed to be missing. There seemed to be so much more room in the creative world. Room to grow, room to prosper. I can't help believing that creative thinking is natural to the human psyche. When you can accomplish your goals and dreams without hurting others (often helping others), it is a wonderful thing.

✎ THE VALUE IN PROBLEM SOLVING

Allow me to repeat:

"If you can solve your own problems, you can be happy. If you can solve other people's problems, you can be rich"

Having said that, allow me to lay some foundation. As I am writing this book we are experiencing some very tough economic times in this country. Unemployment is over 10%. Many companies are closing their doors. We are experiencing the worst inflation in many years. People are asking… "How could this happen in America?" To make things even more difficult the country seems to be divided as to what may be the solutions to these problems. Let's begin with the cause. Once we understand the cause of a particular problem it is much easier to develop a *solution*. To accomplish this we must use a combination of *Truth, Common Sense, Knowledge, and Wisdom*. Keep in mind that if you omit any one of these, your efforts will be in vain.

My dad would always say… "If you want to see the future, sometimes all you have to do is look back. We live on a round thing" As crude as that was it made sense. We've all heard the saying… *"If we don't learn from history we'll be forced to repeat it."* So let's go back and see if we can get some sort of frame of reference. Has anything like this ever happened before? Ah, yes the 1920's. What was the cause? Don't say it was the stock market crash. That was a result; something caused that. I made that mistake myself once and my dad (who lived through those years) was quick to correct me. He said the general cause was "People against People" This in and of itself will cause *collapse*. "People helping people" creates *prosperity*.

Remember, "When you divide you have to subtract, there is no addition to division."

The common sense here is by dividing you end up with less. Everywhere we go we see one group against another. These days it's totally out of hand. So let's go deeper. What caused "People against People?" It seems that when times are extremely good economically, people are having a good ol' time — the Roaring Twenties, for example. People become more independent and have less need for each other. Greed runs rampant and *Integrity* seems to lose its value. Gluttony dulls the mind and few new ideas are born in this environment.

"It's been my experience that an empty belly will indeed stimulate the mind."

Eventually, inflation creeps in and the dollar loses its value. The less the dollar is worth, the more working folks become slaves, and unfortunately many thinkers often become thieves. No one escapes the wrath of inflation. Even the street mugger; instead of accosting one person a day he must rob two or three. Crime escalates. Your savings evaporate before your very eyes and you can do nothing about it. I've used the word "inflation" in conversation many times over the last five years deliberately looking for a reaction. It was clear most people didn't have a clue what that word truly meant. Listen I'm not an academic, but common sense dictates…

"Inflation is like 'Percentage;' it affects the whole thing"

Let's get back to the cause. *Inflation* "*triggered by*" as well as "*triggering*" *a loss of Integrity*. When integrity diminishes, one leg of the economic table is gone and it can no longer stand. Also, if there is the absence of *Truth* in leadership, it's the equivalent of heading out into unchartered territory without a needle in the compass, and a crash is inevitable. If a person in leadership is lacking in integrity, where would he or she stand regarding the *guidance system* (Truth)? Remember Truth is an **absolute, the benchmark**. It's the only thing that is **real**. It's the very foothold you'll need to gain any leverage. Again, *THIS IS COMMON SENSE based on some very old PRINCIPLES.*

Tell me, have we seen any LACK of INTEGRITY with leadership in these economic times? How about TRUTH, any problem with that these days? It's strange that when one thing becomes devalued something else gains in value. As the dollar loses its value, gold gains value. Why? Because gold is stable, tangible. Remember that the American dollar was once fully backed by gold. What backs up our monetary system now? Our economy? American integrity? Believe it or not, it is backed basically by our consumer "might," because we are the world's largest consumer. How's that for stability? Oh that's power for sure but what if another country like China or Germany takes over that position. What if the *dollar, the primary tool* of the consumer continues to drop in value? What then would we have to offer the world in exchange for the safety and the lifestyle we enjoy today? You do realize we have to *give* something in exchange for all of this. What would that be?

Right now gold has a tremendously high value and is expected to go higher. I personally think that *Truth* may indeed be worth *more than gold*. It's rarer, more difficult to find than gold. Lots of folks are selling gold; how many are speaking even a word of truth? As times get worse, the *dollar* (the *primary tool* of the consumer) shrinks and the more people will lie and connive to make up for what they are losing. Think about it. If gold is selling for over thirteen hundred an ounce, what would one sentence of absolute Truth *spoken at the right moment, by the right person, at the right time, under the right circumstances* be worth? Maybe *several million per sentence*? If you have any doubts about this, what would it be worth to you personally to hear the absolute truth from, a politician, a president? How about a doctor, a lawyer, a witness, or a business associate? Remember I said under the **right circumstances**, and at the **right time**. I'm talking about the people who control our lives and many of them tend to put truth and integrity aside during tough economic times. "Your well being" may not be quite as important as their own needs. After all, they have worked long and hard to get where they are. Just staying there is difficult these days (Or so they say, justifying their actions in their own minds.) We go through lengthy agonizing court trials, costing hundreds of thousands of dollars and a serious inconvenience to all involved, just to get to the TRUTH. Recently on the news I saw where a man had been released from prison after being wrongly accused and convicted of a crime he never committed. What do you suppose truth would have been worth to that man?

There is tremendous *value* in *Truth,* it's the *main ingredient needed in solving problems.* If you think that you can solve the problems in your life, your business, your country without embracing truth, you are seriously misinformed. Unless and until we come to this realization we will continue to flounder in all aspects of our lives. Much like gold, the more *rare* truth becomes the more *valuable.* Is it obtained without cost? Certainly not. Many have paid for it with their lives.

We vote for politicians because they are handsome, brilliant, and have charisma. But if they lack integrity they have no political value, especially during difficult times. We have become a *Self Centered, Pleasure Driven, Image based society*, with a *Hollywood mentality, Educated through advertising* and we are paying the price for this foolishness. Can you imagine Abe Lincoln running in an election today? Why, who in the world would vote for such a homely face?

Some of you reading this book may think that I've drifted off a bit with this discussion on problem solving, truth and all this. Allow me to wake up a few brain cells… Do you remember the little lemonade stand? Did Happensburg not teach me about Truth, Common Sense, Knowledge, and Wisdom? At the side street location the *"problem of thirst"* did not exist. At the bus stop the *problem* of thirst existed and I *prospered* by satisfying it. Later at age fourteen did I not understand that the race car guys had a *problem* getting the lettering on the cars repaired and replaced each week? The **Truth** was that the sign painters would letter the car once but couldn't be there each week to touch it up and replace lettering. **Common Sense** told me I could solve that problem with the **Knowledge** I had of lettering, and **Wisdom** dictated that I would eventually take over the entire business of race car lettering and all of the race car owner's truck lettering and signs that went along in the bargain.

Then there were romantic problems, motorized problems, and business problems, I guess you could say my life was just filled with problems! That's what it's like living in the "creative world." A world filled with problems. Interesting, challenging, adventurous, exciting, often job creating, money making problems.

I can go on and on but you read the pages, come on, you've seen the ideas, problems solved, the creative world, how it's done, you get it don't you?

☙ *DO YOU STILL WANT TO SOLVE ALL OF YOUR KID'S PROBLEMS FOR THEM? YOU WILL SERIOUSLY DEVALUE THEM AS CREATIVE HUMAN BEINGS IF YOU DO.*

Entrepreneurs and creative people make money solving problems. They create concepts, inventions, literature, and a slew of things, to accomplish this. There's something else you need to understand…

A problem cannot be solved at the same level it occurred.

"In solving the problem we grow immensely. Intellectually, Creatively, often Financially, and I would hope… Spiritually."

There are so many problems to be solved and *rewards* are connected to each and every one.

This is not just talk. Each and every time I solved a problem in my life I grew immensely. Had I been a money person, I could have been a millionaire no doubt. I had issues about money and how it affected people and it took some time to overcome that. I decided to reap my riches in other forms.

People want money so they can better enjoy life. Most of the time working at jobs they hate. To relieve some of the pain of all of this they surround themselves with *things*. This causes debt and they *get stuck*. They never feel they have enough, so *giving* becomes out of the question and it's the one ingredient that could help them find their way toward true contentment. They don't realize…

"True contentment will never come from an external."

စ *UNFOLDING*

I would like to take a moment to speak personally to you (the reader.) Although many of my friends may be reading this book, you and I may not know each other. However, if you have been with me this far I have to feel we may have become at least spiritual friends. I hope you have learned a few things that may enhance your life. The subject matter in the chapters to come will be purposeful, powerful, and often personal. The road ahead is paved with the substance of my past. I believe it has tremendous value to those who will have the capacity to retain it.

Unfortunately that will be a very small percentage of the population. This book was not written to become a "best seller." It was however, written for a small group of people. They are…

- Those who are always there for a friend.
- Those who get married for the right reasons (because they fall in love.)
- For those who will play in life with the cards they're dealt, and are not concerned about what anyone else may be holding.
- For those in that small percentage that still have integrity and care deeply about this country and cherish its history.
- For those few people who "make things happen" not just watch things happen or wonder what happened.
- For those who put on the bake sales and the church suppers doing all the work while others just "fill in."
- For the coaches of the little league games, not the winning team but the losers, where real learning takes place.
- For those few left who still save and wait patiently for things.

- For those special creative types lost in the shuffle, but should seriously be recognized for their talents and abilities.
- For those great inventors, the "real job creators" that are so rare.
- For those who serve this country and need to find a niche for themselves when they get home.
- For those few who are truly there to protect us from harm and not there only for the pension.
- For those very few doctors who truly understand how much Spirit has to do with Healing and want to be a part of it.
- For those few left who are not so concerned about getting ahead of others as they are about getting ahead of their "old selves."
- For those few who still believe in God and try to follow His word.

Also this book is written to keep alive the memory of all the Masters and Mentors that came into my life and took the time and effort to share their knowledge with me.

I hope that you hear through these words my Heart, my Mind, and my Soul. I write for you. You are the very threads that make up the fabric of a True America.

This book is about Creating Value, in ourselves, in our work, and in our world. I would hope you caught that. The chapters ahead will require a certain thinking process, and are not for the shallow minded. As the next chapters unfold I expect to lose a large number of my readers. This book is not for them. They will be members of the large group who choose Entertainment over INSPIRATION.

I will be expressing strong opinion and very serious concepts. Many won't be able to follow through the last few chapters simply because they have not been conditioned for it.

Behind the Lines…

Before Happensburg passed away, he revealed something to me. He told me that in those early years he wondered himself whether or not there was hope for me. A kid, basically on my own most of the time, alcoholic parents, little or no discipline, loaded with enough anger to set the world on fire, and enough creativity and talent to pull it off. But he told me that I had one very rare characteristic that he could build from. And with that, he could raise my level of consciousness regarding the really important things that would not only change my life, but that I would then be able to change others as well.

I'll let you *think* about that for a little bit before I reveal what that was.

Chapter 31:

THE ARTIST

If you profess to be an artist or an inventor, and you may be introduced to the creative world, will you receive the support you'll need? Or will you have to become a non-conformist and carve your own path? Artists, inventors, musicians, writers, are often looked down upon unless and until success comes their way. I have often seen where a person who has artistic ability is often discouraged by well meaning family and friends because of the "starving artist stigma." This is understandable, but why not allow the art to open other doors for them as it did for me. Using art as a path to greater things.

Painting on canvas may lead to clothing design, or sketching may easily lead to writing. Art and inventing go hand in hand. Not to mention how therapeutic art can be. Art can provide the entrance to the creative world and once inside, go where you need to go. But to kill such an embryo before it has a chance to form? This causes many a creative person to head down the wrong road, never fulfilling their dreams.

❧ A PERFECT EXAMPLE

One day I was talking about this very subject with a friend of mine, *Mike McKeon*. Mike has a business smack in the center of town for the past thirty years. He's very intelligent and quite a conversationalist. He'll talk to you about everything from religion to politics. This particular day, I had been telling him about the chapter I was writing about artists. What he said is worth sharing.

His daughter is an artist and he said he was concerned that she might be discouraged for many of the same reasons I had discussed in the earlier chapter. She told him that she was most happy when involved in art.

All of a sudden, he asked everyone there who they thought was the greatest person of our time (our life time)? Everyone thought he was trying to change the subject, they immediately started throwing out names; Martin Luther King, The Kennedy's, someone mentioned Ronald Reagan, Bill Gates, then came Barrack Obama, and a host of others. Mike then brought it to our attention that no one had mentioned Walt Disney. Mike then went on to elaborate on the accomplishments of Mr. Disney and the affect he had (and continues to have) on our world.

Although most folks liked Martin Luther King, some didn't. Many folks admire the Kennedy's. Some have questions that are yet unanswered. Many people thought Reagan was one of our greatest Presidents, some didn't. Bill Gates certainly deserves respect; we don't have to discuss the divided opinions over Obama. But anywhere you go on this globe, when the name Walt Disney is mentioned a smile will come to a person's face. Have you ever met anyone who didn't like and respect Walt Disney? Wounded soldiers returning home, when asked what would make them happy, they'll always say ... I'd love to go to Disney World. Children battling cancer, when involved in "Make a Wish" often ask for a trip to Disney. Then, for the moment, can truly forget their troubles because of the creative mind of the man, Walt Disney. No matter what language is spoken in whatever country, the universal characters of Disney are loved and understood.

Mike continued... There has never been a "Walt Disney Day" when banks would close or kids would have a day off from school, but it doesn't matter, because each and every day all over the world people smile and think of "Disney." The many dignitaries mentioned certainly are respected and have accomplished much, but no one in our lifetime would be as popular, loved as much, and have directly affected as many people in a positive way, as Walt Disney. Disney passed away but his ideas and concepts continue on. Mike then concluded... "The Disney Empire had its beginning in the creative mind of an Artist."

If you work with your hands, you're a Laborer.
If you work with your hands and mind, you're a Craftsman.
If you work with your Hands, Mind, and Heart, you're an Artist.
(Author Unknown)

Now think about the many problems Walt Disney solved and are still being solved each and every day through his ideas and his way of thinking. Would you say he was a man of *Integrity*? Do you think he was a man who used common sense as a basis for creative thinking? Do you think that these qualities may be what separated Disney from other artist/entrepreneurs? Incidentally, the early animated drawings that Disney made of Mickey Mouse are worth as much as a Picasso Painting.

Let's look at the combination of Problem solving and Integrity from a very different angle. I'll even add a little humor to the mix.

❧ *WHAT MAGIC CAN MAKE BAD GUYS TURN GOOD?*

In my business I still do a lot of truck lettering, most often painting "free hand" the old fashioned way.

Some of my best customers are farmer-truckers. Usually they're hay haulers, milk haulers, cattle dealers — those great hard working folks. Whenever I can, at least in the summer months, I go right to their place and do the trucks. I've lettered them in barns, and often under a shade tree in their front yard. This helps them from having to take two people and two vehicles and drive to my place and then come all the way back to pick the truck up (going to their place is something I can GIVE them.) Also, they don't have to tie the truck up for long. If it's just lettering, half a day usually does it and they're back in service. In this economy many trucking companies are really suffering. One well-known trucker who happens to be a good friend as well as customer just added two new trucks and two new drivers to his fleet. That's rather unusual in this economy. I lettered and pinstriped both trucks recently.

My friend's name is Mike Crewell. He, his wife *Amy*, and brother *Scott*, own *Crewell Bros. Trucking* in Schoharie Valley, N.Y. Today Mike is a very successful, highly respected businessman with a fine reputation. However in his younger years, he had a very different kind of reputation.

If you were to frequent any of the more popular taverns in the area, you might see Mike in there beating up half of the population. The interesting thing here was that Crewell didn't look like your typical "bar fighter" he looked more like a movie actor. So with him you had no warning. Piss him off and he could knock you out with either hand, and most never saw it coming. He did do some "good" from time to time though. I remember hearing about the time some "punks" were thinking about making a career out of "bar hopping" and happened to investigate the opportunities available in the taverns in Schoharie Valley. Well, as luck would have it, they ran into this good ol' boy that had that position covered. The details of what happened one night were not all that clear, but from what I heard one of the punks actually had a life changing experience. After going a couple of rounds with Crewell, they say the guy gave up drinking and bar hopping entirely. He actually took up "Horticulture." Yep, he said he never realized how exciting it was watching flowers grow all by themselves. That was of course after coming so close to his possibly pushing them up.

You might be wondering how does a guy like Mike Crewell go from bar fighter to respected businessman? Well, he met "Amy." And Amy captured his heart. After a while Mike actually began listening to his heart. He also started to realize that the more he would listen to his heart, the less hits he was taking to the head. This was great. Amy was great. Mike's life started to change. Was all of this easy for Amy?

Try hooking a race horse to a wagon and maybe you would realize what it takes to harness that kind of energy. But somehow she did it. Today they own several businesses,

All of them worked by Mike (and run by Amy.) Amy Crewell is one of the most admired and respected people I know and with all of the talent and ability she has, the one characteristic that stands out most is her Integrity.

Why does it seem like all the bad guys get all the good girls? I don't know either, and that's one problem I'm glad nobody solved.

Many of the products that the Crewell Bros. haul are "organic." Organic food is simply food that has "Integrity."

Chapter 32:
CONSTRUCTIVE CRITICISM

A re you still wondering what that characteristic Happensburg mentioned was? It was my ability to understand and accept Constructive Criticism.

"Constructive Criticism" is intellectual medicine, and although it may be tough to swallow, you will be better after having taken it."

Happensburg would give it to me straight up. It hurt yes, but I always "respected the process" He knew he could build from that and he was right. It was one of the reasons I was able be in the presents of older, more experienced people in my younger years. Some of those guys were brutal. Corey was one of the toughest of them all. But I learned so much from them, mainly because I could handle corrective constructive criticism. Today if you try to criticize someone (especially a young person) to correct their path, you have a war on your hands. The people in my life were much older and wiser and I was fortunate to be able to be in their presence. They were sharing life changing information with me. I would have to have been a fool not to realize the value of their knowledge. It far exceeded any discomfort I may have been experiencing. So, once again Happensburg was right. This was a rare characteristic. Only a small percentage of people possess it, I realize that now. Strangely enough, almost without exception, those "few" folks mentioned earlier, the ones I admire so much, possess that same characteristic. If they did not, they would not be who they are.

"With constructive criticism you will feel the heat, but it can help you from having to go through the fire."

Let me ask you a question… Do you think that by spoiling a child you may be damaging, if not destroying that very characteristic?

Did that hurt? Maybe you should close the book now. Listen, for what you paid for the book, you've been entertained, probably picked up a couple of things here and there that you can use, so bail now, because if you think **that** hurt, you may not like what's coming. . Can you take it?

I owe it to those great people, my true American brothers and sisters, to separate the wheat from the chaff right now. In the past chapters I spent a considerable amount of time and words outlining my feelings about the "spoiled child." Also I put a fair amount of emphasis on the value of truth and integrity, (admittedly I've been on the opposite end myself. I don't pretend to be a "saint" in any sense of the word.) The truth is, I look up to those who possess integrity.

"Whenever someone I respect criticizes me I always assume they may be at least half right. From there we can discuss the other half so that I can be corrected without being destroyed."

The larger picture is that America is a "Spoiled Child," and restoring Truth and Integrity will represent the first bricks needed to rebuild the crumbled foundation. They are the "Cornerstone" to this monumental endeavor. We will restore the compass that will lead to new horizons, with new IDEAS that will net new manufacturing and all necessary ingredients to rebuild this great country. And all will be accomplished by that unspoiled select few who are so very accustomed to doing all the work anyway. But first we must get around all those that are currently sucking the system dry.

If you doubt the importance of Integrity understand that if we…

- Remove integrity from food we have Poison.
- If an airplane loses its Integrity it will crash.
- Remove Integrity from any situation, circumstance, or thing and we'll have a problem.

A person lacking integrity cannot be trusted.

"If you cannot be corrected by Constructive Criticism then there is a good chance you will be corrected by Crisis"

I have some answers, and if the right people can digest them, maybe we'll be able to get closer to fiscal regularity. I don't pretend to have all the answers but these things have a way of "unfolding" and revealing more and more as **would be deserving for a diligent effort**. Ideas providing **Answers** have been unfolding in my life for more than half a century.

I'm about to stretch your mind in several directions. If you can stand it you'll be a larger person at the end. If it hurts too much and you close the book I'll fully understand. Here we go...

Chapter 33:

TRUE BALANCE

The Universe is perfectly balanced. From the rotation of the earth to the position of the planets, we see perfect order. We humans live in chaos. Instinctively we strive for balance. Balance in our lives, our families, our businesses. You know by now that I believe many things are connected. I grew up around automobiles, and my references throughout this book have often been comparing situations and people or concepts to the building, maintenance, or operation of an automobile. As a kid I was able to see a race car being assembled completely from scratch. Watching this and listening to the terminology actually helped me understand much about life.

I saw a pile of nuts, bolts, rods, pistons, a crankshaft, etc. become a living, breathing engine. I saw ideas and techniques used to make engines more powerful. One of those techniques was the "balancing" of an engine. I won't go into all the details of how this is done, but by just balancing an engine (not adding any other parts) you can gain horsepower. I thought that was amazing.

One time after Pete Corey had won a big race, he said that he would have to tear the engine down and check it out because during the last twenty laps it had developed a vibration and he really didn't know if he would make it to the checker flag before the engine came apart. Something threw the engine "out of balance" and that usually will *tear things up.*

So I learned that *"balance gives you power"* and being *"out of balance can tear you up;"* does that make sense? Actually it's *common sense.* At least it is to me. I saw people whose *lives* were "in balance" and clearly they had **power.** I watched those who were "out of balance" being "**torn up.**"

All I am doing is making you **aware** of some *basic common sense* principles here. The key to achieve balance (as in the engine balance) is to properly organize all of the working parts. Success (or power) in life is accomplished much in the same way. Organizing parts such as your thoughts, your resources, which may be in the form of talent or ability or people, and also your finances as well. By organizing these key components you can achieve balance and power over much of the world around you.

I know "they" told you that you have a high **IQ**, But if I may quote Dr .David Hawkins M. D., Ph.D.

" *IQ is only a measure of academic capacity for logically compre- hending symbols and words." (Hawkins)*

Without common sense as a foundation to back this up, how could you **logically comprehend** anything?

How do we measure "*Creative Intelligence?*"

"*The ability to use the mind to bring into being that which is not yet created*" or "*To have the intelligence to be able to gather what is necessary to take abstract thoughts and turn them into tangible form.*"

"*Creativity is, among other things, the ability to think in alterna- tives" (Pastor Bob Smith)*

I'm working on a **measuring system**, but that's for another book. Let's see if you can survive this one first. OK, I'll repeat it again…

"*As we stretch ourselves intellectually, we MUST drag along our base common sense or we run the risk of becoming Educated Idiots.*"

Listen, "**educated idiot**" is not some slang term I made up just to be mean. It represents real **people** in our society today. Many of these people are making decisions that affect our lives. They are **educated** people who **lack common sense** and conduct themselves as **idiots**. OK, I'll further prove my point. I want you to turn to anyone that may be in the room with you with the exception of small children, or if no one is there with you, call someone on the phone and ask them if they would tell you the definition of "TYRANNY." (without looking it up) Go ahead; I'll wait for you here.

Well you and everyone around you are supposed to be so damn smart, what was the problem? Were you surprised how many people don't know the correct definition of tyranny? By not understanding the meaning of tyranny you could be left wide open to losing all of your "conspicuous consumption," (all the obvious stuff you have accumulated.) Are you even remotely aware of how much liberty we have lost in just the last twenty years? Tyranny has the same bloodline as termites and cockroaches. It doesn't come in and boldly just take things. It comes in slowly, often under cover of darkness, gradually ruining little by little the things that we have enjoyed for years. Things that were built by hard working creative craftsman.

Tyranny: "Cruel use of power. Oppressive government. Injustice in the exercise of power over others. A country or state under the power of oppressive rule."

When the government has fear of the people, that's **Liberty**.

When the people fear the government, that's **Tyranny** (*Thomas Jefferson.*)

"The accumulation of all powers, legislative, executive, and judiciary, in the same hands, whether of one, a few, or many, and whether hereditary, self appointed, or elective, may justly be pronounced the very definition of tyranny." (James Madison)

How do you feel when a government vehicle pulls into your driveway? Or a couple of tax agents walk into your business? Do you say… "Oh honey, put on some coffee, the folks from the Government are here to visit!" I don't think so.

You will have to hire people who understand their language. Their salaries are paid with your taxes so they have not only unfair advantage but unlimited resources as well. Admit it, you fear them.

"We are many, they are few. Why do we allow them to do what they do?

As a society we have become so complacent, so removed from community involvement that corrupt politicians have an opportunity to move into positions of power without having had to deal with any resistance. These people make laws that benefit certain groups but seriously hurt others.

What does all this have to do with balance? Need I remind you that when things go out of balance they shake apart? Can you see where things may be seriously out of balance in our political system?

Do you have common sense? Of course you do. Then a little constructive criticism shouldn't bother you. Let's find out.

Regarding your current job, are you giving your company or employer **more** in **value** than you are accepting in **payment**?

What was your first reaction to what I just said? Sound stupid? You say why would I do that? So then, are you giving the company very near the amount of value for what you are accepting in payment? Oh no! You're not giving **less** value for what they are paying you? Yes or No answer please.

How are you doing with the *constructive criticism* so far?

And what about integrity? (Don't you wish you closed the book when you had your chance?) It gets worse. But I will bring it all together as we move on. I'll prove how when integrity is missing it can throw a whole community out of balance and literally shake it apart. I'll make my point with a couple of examples. One **simple** and one **extreme**. I'll begin with you and your job. Let's say you found your soul and admitted that you may not be doing quite as much as you are being paid for. You ask what's the big deal? Does it really matter? I work for a big company, they have plenty of money. Well, let me say this…do you remember our talk about inflation in an earlier chapter? How devastating it can be to an economy? Maybe I should have gone into more detail about its origin.

❧ RELATION TO INFLATION

You see, the *space* between the amount someone is *receiving* and the goods or services they are *producing* is an excellent example of *inflation*. Small space, little inflation, big space, big inflation. Now multiply this by millions of people working in thousands of businesses conducting themselves in the same manner. You've heard how the electric and gas power companies have these advertisements on TV on how, by just doing a few little things, we could help in the monumental task of keeping costs down. I would expect these companies have integrity and they are telling the truth. Correct? Then the opposite would have to hold true as well, would it not? Or one would discredit the other. A few little things nibbling at integrity could make a serious difference as well.

The truth is, when we are **not** doing all that we are being paid to do, we are actually **feeding** inflation. The person (company) handing you that dollar is being "short changed." I'm sure you haven't realized it but people doing this may well become a member in good standing of the "**Inflation Party.**" A group that *takes* considerably more than it *gives* therefore becomes a drag or burden on society. Inflation tips the scale and causes serious imbalance. So what if folks are so arrogant to think "So what! I don't give a damn; it's too late for anybody to do anything about it anyway. I'm retiring!" Let me inform them that it is not "anybody" who will bring things back into balance. It's corrected by something much larger than "anybody."

Now the extreme example . . .

There is another level to all of this. People tend to adjust their lifestyle to their income and when people are paid for more than they produce, there can be some very serious ramifications. Let's say, based on current income a person is paying for a beautiful home, a couple of new cars, and a young person in college. The company they work for runs into problems and they end up unemployed. They try for other jobs but there aren't any available that would pay them the kind of money they were making for doing less than what would be needed. Things were not in balance. After coasting for a period of time and not picking up any new skills, or having a change of heart, what would be expected? What can they GIVE society in fair return for money? Not much.

I mentioned "serious results." Allow me to elaborate… Under these circumstances it wasn't just a person's job that was taken away from them, but their life. They had been in a situation that was not grounded in Truth. Once the person realizes there are no jobs for them and they are about to lose everything they have, God help everyone back at the old office. They're about to experience new meaning to "Unbalanced."

A large number of the phony lawsuits that fill our court systems and cause insurance rates to skyrocket are rooted in the same soil. People living above their means, trying to "hang on" to a lifestyle they never truly earned. How could a person take more than they give and at the same time create value? That would be impossible. Impossible in business, in relationships, in spirit.

✎ THE OTHER SIDE OF THE COIN

So what about the other side of the coin? Those folks who actually do more than required of them. Those special folks I mentioned in the earlier chapter. I suppose they throw things out of balance as well, but in an entirely different direction. The fact that they are doing more is usually **obvious**, and balance is generally accomplished through promotion or some sort of compensation. If this type of person is ever unemployed they are usually picked up quickly because of the *value* they can add to a company or business. They simply give more bang for the buck and therefore are a good investment.

Inflation **takes away** the *value* of your money. These good people **give you more value** for your money. *Common sense* dictates a person doing more than is required of them will also have a fair amount of job security. *They would be the last person a company would want to let go.* In their case, the space between the more they do and what they are paid for is an investment in their own **personal value,** and there are many places where they can turn that into cash.

Where do you fit in the scheme of things? In the negative? Or the positive? Having dealt with corrective criticism at least you've found out where you stand. How much respect you have for **truth** and **integrity** will determine how much **value** you'll put on the concept of *"change."*

Are you still there?

Let me explain that everything I'm laying on you is coming from my heart, and this isn't anything my own kids haven't had to hear from me. Corrective constructive criticism has much to do with people developing common sense, becoming intelligent, creative, resourceful, appreciative, spiritually and emotionally strong, as well as helping them to work diligently at developing and maintaining integrity in their work and hopefully in their lives. This is not to say we don't make mistakes, but it is this foundation that helps us to **overcome** and **recover** from our mistakes, difficulties, and problems. Constructive criticism helps us take a good hard look at ourselves. Won't you agree that this would be necessary from time to time?

Many people are so afraid to say anything to their children that may hurt their feelings that they (the children) go through life never to be corrected. Did you ever notice that the "strict" parents have the closest relationships with their children? Somewhere **beneath the surface** there's a message that says… "I really care about you." The parent that allows anything and every-thing is sending a message very much **on the surface** of… "I need you to love me."

Picture a platoon of young men in Army basic training. They're carrying forty pounds of gear and are on a five mile run. About a half mile into the run the Drill Sergeant directs the group down a path to a creek, where there's a pleasant little swimming hole. Then he says…

"OK guys, take those heavy packs off and jump in for a swim. This is what we'll do each day. How's that"?

They would think, wow did we luck out or what — we've got the best "Drill Sergeant" anybody could ask for.

But six months later when they're in the jungle fighting for their lives, they come to the realization that they had the **worst** Drill Sergeant they could possibly have had. He never prepared them for what was ahead.

Parents who don't prepare their children for life are more concerned with being their "buddies" than guiding them toward **serious purpose**. This is not only selfish, it can also be destructive. This lack of preparation is revealed in the "professional student." The young adult that found "success" and "recognition" within the confines of learning institutions and then continues in one school after another gathering more and more knowledge while secretly frightened to enter a much larger unknown world.

This is precisely why many children have resentment for their parents later in life. They realize they never prepared them for what was ahead. They realize although it was nice to have a "buddy," what they really needed was "strength." Something else to consider…those who had the more strict, purposeful parents always seem to return some form of **intrinsic love** to them in their elder years. These are not just my thoughts on this. I have seen this play out over and over again.

If I don't tell you this stuff, who will? Seriously, who will? Do you understand the presence of that empty field in the mind and the importance of allowing the **right** people to plant there? In a politically correct world this stuff gets buried. "Corrective criticism" and "politically correct" are in conflict. I've presented my case for constructive criticism and I see serious flaws in political correctness. I understand clearly how people use this concept to mix just enough good with evil to make it palatable. I can only imagine my dad and those who helped shape my life having to be politically correct while trying to straighten me out. My dad would probably add his wisdom to all of this by saying something like… **"Please don't piss on my head, and then tell me it's raining,"** and I guess that would cover it.

"Common Sense indicates to me that much of what is called "political correctness" is not only an insult to our intelligence, but a vexation to our spirit."

Have you learned anything in these last few chapters? Did it hurt? I'm not going to apologize for giving you **valuable** information. That would only make me your buddy. I would rather strengthen you. I warned you that these chapters will not be for the shallow minded. It gets worse; maybe you should exit now.

Chapter 34:

AMERICA "DUMBED DOWN"

When I was in school, girls were smarter than boys. In those early years, they were two to three years more mature, intellectually and emotionally. In school if I needed help with an assignment or information about a test coming up, it's for sure I didn't ask another boy for help. Even years later, when I registered my car, I registered it in Linda's name because back then girls got a better break on insurance. They were better drivers. In my teenage years, it was very unusual seeing an intoxicated girl. And then, there were lots of guys that were BS'ers, but really, back in school, I didn't know many girls that were liars. I remember distinctly how difficult it was trying to get them to lie for me to get out of some situation. They just would not do it. This has all changed. Today a startling number of teenage girls are so stupid it's frightening. They no longer get a break on insurance because they are no longer more careful drivers. It is not unusual at all to see teen girls drunk today. I'm not just picking on girls (I'll get to boys in a moment), but I just want you to see what we have lost regarding these precious jewels. If you look back in history and think of the great women of our time, I can only imagine how they would feel about this travesty.

Late night talk show hosts have done random sidewalk interviews with young females making sport of their stupidity, having them look like fools in front of the entire world. Keep in mind that I am talking about only the mental condition of the female. I have no case to present against the physical condition of women today. They have done a spectacular job in this area no doubt; actually making a bad situation worse.

"The MIND is the one thing that distinguishes the HUMAN from the ANIMAL, everything else can be found on a HORSE or a COW."

Many bright young women today, who manage to trudge through this muck and make it to high positions, often become defensive and angry with being stereotyped and having had to fight for the respect they deserve.

What day did this all change anyway? We all know that this didn't change in a day. It changed gradually with the introduction of the "BIMBO." After *loss* **of** *integrity*, the devaluation of the female crept in just like the termites and cockroaches mentioned in the earlier chapter. In every sit-com (situ-ation-comedy) on television we saw the blond bombshell that was abso-lutely gorgeous portraying a girl that was as dumb as a box full of rocks. This became so popular that even today just about every comedy show has at least one. Young girls were seriously affected by this and began to think that "we don't have to be smart, we just have to look like that!" This also launched the "Barbie syndrome." Look around, they're everywhere! TV and advertising producers know what is appealing to the eye and exactly what will hold your attention. The concept of *"A drop-dead beautiful idiot"* took off, became **"vogue,"** and actually set the standards for young girls today. You would often see them "acting dumb" even if they were bright! As I said before, we have become "image-based," and it's all about how you "look." This puts a tremendous amount of pressure on young girls. Often if a girl is not pretty or particularly attractive, she feels she has little, if any self worth.

This is all about "Shallow." Shallow thinking, shallow people, shallow lives. To me "intellect" is extremely attractive, and can deepen the quality of any relationship. Stupidity holds nothing of genuine value.

I have a friend who has been with more women than anyone I know person-ally. Most of them short term relationships, with "Bimbos." I once asked him, "What is it like making love to a woman you can hardly have a conver-sation with?"

He said "They're beautiful!"

I told him I understood, but there seemed to be nothing beyond that. He just shrugged his shoulders. Then he continued…

"Would you like to try one?"

He was offering one of these girls like offering someone a beer. I said "No thanks, I'm so accustomed to sipping **vintage wine** from my own cellar, that the thought of guzzling beer doesn't do anything for me. Besides, I never drink from somebody else's bottle."

What about **respect**? Did the termites and cockroaches of "change" chew that up too?

What about the "**courtship?**" That's pretty much gone these days. I think the way they dress today sends the "*No need for that, I'm ready*" message.

Oh, I forgot, they're **not** sex objects! They look like sex objects, they even move and conduct themselves like sex objects, but they're not sex objects? OK, I know what you're thinking, "Don't go there!" (I think I feel something trickling on my head; maybe it's raining?)

Guess what? "*Corrective criticism* **goes there!**" And **not** "*going there*" *is what got us* **here!**

If you still don't understand, then try this little "brain stretcher."

Take some bird seed and toss it out into your back yard. Then wait and see what happens. Cute little birds will come.

Now take *raw meat* and throw that out into your back yard. Wait and see what comes now. Better yet, throw it out there at night; you'll get even better results! It's called "**cause** and **effect**," a concept that "**goes there**" and has been around long before "politically correct."

I told my daughter when she was a teenager… "When a woman leads with her body, she's diverting attention away from her heart"

In this environment boys don't fare much better, they lack skills and laziness is like a plague among them. TV and video games have taken up valuable brain cell function. What will these young men be able to GIVE society? Some become dependent on their parents well into their adult years. They have been robbed of enjoying wonderful discoveries and exciting times. In the spirit of fairness, I'll call the young men "BUMBOS!"

Is it possible that complacency could be connected to a number of mental problems? "*The idle mind being the devil's workshop*." My slant on this would be…

"If we hang out with Lazy long enough, at some point you'll meet its closest friend… Crazy"

I'll let you digest that last chapter as I explain where all this stuff comes from.

In my lifetime I have seen so much. My craft has taken me so many places. Never in my wildest dreams could I imagine where that little pinstriping brush would take me

For over half a century I have had the opportunity to have pinstriped or painted some vehicle or object for…

Sophisticates, Aristocrats, Insta-Grat's, Intellectuals, and Spoiled Brats. Liars, Flyers, Piker's, Hikers, and Bikers. White collars, Blue collars, Idiots, and Scholars. Whores, Virgins, Psychiatrists, and Surgeons, Teachers, Preachers. Ramblers and Gamblers, Law Makers, and Law Breakers, Punks, Drunks, Patriots, Politicians, Parrots, Pigeons, Eagles, and an occasional Dove; some people I have hated and many I love. Lots and lots of Truckers, and a few Blood Suckers, just to name a few, all kinds of people, maybe even you. Some came from Heaven, some were from Hell, but with each one, there's been a *story* to tell.

I once painted the "Flying Death Head" (Hell's Angel's logo) on a couple of members' motorcycles and embellished the alter of a church for a carpenter friend in the same day using the same brushes. It was a spiritual rollercoaster ride to say the least. I wonder how many artists have had an experience like that.

Chapter 35:

THE "BRIDGE"

The fact that I had been utilizing mostly my father's skills, the art, inventing, mechanical skills, etc., had certainly brought me a long way, but the stories that were spinning off of the experiences I had been having were becoming more and more valuable to me. I was about to enter my mother's sphere of influence.

I loved writing and the experiences I was enjoying were worth writing about. As I mentioned earlier in the book I became a "closet writer." Again, the circles I was traveling in were not the kind of places you could talk about poetry, writing or culture. So I would get home from striping some guy's antique car or from a motorcycle rally and often write for hours about the experience.. The question now was …"What do I do with all of this stuff?" Help with that answer came when I met Dr. Arthur Salvatore.

Dr. Salvatore happened to be the brother of a good friend of mine, Richard Salvatore, who was (and still is) a serious car buff. I met Richard through the pinstriping and we hung out together for a time before he went off to college and eventually entering the field of dentistry himself. Anyway, one night Richard and I were heading to a car show and he had to stop at his brother's house to pick up some papers or something. While he was looking for the papers I waited in the hallway and happened to hear someone playing a piano in the next room. I curiously peeked around the corner. The man sitting at the piano would play a few bars then stop to write on a tablet, and then continue. He was composing music. At one point he noticed me watching and immediately got up from the piano, walked over and introduced himself. "Come in, sit down" he said "tell me what you think of this." He played a few bars for me.

I said "I'm not familiar with that one"

He smiled and continued, "That's because it's an original. I just wrote it. Well, this part of it anyway, it's not finished"

I told him I was honored that I'm the first person other than himself that has ever heard that. We both laughed.

I told him it was very good and that I would love to hear it when it's complete.

He then explained that he was stuck on this one. "I seem to get to a point and then it stops,." he explained.

I asked him if he had any words to this.

Lyrics, no I hadn't thought much about lyrics right now. I'm just composing the music.

I then said…"Maybe if you put words, I mean lyrics to that, it might just help you take it further... like a story unfolding. Words are triggered by thoughts and then the words often trigger more thoughts themselves, at least for me they do. In this case words might be triggered by music or vice-versa."

I remember thinking … "I'm getting in way over my head here; what if this is just a melody or just music, maybe he doesn't want it to be a song." So I quickly continued… "You could use the words only to get you further into the melody or whatever you call it, then just dump the words and keep the music part..."

He laughed. Then said, "Let me play what I have and you see if you can come up with some words."

He played what he had written several times. I started with a few words (looking for a theme actually) and then they came. I won't go into all the details of this particular piece but we were able to come up with what is known as a "bridge" that allowed the continuation to another part of the composition.

What happened that night began a wonderful friendship that changed my life in many ways and from that moment on the word "Bridge "held a very special meaning for me. Over the years Arthur Salvatore has written and arranged many beautiful pieces and on occasion I was fortunate to be involved with the lyrics.

I never thought that I could ever venture into my mother's sphere of influence, her being an academic, educated beyond anything I would ever experience. But I also knew that I controlled a certain amount of talent in this area, although until this point it had been basically dormant.

One day Dr. Art and I were on his boat enjoying a "get together" with some of his friends. There were primarily doctors, lawyers, and high-level businessmen present. I felt quite "out of place" He introduced me to the group as his "lyricist." Not as an artist-painter. It took me totally by surprise. He went on to elaborate on our accomplishments working together. I will never forget that day and how it made me feel.

Later one of the dignitaries asked if I was related to "Davies" the artist / pinstriper. I just said yes and left it at that.

Dr. Salvatore is a very special person. Everyone who knows him would agree on that. It was his encouragement, and inspiration that gave me the confidence to take my writing seriously. He also completely changed my view of the educated class.

Arthur Salvatore and Dave review a few bars late one night in 1976.

Neil Schwartz looks on as Arthur Salvatore and Dave composing music.

✎ WRITE ON!

Time for some more brain stimulation…

Chapter 36:

THE GREAT TRAIN

Visualize that we are standing in a train station. The train is stopped and the doors to the cars are all open. No one seems to be in any of the cars. The cars are labeled with "free hand lettering" (can you believe it?) only because they were lettered a long time ago. This train has been in this station before, many times. The lettering displays a different word on each car. On the first car directly behind the engine we read the word "OPPORTUNITY." On the car behind that one we read the words "NEW IDEAS." On the next car we read "HOPE." Another car displays the word "GRATITUDE," another with the words "KNOWLEDGE" and "WISDOM," and then came the "HEALTH" car, "RESOURCES" car, the "SECURITY" car, etc.; the train stretching as far as the eye can see.

We are wondering when people will start boarding the train. Everyone is in the station bickering about the economy and how tough times are. We see a small group of individuals standing on the platform near the front of the train. They are made up of creative types, idea people, inventors, writers, artists and thinkers. They are not complaining. They are planning. A few are about to start up the engine. These are obviously very special people. Just as soon as the engine starts to fire, a group starts entering the car labeled "Opportunity." The car lettered "New Ideas" fills up immediately. Several Church groups enter the car labeled "Hope." As the engine begins to warm up more and more, people begin entering cars. The "Knowledge/Wisdom" car is filling up as well. Just the sound of the engine is exciting people and they are getting on board.

Another group in the station is now starting to complain about the noise, and some are complaining that there is smoke coming from the engine's exhaust and it should be stopped immediately. A response comes from the engine department. "There will be much more smoke and noise, especially when this whole thing starts moving." The folks in the engine area offer no apologies. They say it's the smell and sound of progress, and refuse to respond to any more ignorance.

Soon the train of Opportunity, New Ideas, Hope, Gratitude, Knowledge, Wisdom, and all the other cars, starts to roll across this great country. With each stop more and more people get on board, entering their respective cars.

The people in the station that were complaining never got on board. This seemed strange. Why would the people not get on board? After careful thought we realize a couple of things. They were all holding "Get" tickets. The folks boarding all had "Give" stamped on theirs.

We realize that those still standing there as the train pulled away, hadn't had enough common sense to turn their "What can I **GET** tickets" in for the "What can I **GIVE**" tickets. These folks didn't have a clue where the train was going or why it was there in the first place. I might add that the people getting on board were people of **integrity** and it would be very uncomfortable for those who don't understand **truth** and **integrity** to mingle with those who do.

This is of course an over simplification of where we stand in this country today. These are difficult times but the opportunities are immense, and once again "problem solving" opens up another great frontier.

Most people, if you were to approach them and ask if you may discuss some problems with them, would quickly back away and probably say "I have enough problems of my own thank you, I don't want to hear about any other problems." But if you were to approach some of the "big guns" in business and finance, they may not back away but may even ask "What kind of problems exactly?" Simply because they know there may be many benefits tied to solving them. The government would love to solve your problems. The cost: much of your liberty. The pharmaceutical companies have been onto this for years and take a slightly different approach. They play "name it and claim it." They come up with fancy names that clearly identify just about any ailment (problem) and then give you something in the form of a pill to **service** it (I didn't say "solve it.")

I'm sorry to say that there is evil even in the creative world. There is nothing that says the creative mind is an "only for good" mind. We have choices.

My dad always said… "If you do good, you'll feel good." I've found that to be true for the most part. I began doing good and it felt very good. It's true when you do the right thing, take the correct path, etc. you will "feel" good. But it is very important that you don't put too much emphasis on the "feeling good" part. Doing good and feeling good are not always related. It's great if feeling good is part of a process, but feeling good about "end results" should be the **goal**. That's the good feeling that actually "**stays**" with us. There is something else you should know…

Chapter 37:

OUTSIDE OUR COMFORT ZONE

"We make our greatest progress while outside our comfort zone"
(Dave Jr.)

David Jr. came up with that phrase one day when we were working at a motorcycle rally. "Sturgis." It's the largest motorcycle rally in the country and takes place in South Dakota. It's a great event but always difficult as well. With 105 degree heat, storms that pop up out of nowhere, and hundreds of thousands of people, you can imagine what someone applying paint to motorcycles goes through. People attending the rally love it. For us it's not all fun. It costs us a fortune to attend that event and if we don't really push ourselves, we could go backwards real fast. Our work has no room for error. It's the equivalent of shooting a gun into a target and you don't get paid unless you hit the bull's eye. After the rally we enjoy ourselves but during the event at Sturgis, there is no comfort zone.

David was right; when we step outside our comfort zone we "stretch" ourselves. This is progress. When you can conjure up the strength to step out of that comfort and actually function, the growth can be tremendous. Can you imagine how difficult that would be for the spoiled child? How about a second or third generation welfare person having to find work? What about a kid that has been making a considerable amount of money selling drugs on the street, having to change his source of income to something legitimate? I'm just outlining a few problems needing to be solved, that's all. In this day and age, less and less people are willing to step outside their comfort zone. Less and less people are getting involved in understanding government and politics and how it may be affecting our everyday lives. The luxuries and comforts we enjoy everyday are the results of someone's efforts while operating outside their comfort zone.

When I first began learning freehand lettering and pinstriping, I would often try to get my friends involved. I was having a tough time myself learning this skill. It was very difficult at first and very uncomfortable trying to get my hand and brush to do what I needed them to do. My friends would give it a try, but when it became uncomfortable and much less fun than they anticipated, they quickly gave up.

If you view anything on military history, you'll clearly see many brave souls fighting in situations where they had not an ounce of comfort. We owe these people so much for their efforts. Yet we have been so complacent that many of us allow politicians to change laws that we know will adversely affect our lives and we do nothing. It would be too "uncomfortable" to get involved. This concept is what often "overrides" our common sense. Inside our heads and hearts we may know something is not right, yet we allow our comfort to dictate the decisions we make. This is deeply rooted in a lack of discipline. Something *"that important"* should "shake" our emotions enough to get us to take action, but because of our lifestyles, television, movies, etc., we have been so desensitized that nothing "moves" us. We just change the channel and it goes away. But in real life it doesn't "go away." The world is changing right before our eyes and yet most of us do nothing to hold onto many of our cherished customs and ideas. We see just a few people changing rules and laws that affect so many of us. It's obvious what a few can do working diligently while others lay in comfort and fail to get involved.

The sad thing is that few people realize that after certain liberties are gone, the only way to get them back is to fight for them. These things we love so much "slip away" and then it costs **human lives** to get them back.

Complacency is a very destructive disease. We take for granted that our children understand how great freedom and liberty are, but if they have never experienced anything else, how would they really know? Kids today see plenty of horrible things on TV, but then a commercial comes on and when you go back to the program, everything is as if it never happened. When children **actually experience reality**, they often need a drug to be able to cope with it. I'm aware of how fast technology is moving forward but if we don't look back once in a while, how will we know from where we came? We must be careful of being "swept up" in all that the world has to offer these days, lest we forget how many battles were fought to give us all that we are enjoying right here, right now. Counting my many blessings has given me many rewards, as well as provided the spiritual strength to handle difficulties. The majority of Americans are not counting their blessings. They don't have a clue as to what is at stake and what we could lose.

This also leaves a door open for CORRUPTION to enter.

"Contrary to popular belief, CORRUPTION is not born of intelligence. It is however, a highly refined form of ignorance."

How do we get rid of Corruption? The answer is quite simple... "Accountability"

"Accountability" extinguishes corruption like a fire extinguisher extinguishes a fire"

It's amazing how words like *"accountability"* and *"initiative* and *referendum"* will make a corrupt politician shake in their shoes.

It's time to lighten up a bit and change the subject.

❧ *JOY BEYOND UNDERSTANDING*

Have you ever been in *The Right Place at the Right Time, doing the Right thing for the Right Reason, with all the Right Stuff?* If you have, then you have experienced a **JOY** that is indescribable, a joy beyond all understanding. When all that you have worked for, hoped for, or waited for, comes in to you. That moment in time, when it all comes together just for you or someone you love. I have experienced that moment several times in my life. Though before I had experienced this personally, I had been present when some others I had known had experienced this for themselves. Several times I had the opportunity to be part of the process and thus shared some of the joy. I'm talking about achieving goals, in my case getting national recognition for my work in magazines, or winning "Best Paint," "Best Use of Color" at car shows, that sort of thing.

Then there are the times when a great Idea works out and brings home some needed cash. Or a new concept takes off and feeds the business for a length of time. It's wonderful! It's also something that everyone wants and needs desperately in their lives. When our children started receiving awards for their work we felt that joy all over again.

Just look at the contestants trying their hearts out on talent shows or those with the discipline to be able to compete in the Olympics, or race at Daytona, or play in the World Series, or Super Bowl. The joy they experience is so powerful that you can feel it, emotionally, through the TV or from a radio broadcast! Now let me ask you, do any of these people achieve this degree of success completely on their own? I think not. I think you would agree that they have much help in the process. I know I had help in my accomplishments, that's for sure.

So what kind of "help" are we talking about? It wasn't just "finances" or "coaching" that put them there, although that was certainly part of it. But where did the "finances" and the "coaching" come from? Can you understand where I'm going here?

If you were to talk to most of the individuals that have experienced the level of joy and accomplishment we have just discussed, they would probably admit that something much larger than them was indeed involved. I myself would have to be a fool not to admit that in my life there were many times when I had no control over outcomes that I had benefited greatly from. As I explained early in the book, I felt something was watching, protecting, and even guiding me along. We all have opposition to deal with. But over the years our family has always been protected and preserved so we could move on. I think by now if you have gone this far with me you will see that I need to give credit where it's due and acknowledge where all this comes from. How in the world could a kid with as many problems as I had, make his way through life, Linda and I married in our teens, and have the joy I have and the family and friends I have, the talent we share, continuing to unfold as I grow older, without serious help and guidance from a Higher Power? (I know what some of you may be thinking but "luck" only goes so far.) We're talking over a lifetime here.

So many people entered my life at just the right time and just the right place to give me what I needed at that time. The key to this was that I was receptive to all of this. Many of my friends who I grew up with did not seem to hear what I heard or see what was so evident to me, and this was unfortunate because they went in a different direction.

Those who Happensburg represented were not much when it came to "looks" or "style." When I met them I thought they were just very nice older folks. As I got to know them better they turned out to be much more than that. Many of my friends were not receptive to this wisdom and I could never quite understand why. What I learned opened my mind to so many things. I know now that these people (and even certain circumstances) are put in front of us from time to time so that we may learn from them. This is exactly what gives "**overcoming**" such credence. Also, it was always on my heart and in my mind that all things were somehow connected. This proved to be true over and over again. The fact that "art mimics life" holds true and I was onto that early on in my career. Happensburg made it clear that as long as I would listen, he would continue. If I stopped listening then what would be the point to continue? The Higher Power acts much in the same way. Stop listening and it stops. Sever those connections and you are on your own. I hope you understand that I'm painting here with a broad brush. If I were to jump directly into specifics and tell you that what I'm speaking of is a relationship with God, you might be closing the book yourself. But what other answer would suffice? Being "creative" and connecting with "THE CREATOR" makes perfect sense. I thought this would merit further research so I started studying the Bible. At first it was difficult so I got into Bible study classes. I wasn't surprised to find that much of what had happened to me was Biblical. I learned as Christians that we have a Savior; that a great sacrifice was made on our behalf. I also learned that the Holy Spirit would watch over us and guide us. The more I learned, the more it all made sense. I found out later in my life that when I was a child, many of my relatives had been continually praying for me. Prayer can be very powerful. Also Christianity has within it the concept of "forgiveness." The ultimate being Christ dying on the Cross for our sins, and this was very comforting, given my past and the many mistakes I had made. I had made many mistakes yet **He** never left me, I knew that to be true. In fact, the more I saw and the more I learned, the more it all seemed to hold true.

Interestingly…

"JUSTICE" You get what you deserve.

"MERCY" You don't get what you deserve.

"GRACE" You get what you don't deserve.

— Dr. William Grosso (pastor)

As for me… I owe *Justice* nothing. I owe *Mercy* and *Grace* everything!

"Jesus came not to "put us away" but to "show us the way."

Here I am writing a book and with every intention of writing several more. God has provided me with an endless stream of "new beginnings." **My world is still unfolding** and continues to be fascinating. I intend to strengthen my connection with God and learn more about the Great Creator who became my friend even before I knew Him.

"We can build the ship with our ability and our talents, and use our Creativity to set the sail, but only GOD can provide the wind."

Chapter 38

NEW BEGINNINGS

I mentioned earlier in the book the "value in problem solving" and, under the right circumstances, just how lucrative it could be. I also explained how the government and "pharmacia" have been onto this for some time now. My wish is that they could grasp the concept of God providing "new beginnings." We could then **solve** many of the problems in this country, and *cure* many diseases instead of merely **servicing** them. Can you imagine if we, as a nation, decided to put forth every effort and every resource to **cure** every disease known to mankind throughout the world! We would become the "World's doctor." We would be *loved* and *respected* by every nation on earth. Every industry would be affected. The medical research industry, the plastics industry, the many transportation industries, trucking, airlines, railroad, etc., construction industries, material industries, colleges would prosper, just about anyone with a brain would be employed doing something. When employment is up, crime is down.

This is a monumental task and throughout history, as many diseases have been cured, others still "pop up." Therefore, we don't need to fabricate fear of "global" this or that, or create false enemies, we have enough already in place. We need to address genuine issues that are affecting us right here, right now! Remember we will need the help of **Almighty God** to achieve this. We will have to show diligence by clearly displaying that we have set the "cornerstone" of *"integrity"* in our efforts. Without that **ultimate ingredient** it won't happen. Man cannot accomplish such a huge endeavor alone. History has proven this again and again. Just think how different the world would be if governments embraced the concept of integrity, followed by the medical industry, the food industry, the school systems, etc. We are living now in its absence. How do you like it so far? We desperately need God's help in these matters and I know from actual experience that He will never load a "loose cannon" or help with some "hare-brained" idea that man concocted. We must show that we have "**integrity**" first. Then **"our creator"** would have the right "**substance**" to work with and indeed, the **miracles will come.**

Don't be Ignorant!

"Deep in the roots of suffering you'll often find some form of IGNORANCE"
So what is it that is being *Ignored?* or should we be asking *Who* is it we are ignoring?

Ignorance in and of itself is bad enough but when you combine
Arrogance with Ignorance you'll experience a creature "un-civilized."

Learn to LOOK and LISTEN for the LESSONS.

Chapter 39:

SPIRIT CONNECTION

As Humans we are much more than just flesh and blood, we are also spirit and energy. Our spirit has everything to do with who we are. Think about what it is you like about another person. Providing you are not shallow or stupid, I would think it would go beyond their looks or their financial status. You know what I mean. There's just something about some people that makes you feel good when you're around them. Would you agree it's their "spirit?"

I believe that this spirit controls the "energy" they project. I also believe that this spirit, although very powerful, is also very delicate as well. It can be swayed or even damaged much easier than we think. It is constantly bombarded by everything from advertising concepts to political rhetoric, and influenced by environment and even the people around you. Any of these, as well as a host of other things can affect the spirit, often changing the "polarity," resulting in good, well-meaning people getting swept up into doing bad things.

We can all give examples of friends, relatives, even ourselves, doing things that were completely "out of character." I believe that before this can happen the *spirit* has to "*take a* **hit.**" With a damaged spirit, the energy becomes misdirected, causing results that are **not** normal to that person's persona or character. Therefore we must not only **nurture** our spirit, but **guard** it as well. I only hope this is making sense to you and this understanding can be of value to you. This is why it is so important to have Spiritual and Life Centered Values.

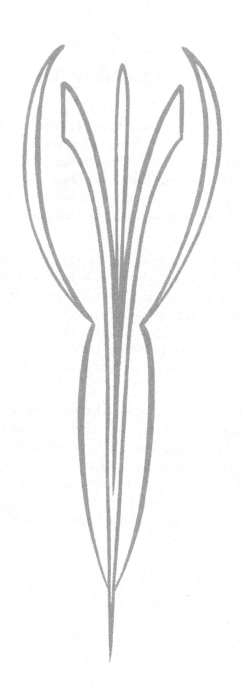

Chapter 40:

SIMPLY UNDERSTANDING
A COMPLEX WORLD

We live in a very complex world getting more complicated every day. It often takes four paragraphs for a person to say what can be said in one sentence these days. Is that intelligent? Is that knowledge? Is that wisdom? I think not. Allow me to prove my point. It's been my observation that "**too much**" has always been the sign of an amateur. "**Simplicity**" is the hallmark of a master. The reason being that simplicity has within it a "**secure foundation.**" "**No more than necessary**" is the theme. This can be achieved only through **time** and **experience**. Let me give you a simple example. Think of when a grandmother makes a pie. A pinch of this, a tad of that, and the results... perfection! Now, have a grand*daughter* make a pie. I will guarantee you there will be "**too much,**" not "too little." To the amateur there is never quite enough.

This stems from a lack of security regarding the task at hand.

I recently heard of a bill presented before Congress containing thirteen hundred pages. Who made that "pie?" We'll all have to eat it. This is typical of "man" operating without any guidance system.

✎ THE IMPORTANCE OF A GUIDANCE SYSTEM

We have seen in our lifetime man walk on the moon. That endeavor took tremendous effort by some of the most intelligent people on earth. The astronauts are indeed among the most highly respected individuals. You realize that, from the launch to the completion of their mission, at no time are they ever *disconnected* from Mission Control in Houston. If at any time they became disconnected they would risk being "lost in space" (literally.) As humans we have the natural desire to be connected, to belong, to follow. I think it's safe to say that all of us at one time or another have felt what it is like to be disconnected, and how lost we felt when that happened. But we must understand how important it is to be connected to the right principles. The ultimate is a connection with God. This connection can provide a very special love to be instilled in our hearts. I believe that this "special love" is directly connected to health, and produces a unique form of happiness. To have love, health and happiness in your life as a child is certainly wonderful, but to enjoy these gifts in your elder years is to experience a joy that truly surpasses all understanding.

If you don't understand or even possibly disagree with what I just said consider this…

Less God = More Hell, and in case you haven't noticed…there has been a lot **less** *Healing* as well.

Proof of this is evident in our homes, our schools and our government.

As crazy as this world can be, the old school principles written thousands of years ago still serve as a guidance system to take us out of the wilderness. The past can be extremely valuable regarding the future. Our past does not dictate our future, because we have the ability to change our minds and our hearts. The one thing the past may dictate is the **need** for us to change. This is why a study of history is so important.

To be specific, HIS-story. It's very much like looking into the past and seeing the future. If you look into the Bible you will see that much of what we are experiencing has been experienced before, often over and over again. Those smart enough to grasp this can have tremendous power and control over their lives, not to mention being able to avoid much pain and suffering.

"Education trains only half the person, developing their intellect but not their will, their mind but not their character. It gives them knowledge of facts, but gives them no purpose or destiny. The missing link is Devine Truth." When Divine Truth is denied, there is no final determinant of truth except "power," which has enslaved one-third of the world. **(Fulton Sheen)**

If any man lack Wisdom, let him ask of GOD… and it shall be given" (James 1:5.)

All I could possibly do with the life and talents given me would be to make you **aware** of our spirit nature, and what is available to you. As a person who has walked the walk and been on both sides of the fence, I assure you that **good** certainly holds more value than evil.

"It seems to me that "Good" needs constant maintenance, in order to prosper, where "Evil" only needs to be left alone." But relax it's the presence of EVIL that gives GOOD its value.

Just in case you are not familiar with what can be clearly defined as EVIL let me list a few examples;

Anger, envy, jealousy, regret, greed, arrogance, self pity, guilt, resentment, inferiority, lies, false pride, superiority, and ego.

Representing GOOD would be;

Joy, peace, love, hope, serenity, humility, kindness, benevolence, empathy, generosity, truth, compassion and faith.

I spent over half a century living out old-fashioned values, and some very basic principles, amidst constant change. That is what Creativity is all about. The "mixing" of ideas, old with new, thinking in alternatives, taking abstract thoughts and creating tangible form, inventing, writing, artistry, music, it's all interconnected, all related, and it is indeed a different world.

Be especially careful giving all of your attention to what everyone else is doing. You have your own universe. "But seek ye first the Kingdom of God, and all his righteousness; and all these things shall be added unto you." (Matt. 6:33)

Chapter 41:

LOVE

Love. A word so often misused and misunderstood. I believe that *genuine love* is a very important part of human existence. Like the air we breathe, the water, the nutrients we must have to exist, we also **need** Love. It is very clear in the beginning, that in my less than perfect efforts at this thing we call life, had it not been for love presenting itself over and over again, I could not have made it this far. Love has been the main ingredient holding everything together. I could go on and on about all of the aspects of love but let me touch on what I feel may be most important.

I think most humans are equipped with love in their hearts, although it must be understood and developed much like talent. For some it is very difficult to express love, especially if it has been void in their lives from the beginning. It is difficult to embrace something you know little about. Living without love can affect your health and well being. From what I have seen in my lifetime, I personally believe that the presence of true heart-felt love can positively affect everything about us, even such things as our immune system. When love is present in your life you can feel it deep in your heart. Love should be the main ingredient in a marriage. Fifty percent of the marriages in this country fail. Why? Because many of these folks should not have married in the first place. They married for what they thought was security, status, comfort, sometimes because all of their friends were getting married, and a host of other reasons, none of which included heartfelt love. When love prevails in a relationship, there is a special strength to draw from that can get a couple through almost anything.

"Love is the Ultimate Renewable Energy"

The power of Love extends far beyond relationships. It should be present in your health, your work, your attitude toward your country, and almost every aspect of your life.

My love of Creativity allowed me to live in a Creative environment. My love of my craft allowed me to spend over half a century working Ideas and meeting some of the greatest people in the world. My love of writing is allowing me to share the stories and philosophy with you and also providing even more Ideas with new beginnings.

"Love flourishes wonderfully, in an environment where God is present, there is a high level of creative thought, a reasonable sense of humor, and totally free of corruption."

The ultimate goal of this book has been to raise a level of consciousness regarding the existence of some very solid "Old School" Values. Clearly I put a fair amount of emphasis on the importance of a sound belief system and its effect on our values and virtues. My own experiences have revealed that with age old tried and true values in place...

Order will emerge from chaos, Life can be meaningful,
Hope blossoms and Joy is attainable.

It would be advisable that after reading this book, to let some time pass and then read it through again. As you experience the writing a second time many secrets will be revealed as you increase the quality of your attention toward the depth of its content.

THE LINE CONTINUES...

"Wherefore by their fruits ye shall know them."
—MATTHEW 7.20

DAVE SR.'S WORK

Dave was asked to pinstripe a Thomas Edison exhibit for General Electric.

In the early years Dave would paint almost anything; from signs, to cars, and even a complete paint job on an airplane.

Dave Sr. & Dave Jr.

Dave Jr.'s illustrious racing career.

Dave Jr.'s work ranges from customizing trucks to refinishing rare vintage bikes, like this British 1955 Ariel motorcycle.

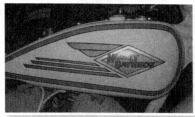

Dave Jr. and Michael work jointly on Dad's Pet Care promotional motorcycle.

Michael paints it all, even "hard core graphics"
like this motorcycle frame and fuel tank.

Michael painted this for a customer on his garage wall using only black and white paint and the brushes seen above.

Motorcycle owned by Simmons Machine Tool Corporation and customized by Davies Custom Cycles. The airbrush work was done by Michael Davies.

These three trains were hand painted by Michael on each saddle bag.

Michael painting the Town of Deadwood, SD, in complete detail on the back fender.

*Michael (in Kauai "the Garden Island," Hawaii) painted this mural for the
U-TURN for CHRIST church in of May 2015.*

Dave Jr. and Sandy work jointly on Dads Pet Care Promotional Motorcycle. David built and painted the bike while Sandy did the custom art work.

Sandy, the newest blossom in the orchard, puts her spin on custom art through Artistic Linez.

For more visit the "Orchard"

DaviesCustomPaint.com

There is a place where there are no lies

<u>*Only Truth*</u>

there is no anger — <u>Only Energy</u>

there is no hate — <u>Only Love</u>

To get there we must seek KNOWLEDGE FROM GOD

HIS knowledge will lead us to <u>Wisdom</u>

Wisdom will lead us to that wonderful place called

<u>Understanding</u>

I'll meet you there.

David Holland Davies

CPSIA information can be obtained
at www.ICGtesting.com
Printed in the USA
BVOW06*2046041116

466990BV00002B/2/P